"I want the whole thing, Nate. I want a family. I want kids—and a husband. The whole package."

Nate leaned in, so that they were nearly nose to nose. "Since when, Josey? You love being single. How many times have you waxed philosophical about how impossible it must be to find the right man and so you weren't going to bend over backwards to do it?"

"So what?" Her voice turned stubborn. "I can't change my mind?"

"You can change your mind, but this is a complete about-face. It's weird."

"Oh, I'm so glad you think I'm weird."

"Josey, I'm sorry," he said, grabbing her hand. "It's just surprising. But I think it's wonderful. I wish you luck. I really do."

"You do?" she asked, her voice tripping with excitement.

Nate wondered why she was getting so emotional. "You know I do. You're my friend and I'll do anything to make sure you're happy."

A huge grin spread across her face. "I'm so glad you said that, you have no idea. Now I can get to what I really wanted to ask you tonight. I need your help...."

Dear Reader,

Well, the new year is upon us—and if you've resolved to read some wonderful books in 2004, you've come to the right place. We'll begin with *Expecting!* by Susan Mallery, the first in our five-book MERLYN COUNTY MIDWIVES miniseries, in which residents of a small Kentucky town find love—and scandal—amidst the backdrop of a midwifery clinic. In the opening book, a woman returning to her hometown, pregnant and alone, finds herself falling for her high school crush—now all grown up and married to his career! Or so he thinks....

Annette Broadrick concludes her SECRET SISTERS trilogy with *MacGowan Meets His Match.* When a woman comes to Scotland looking for a job *and* the key to unlock the mystery surrounding her family, she finds both—with the love of a lifetime thrown in!—in the Scottish lord who hires her. In *The Black Sheep Heir,* Crystal Green wraps up her KANE'S CROSSING miniseries with the story of the town outcast who finds in the big, brooding stranger hiding out in her cabin the soul mate she'd been searching for.

Karen Rose Smith offers the story of an about-to-be single mom and the handsome hometown hero who makes her wonder if she doesn't have room for just one more male in her life, in *Their Baby Bond.* THE RICHEST GALS IN TEXAS, a new miniseries by Arlene James, in which three blue-collar friends inherit a million dollars—each!—opens with *Beautician Gets Million-Dollar Tip!* A hairstylist inherits that wad just in time to bring her salon up to code, at the insistence of the infuriatingly handsome, if annoying, local fire marshal. And in Jen Safrey's *A Perfect Pair,* a woman who enlists her best (male) friend to help her find her Mr. Right suddenly realizes he's right there in front of her face—i.e., said friend! Now all she has to do is convince *him* of this....

So bundle up, and happy reading. And come back next month for six new wonderful stories, all from Silhouette Special Edition.

Sincerely,

Gail Chasan
Senior Editor

Please address questions and book requests to:
Silhouette Reader Service
U.S.: 3010 Walden Ave., P.O. Box 1325, Buffalo, NY 14269
Canadian: P.O. Box 609, Fort Erie, Ont. L2A 5X3

A Perfect Pair

JEN SAFREY

Silhouette®

SPECIAL EDITION®

Published by Silhouette Books

America's Publisher of Contemporary Romance

To Bobbi Lerman,
a fantastic writer and friend, who coaxed this story
out of me even when it felt impossible. We did it!

 SILHOUETTE BOOKS

ISBN 0-373-24590-4

A PERFECT PAIR

Copyright © 2004 by Jen Safrey

This edition published by arrangement with Harlequin Books S.A.

® and TM are trademarks of Harlequin Books S.A., used under license. Trademarks indicated with ® are registered in the United States Patent and Trademark Office, the Canadian Trade Marks Office and in other countries.

Visit Silhouette at www.eHarlequin.com

Printed in U.S.A.

JEN SAFREY

grew up in Valley Stream, New York, and graduated Boston University in 1993. She is a nearly ten-year veteran of the news copy desk at the *Boston Herald*. Past and present, she has been a champion baton twirler, an accomplished flutist, an equestrienne, a student of ashtanga yoga and a belly dancer. Jen would love to hear from readers at jen02106@lycos.com.

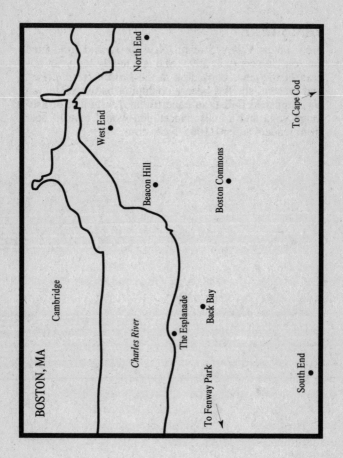

Prologue

Nate heard a woman shout in the apartment above, but he couldn't make out the words.

The abrupt, angry sound pierced the silence in which Nate had been sitting at the kitchen table, spooning up Cheerios. He jumped slightly and a few Cheerios dripped onto his lap. He lifted the window curtain, opened the window and peered out. Squinting and tilting his face up to the early afternoon sun, he saw the open windows above him. After a few weeks of crisp, cold weather, the unusually mild November day had likely prompted his neighbor to air out her place. Nate silently waited a few moments. Nothing.

Slightly tense, he picked the Cheerios off his lap and reluctantly went back to eating. Still hearing nothing, he slurped on the spoon a little, quickly intercepting a stream of milk down his chin with a napkin. He hoped that one shout was the end of whatever was going on. As he scooped up the last Cheerio, he caught himself trying not to tap the bowl with the spoon, trying to stay quiet, his ears alert as a fox's for another sign of discord.

He forced himself to relax his shoulders, to breathe normally. He reminded himself that one distinct drawback to living in Boston was getting to know neighbors intimately, whether he wanted to or not. And today, like most days, it really was "not." He'd allowed himself the Sunday luxury of sleeping in as long as he could—until after noon—then he'd cracked open his briefcase and worked about an hour before he'd realized he'd forgotten to eat breakfast.

Nate put the bowl to his lips and drained the rest of his milk, feeling the sweet coldness slide down his throat, before carrying the bowl to the sink. He washed it carefully and rubbed it with a clean towel until it squeaked. He did the same with the spoon and replaced both in the overhead cabinet.

But then, there it was again.

Another wordless, indignant female scream echoed through the alley between buildings and into Nate's kitchen. He stood motionless and tried again to talk himself out of his discomfort, this time attempting to be annoyed at the noise, the way a normal city dweller would be.

At least he'd already been awake and the racket hadn't dragged him out of slumber, he told himself. Who was she yelling at, anyway? He didn't even hear another voice.

He took the three steps to his sofa and fell onto it. He fumbled underneath his butt for the remote. A little channel surfing for half an hour wouldn't put him too far behind, he thought. He needed a little downtime in his week. Besides, the TV would drown out his upstairs neighbor until she quit for the day, which, Nate hoped, was before he had to get down to serious work.

But before he could press the On button, there was a

loud crash over his head, accompanied by an incredulous shriek.

Then silence.

Nate jolted upright.

There *was* someone with her. And it sounded like someone she'd pushed too far—someone who was going to hurt her. If he hadn't already.

Nate tensed, waiting, his senses at attention. Then he heard another crash, like a piece of furniture hitting the wall, and another cry of outrage.

An image of the woman he'd never met flashed in his mind. Her features were unrecognizable, but there was terror in her eyes as she cowered, fearful of the next blow that was sure to come. He felt her terror now.

He had known it himself, long ago.

Nate leaped off the sofa and ran to his open window. "Hey!" he yelled, aware that his interference would be ineffective against someone like his own father, but hoping the man upstairs was a different kind of coward. "Hey! What's going on up there?"

The woman yelled again, but what he heard couldn't be right: "What is this freaking *game?*"

Game? Still at the window, Nate stared out at the parking lot, his thoughts tumbling over each other. Was someone playing some kind of sick "game" with her? Some twisted sex game, maybe? He knew one of his colleagues in the D.A.'s office had had a case like that a few months back. A man had inadvertently killed his wife while trying some kind of sadistic—

Over Nate's head, the banging became rhythmic, like someone pounding the floor. "Come on!" the woman screamed. "Come *on*... Oh, God! No! *No!*"

Nate's fury overwhelmed him. He dashed into his bedroom and blindly grabbed his baseball bat out of a corner.

Then he ran down the short hallway, slipping a bit in his socks on the hardwood floor, and threw open his door. He raced up the stairwell, one flight, and without knocking, pushed open the door to the apartment directly above his own. He slid into the middle of the living room, bat raised, and the woman, sitting alone on the floor in front of the television, jumped to her feet and screamed.

"Are you okay?" he demanded.

The woman dropped her hands from her mouth. "Who the *hell* are you?" she shrieked.

Nate momentarily ignored her, scanning the room and the adjoining kitchenette, then stomping into her bedroom, then her bathroom, despite her cry of "Hey!"

Empty. Confirming she was alone, he returned to the living room, where she still stood, eyes wide, and he finally answered, "I live downstairs. I heard you yelling and—"

"And so you just rushed in here? Into *my* apartment?" The woman stared at him a minute. "Well, I'm sorry, I didn't mean to disturb you. It's just that I get very emotional about—"

"Are you okay?" Nate repeated. Frankly, she looked fine to him. Better than fine. She was gorgeous. Her blond hair was cropped short, like a boy's, but her face was nothing but feminine—small turned-up nose, full pouty lips and enormous, milk-chocolate brown eyes.

She made some kind of sound, which sounded to Nate like part relieved sob and part laugh. "Well, a half-naked man just crashed into my living room with a baseball bat, apparently about to beat me up for making too much noise. Not a usual Sunday afternoon occurrence, but yeah, I'm pretty okay."

Nate looked down at his ratty old jeans, only realizing now he was shirtless. "Where is he?" he asked, but his tone had softened a little bit.

She shook her head in confusion. "Wh-what? Who?"

"You were yelling. I heard you. And there was all that noise, banging around. Someone was…hurting you?"

"Oh, no." She covered her mouth with her hands again. "Oh, no, I'm so sorry." But her eyes were suddenly laughing. "It's the game."

"Yeah, I heard that, too—a game. What game?"

She pointed at the television. "Football game."

Nate tore his eyes away from the woman's enchanting face to the TV, where the announcer was saying, "And at the end of the first half, the score is the Denver Broncos 13, the New England Patriots 10." Then a commercial, two guys walking through a desert, wishing for some great beer.

Nate kept his eyes on the screen. "The game? This game?"

"Yes. See," the woman explained hurriedly, "I usually watch the game down at the Bull Pen, but my date stood me up. Normally I'd just go solo, because after all, I'm not going to let an inconsiderate idiot ruin my day, but I'm short on money this week anyhow and the Pats game was on regular TV. So I'm watching it here." She gestured lamely at the television, then bent to pick the remote control off the floor where she had been sitting. She muted the set before continuing. "I get a little, um, emotional about my team. There were a few incomplete passes that made me flip a couple of chairs over, and I was yelling no because Denver intercepted the ball and they were running up the field for a touchdown and I couldn't believe it and I kind of started banging on the floor…. Wait, you ran up here because you thought someone was hurting me?"

Nate nodded mutely, then sank onto her ugly orange sofa. He looked back at her, taking in the red-white-and-blue football jersey and jeans she wore, then dropped the bat with a clatter on the floor by his feet. He took in the scantily furnished room, and saw that the couple of chairs in it were, in fact, lying on their side.

"Thank you," the woman said sincerely. "I mean it. Thank you." She studied his face. "Are *you* okay? You seem really upset. I'm so, so sorry."

Nate wasn't sure how he was feeling. He had rushed up here, thinking he was rescuing someone from the kind of abusive terror he himself had had to live with for so long. Now, seeing this woman standing over him, obviously unhurt, was almost too much of a relief. "I'm, uh, I'm just a little embarrassed, is all."

"Don't be," the woman said vehemently. "I'm so grateful—just as grateful as I would have been if someone really was hurting me and you came to save me. Really," she said. "I'm just so sorry for getting carried away in here with the windows open. I wish I could make it up to you…wait, I can. Why don't you stay? I'll make something to eat and I have enough soda and beer for both of us, I think."

"You want me to stay?"

"Sure I do. I mean, I don't know you, but you passed the friend test immediately by running in here to rescue me. Not too many of the friends I have now would do that, I'll bet, including the creep who stood me up today." She walked backward into her kitchenette, talking all the way to the refrigerator. "He wasn't my type, anyhow," she added, yanking a six-pack of diet soda from the fridge and pulling two cans off their plastic rings. Then she slammed the door shut with a nudge of one blue-jeaned hip. "Not that I'm actively searching for my type, mind you. But I digress." She tossed him one can, and Nate reached out for it, the cold condensation suddenly shocking the nerve endings in his fingers. "I'd love to have a friend in this building. Besides, if you were a true psycho, you would have bonked me over the head and taken my two pieces of real jewelry and the six bucks in my wallet by now. Come on, stay. Watch the game.''

Nate was having trouble keeping up with her train of thought, being a little weary from the emotions that had surged through him in the last few minutes. He popped open his can and took a long swig, nearly choking when the woman exclaimed, ''I'm not trying to flirt with you or get a date with you or anything like that. Don't get me wrong, okay?'' She took a small sip of her own soda. ''I mean, nice chest and everything, but that's not why I'm asking you. I value my single status. It's just that you just seem so…nice.''

She squinted at Nate the way he imagined a psychiatrist would scrutinize a patient. He avoided psychiatrists, since he didn't find it necessary to pay someone to remind him that his childhood had been messed up. But this woman's searching stare was unnerving him. ''You're not a psychiatrist or psychologist or therapist of any kind, are you?'' he asked.

''No, sorry, can't help you there,'' she said, then she laughed. ''Watch the game. You can tell me your problems at the time-outs, if you want, and I'll see what I can do.''

Her vivacity was infectious and it was tough not to smile back at her. ''Do you think you can control yourself with another person in the room?'' he asked. ''I don't want to duck flying furniture for the whole second half.''

She gave him a cocky grin. ''No, of course not. Maybe with a guest here, I can try to keep a lid on it.'' She extended her hand. He took it, and her skin felt cool and delicate but, at the same time, warm and immediately reassuring.

''I'm Josey.''

Chapter One

About a year and a half later

The Mother's Day pageant was a catastrophe waiting to happen.

Twenty-seven third-graders ran amok backstage, darting around abandoned, faded backdrops, hiding behind black curtains and giggling as they tripped over their own baggy, assorted animal costumes and landed on the dusty wooden floorboards. Fifty-four little sneakered feet thundered back and forth in a frenzied pre-performance game of demented tag, no one knowing who was it, but everyone joining in, anyway, for the sheer joy of running in circles and screaming.

Josey squinted at her watch, straining in the dank backstage dimness to see the clock. Five minutes until curtain time. The best way to get a grip on this eight-year-old hysteria, she knew, was her piercing, unladylike taxi-hail whistle, the one she used when her pumped-up kids returned to the classroom from either recess or gym class, the one that made them cover their ears in mock terror and shriek, "Miss St. John! That's so *loud!*" But she hated to use it here, aware of the mothers and handful of fathers currently seating themselves out front, and dreading what they would think of her archaic method of crowd control.

"Kids! Kids, settle down!" she hissed in—appropriately—a stage whisper, but no one heard or cared. Arms and legs flailing, they continued their chase around and around until finally, Josey felt forced to take her drastic measure. She put two fingers in her mouth and blew with all her might.

Small hands flew to heads. "Miss St. John! Ow!"

Josey winced, remembering the parents, but then she heard several amused titters and one outright laugh come from out front. She should have known they'd understand—and approve. Relieved, she turned to her class.

"Okay, everyone," she said, widening her arms and allowing all the children to gather around her. She did a silent head count, did it again and was satisfied. "Just remember to do your best. If you forget your lines or a song, it's okay. We're just doing this to have fun, right?"

They all nodded, suddenly very serious in their fuzzy costumes and rainbow feathers and painted-on whiskers. *My kids,* Josey caught herself thinking, and smiled to herself.

"And," she added with a wink, "I'll be right in front of the stage like I showed you this morning, if you need help remembering anything. I'll wave right at the beginning so you all can see me. Our rehearsal today was awesome, right?"

Enthusiastic nods.

"Your parents are going to be so proud. And if your parents couldn't come today—" she focused on a few specific faces "—I'm especially proud of you for being good sports."

Ally Berenson, the music teacher, poked her head through the curtain then. "Hi, Miss Berenson!" a chorus of voices called, and Ally waggled her fingers at them.

"Hi, gang. Are you ready to rock and roll?"

"Yes!" they all yelled happily, even though Josey was sure the expression went right over their heads. Ally was a kid favorite. With her wild mop of brassy hair tumbling around her face and her ability to make up a silly spontaneous song about any student, it was easy to understand why.

Ally flicked her gaze to Josey. "Are *you* ready?" she asked more quietly, grinning. "Full house out there. Somehow, when they dim the lights, I forget it's a gymnasium with folding chairs."

Josey smiled back. "Just soothing some opening-night—uh, make that opening-afternoon—jitters."

"Your own or the kids'?"

"Well," Josey admitted, "I am a little nervous."

"Me, too," Ally whispered. "And I have no excuse. I write songs for every class, kindergarten through sixth, for plays every year. I deserve a Tony by now. Maybe two."

Josey turned back to her class. "Everyone get in your places!" she called. And as the third-grade zoo animals scrambled around the stage, she added in a low voice to Ally, "You're terrific. I thought when I came up with this year's Mother's Day play idea you were going to kill me."

"No, it's great!" Ally said. "I had a lot of fun with them. The tiger song was tough, but hey, I'm a genius."

"Anyway," Josey pointed out, "this audience didn't come here to see you and me."

Ally chuckled. "True enough. Good luck! See you at the cast party. I hear Mel Gibson may show." She laughed and ducked as Josey took a playful swat at her, then disappeared again behind the curtain.

Josey hustled a few children around, and when all seemed in order, she took a small lion named Jeremy by the hand and led him to where the curtain parted. She put Jeremy's hand—now a golden paw—on the curtain in the right spot so he wouldn't have to fumble, then knelt by him.

"Okay, Jeremy. All set?"

"Yeah," the boy answered in a shaky but definitely determined voice.

"I'm going to go out front. You stay here and count to twenty-five slowly, then come on out."

"Okay, Miss St. John. I'm not scared," he added, more to himself than to her.

Touched, she put a playful finger on his now-brown nose. "I know. Okay, start counting!"

Josey tiptoed offstage so as not to make a clatter, then once safely in the wings, she ran down the stairs, leaping off three steps from the bottom. She smoothed her long, swirly rust-colored skirt and tucked a strand of hair behind each ear before pushing open the door and stepping out before the audience.

She opted out of an opening speech, aware that Jeremy was probably counting fast. Instead, she waved an acknowledging hand to the clapping parents and took her place in front of the stage just in time for Jeremy to hustle his way through the curtain. The crowd behind Josey murmured at the adorable costume.

"Moms and dads," Jeremy began, and Josey was relieved to hear he'd remembered to speak very loudly. "Miss St. John's third-graders are proud to present 'Wild

Moms.' We take you now to the zoo. The animals are all getting ready to celebrate Mother's Day.'' He ad-libbed a growl, which elicited an auditorium full of laughter, then moved stage left as the sixth-grader Josey had hired for the day pulled open the curtain.

The play went amazingly well. Ally's songs were perfect; the parents loved the one about the mama tiger teaching her cub how to growl. One child, Jamie Cranston, forgot her lines, and though Josey called them out in a whisper for her, it clearly distressed Jamie, one of the smartest little girls in the class, to have been the only one helped by the teacher. She watched as Jamie slunk backstage in humiliation. Josey made a mental note to talk to the little girl after the play and tell her how brave she was.

But then she saw that she wouldn't need to.

A moment later, out of the corner of her eye, she spied Jamie's parents. They slipped into the side aisle and climbed quietly up the side stage stairs, pushing behind the heavy black curtain. No one else in the audience seemed to notice, all focused on their own children. But the black curtain didn't fall all the way behind the Cranstons, and through the open space Josey saw them approach their miserable daughter, and then saw the father scoop Jamie up in his arms.

Josey turned her eyes back to her job, back to the play, but it was going without a hitch, and she just couldn't help herself from peeking at the backstage family again. Jamie's father lifted his mouth to her ear, blew away a strand of flaxen hair and whispered. Josey watched his lips form words that only his little girl could hear, words that produced a small wisp of a smile. Then the mother leaned in closer and added her own soft comments, which elicited an even larger smile. And then Jamie snuggled her face happily in her dad's shoulder.

And Josey, suddenly distracted from her onstage class, her gaze on the backstage drama, was sure she would never forget, in her whole life, the look on the mother's face. As the woman gazed at her husband and daughter, there was a glowing serenity about her, a sweet combination of love and satisfaction that reminded Josey of a holy madonna statue.

And although Josey couldn't hear her voice, she instinctively knew that when the woman bent her head toward her husband, her murmured words were, "I love you."

Then the pair slipped quietly back to their seats, and Josey returned her attention to her class, and the show went on.

When the curtain closed, all the parents jumped to their feet, clapping and whistling. Josey leaped onto the stage, pushed behind the curtain and lined up the children, holding hands, for their bow. When one little boy and girl in the middle refused to touch each other's hand—fear of cooties, no doubt—Josey alleviated the problem by stepping between them and taking a small hand in each of hers. She nodded at the stage girl to pull the curtain open again, and as cameras flashed and camcorders whirred, Josey took the deserved bow with her hardworking, exhausted kids.

But in that moment, when she expected her heart would swell with its usual pride, it felt achy and hollow—a first for her.

When the last straggling child had gone for the day, Josey looked around the room, abandoned for the afternoon. Rays of sunshine filtered through the window blinds and lit up the desks in the front row. Everything was so familiar and yet felt strange to her. *She* felt strange, really. As if she'd never really seen anything before and now it was all suddenly clear.

Instead of rummaging through her desk for her take-home work—papers to grade, lessons to plan—she just went to the closet, grabbed her spring trench coat and flung it over her arm. She picked her keys absently out of her top desk drawer and left the classroom, slamming the door behind her.

The subway ride home passed in a daze. Josey hung on to the overhead bar, the car's motion bumping her into fellow Boston commuters. She didn't notice. She just stared at her own face, reflected in the window as the train moved through the darkness in between stations. She looked at herself, standing in the crowd, the way someone else on the subway might have looked at her, and she didn't feel anything at all. She got off at her stop automatically, and walked the three blocks to her apartment building. It was a pleasant walk, and usually Josey thought about how nice it was to live in such a historic, if slightly overpriced, neighborhood. But today she may as well have been walking through a war zone, for all she knew.

She turned her key in the front door and without stopping at her mailbox, started up the stairs to her apartment. She didn't bother knocking on Nate's door to see if he was home yet, just dragged up one more flight and let herself into her own place.

The answering machine was blinking—two messages—but Josey didn't care. She threw her coat over a chair and flopped onto the sofa, listlessly staring up at the ceiling. She didn't care at all. She felt…empty. She kicked off her beige suede pumps.

What had happened to her? This day had been turning out so well. The play went off with barely a hitch. She was able to talk to parents without stammering… Even this morning, her kids had done so well on their spelling tests—

Her kids. *Her* kids.

They weren't her kids. They were all someone else's kids.

In the peeling ceiling plaster, Josey suddenly saw Jamie's mother's face again, beaming with pride and love at her family. Josey didn't know what the woman did for a living, but she suspected family was the woman's first priority.

Having a family had never been *her* priority.

She liked—no, loved—being single. She liked having different dates on different weekends, and getting to know a variety of people. Her girlfriends—Ally, for one—thought of dating as a necessary step to finding the right man and getting married. But Josey didn't think that way. It was too much pressure. How could you go out to dinner with a man you just met and be checking him out for commitment potential? Josey knew she wouldn't even get to dessert if her mind worked that way. She just liked talking to new people and having fun. Her dates were platonic, anyway, for the most part. She'd only had two boyfriends that she would have called serious—one in high school and one in college. Both relationships had run their course, though, and Josey, a resilient woman, had gotten over them. Plenty of fish in the sea…

Josey shifted her weight on the sofa and picked the remote control off the floor. She pointed it at the television, but dropped her arm almost immediately and began toying with the device, fingering the rubber keys.

She remembered Ally lamenting once, after a particularly horrendous date, ''I know the perfect man is out there for me, and I can't find him. You can't find yours, either, but it doesn't even bother you. You're in the same boat as me, but if you have a lousy date, you just shrug it off.''

''Sure, I do,'' Josey had said. ''What's the rush?'' And she had believed it, then.

So why was she sitting here now, thinking maybe Ally

and all those other single women were *right?* Thinking that maybe dating really was a means to an end, and she'd never get to that end if she just continued on the way she had been, accepting dates with nice people just to have a good time.

Did she really need more? Were there possibilities she had ignored?

Josey suddenly bolted up from the sofa and walked into the kitchen. She usually had a beer and watched TV before fixing a simple dinner, but when she opened the refrigerator, the thought of downing a beer and yelling at Oprah Winfrey's guests seemed too…bachelorette. She slammed the fridge door and grabbed the mostly unused teakettle off the stove. She filled it with water and set it back down on the range, turning up the heat. Then she rummaged through the overhead cabinet for a clean mug. Tea. Very domestic.

Domestic?

Josey stopped in the middle of the kitchen floor. Was she really considering this? A family? Her? Born-to-have-fun, sworn-to-single-life Josephine St. John?

A husband?

The phone rang, startling Josey so much a small gasp emerged from her throat. She lunged for the phone, not wanting to hear one more offensive ring. "Hello?"

"Oh, you're home early. I was going to leave you a message." Nate's rich baritone filled her ear. The reserved, slightly detached tone of his voice was typical of someone making a personal phone call from work, but then, Nate often sounded like that. Besides, Josey knew he had to be at work, because if he were at home, he'd be knocking on her door instead of calling her.

"Hey, Nate."

"You sound exhausted. The kids wear you out? Oh no, wait, the play. How'd it go?"

"All right. I mean, fine. It went fine." Josey, frustrated with her inability to communicate, pushed back a corner of the kitchen curtain and glanced outside. The bright late-afternoon sunshine made her squint, so she dropped the gauzy material.

"It's Friday once again," Nate continued. "And it's your turn to choose. Japanese, Italian, Thai? Hamburgers?"

Oh, damn. Josey couldn't believe she'd forgotten her weekly dinner out with Nate. But she was in no shape to go anyplace tonight. She was just going to get into her bathrobe and turn on some Billy Joel and stare into space. She was in the midst of some kind of epiphany, and she needed to stay here and sort out her mind. And maybe replan her future.

"Nate, you know what? It's not really a good night for me."

Nate paused, then asked, "What's wrong?"

"Why does something have to be wrong?"

"All right, strike that." Spoken like a true lawyer. "What's going on?"

"Why does something have to be going—"

"Because you never cancel out on me. *I* tried to cancel on *you* twice, but I didn't succeed because no matter how much work I have to do, you always convince me otherwise."

"Mmm…"

"And you know what? You're always right. So, no excuses. I'll stop by in about two hours. I've got a few more things to handle here, then—"

"Nate, I'm serious. I'm sorry. I really can't do it tonight."

"All right. Don't worry about it. I'm not insulted. Just tell me why you're canceling."

Josey began pacing in a slow circle, wrapping the phone cord around her body. "Why do you sound so worried?"

"Because I am worried. No one likes to go out and have fun more than you, Josey. You wouldn't ditch a night out on the town unless something was up."

"Nate," Josey insisted, "I'm fine. Okay? I just have to—well—I have to stay here and…think for a while."

Not normally one for spontaneous good humor, Nate laughed out loud. "That, I have to say, is a new one. Do you usually go through life *not* thinking?"

"Nate, please. I'll talk to you tomorrow about it, okay? Don't get on my—"

"I'm not, I'm not." Nate was suddenly serious again. "I didn't mean to laugh. Whatever this is with you, I hope you figure it out. Do you want a rain check for tomorrow evening? It's a Saturday night. I wouldn't want to impose on any big date plans."

As it happened, Josey didn't have a date. "I'll call you tomorrow and let you know. That should be fine," she added, distractedly.

"Hold on." The sound was suddenly muffled, as if Nate had covered the mouthpiece with his hand, and she heard voices. Then he came back. "Josey, listen, I have to run. One crisis after another around here."

"Yeah."

"So I'll speak to you tomorrow. Don't forget to call."

"I won't, Nate."

They said their goodbyes and hung up, and Josey rested her hand on the receiver for a moment, trying to get control of her thoughts again.

But despite her effort, all that went around in her head was *I want a family.*

Well, she thought, *why fight it? My mind is made up.*

She glanced up at the framed poster on the far wall, of

the Patriots' quarterback. Nate had bought it for her birthday last month, in remembrance of their first meeting. Her mouth turned up slightly at the memory of tall, dark, handsome, subdued Nate crashing into her apartment, afraid all hell was breaking loose, and intending to do something about it. Sweet, reliable, responsible Nate.

Nate, Josey realized with a start, would be perfect to help her.

When she had told Nate she'd call him tomorrow, she had said it automatically, so that he'd stop worrying about her. But, she thought now, he was the perfect person to help out.

If anyone would understand what she was going through, it would be him. He didn't have a wife and kids—hadn't even dated anyone seriously since Josey had known him—but he was goal-driven and ambitious, and she needed someone like that now that she was planning to restructure her own life around a new objective. A family.

Besides, Josey thought, walking down the short hall to her bathroom and shedding her work clothing on the way, good old responsible Nate ought to be able to help her figure out how to do a responsible thing like settle down. She'd just ask for his help. Tomorrow.

Chapter Two

A light tapping on Nate's door startled him.

"Come in!" he called, leaning back in his chair in an authoritative position. The door creaked open, and David Jeffers strode in, his footsteps muted on the soft green pile rug.

"Nathan Bennington," Jeffers said, taking the seat across from Nate without waiting for an invitation. He wouldn't have needed one, of course. To Nate, David Jeffers was the closest thing he'd ever had to a mentor. He was the first assistant district attorney Nate had met and worked with upon arriving at the D.A.'s office two years ago, fresh out of law school. Jeffers was someone Nate strove to impress—even now, after they'd become friends.

"Sir," Nate replied with a smile.

Jeffers picked up a glass paperweight on Nate's desk and studied it closely for a moment before replacing it. "Listen, I wanted to talk to you about a new opportunity you might be interested in. As soon as I heard about it, I had a feeling you might want to be in on it. Kind of a new challenge.''

"Yes?" Nate's interest was already piqued. And it was a good thing, because it took his mind off Josey and that weird little phone call earlier. For Josey to say she wanted to sit inside and "think" on a Friday night was odd, and for the last hour, Nate had been a little distracted by worry. Which was something he was rather talented at. So now he focused his full attention on what Jeffers was saying.

"A small group of attorneys in this office is getting together to work in a specialized area—domestic violence. The number of local cases is skyrocketing, and it's all you ever see in the media anymore. The D.A.'s decided to expand the domestic violence unit—with some additional lawyers. Talented ones. Ones who can handle the type of cases that come through here.''

Domestic violence. "What kind of cases?" Nate asked, his lips suddenly dry. It was a silly question, really. He knew the answer full well. But it was all he could think to say.

"Just about anything you'd conceive of. But the boss wants to specifically—and more publicly—target spousal abuse and child abuse.''

Nate stared at Jeffers's face for a full minute, his heart beating fast, suddenly paranoid that his colleague knew about him, knew— No, his rational mind quickly insisted. Jeffers could have no idea of the kind of gift he was offering. Close as he was to David Jeffers, Nate had never told him—or anyone—about his father, or about the demons that had haunted him ever since he and his brother had run away from home.

He had considered the possibility of getting child abuse cases eventually. He wasn't entirely sure that it hadn't been in the back of his mind all along when he'd applied to

Harvard Law School. But this "task force" would make prosecuting abusers a main focus. He would be personally responsible for throwing abusers behind bars.

With this new position, Nate could confront his demons. And spit in their faces.

Trying to keep the eagerness out of his voice, he said slowly, "That definitely sounds like something I would like to be involved in. But why me, Jeffers? I haven't even gotten a chance to prosecute an abuse case yet."

"You've been very successful here so far, with an excellent record, and it's important we have the city's best prosecutors on these cases, which can become very high-profile. But you may want to think about it. I'm handing over to you a case involving assault on a child. You can work on that and see how you do."

"I assure you I can handle the work."

"Oh, I'm certain of that. I don't doubt your ability in the slightest. Quite the opposite—that's why I thought of you. But I think you should feel out what it's like to see abuse, and deal with it day in and day out, before you actually make a commitment to become part of this team. It's rough stuff, very ugly."

Nate's mouth twisted at the irony of the attorney's words, for he remembered, long ago, dealing with pain day in and day out under his father's roof without any choice at all. But all he said was, "Thank you very much."

"No problem." Jeffers stood and stretched his head and arms back, groaning a little in fatigue or weariness. "Look at this damn place, Nate. It's neat as can be. My office looks like my file cabinet exploded. Do you get a maid to come in here or what?"

Nate forced out a smile, forced himself to look normal. "I can come in and do your office. For a fee, naturally."

"No thanks. I always say, if everything's all over my

desk in plain sight, I won't lose anything.'' His grin easily cut a decade off his forty-five years. "Listen, you need to come by one of these weekends now that the weather is on the steady improve. Simone's been asking about you.''

Nate's smile felt more natural at the mention of Jeffers's sweet but mischievous wife. "Because she misses me or because she's got a girlfriend she wants to set me up with?''

Jeffers spread out his hands, palms up. "I didn't say a word.''

"You didn't have to." Nate stood to open the door for his friend. "I will come by, but be sure to tell her it's for the mere pleasure of *her* company.''

"She'll love it.'' Jeffers moved toward the door, then hesitated. "Come by my office when you get a minute and grab that case file, all right? I'm happy you're interested.''

When Jeffers left, Nate closed the door, vowing to open it in five minutes. After some privacy and head-clearing. He sat back down in his chair, rested his elbows on the desk and raked his fingers through his hair. Then, in a swift move, he swiveled his chair around to stare at the busy streets of Boston from four floors up.

Out of nowhere, he'd been handed the opportunity of his lifetime.

"I'm going to have a baby,'' Josey said.

Nate stared at her for a fraction of a second, then promptly began to choke on a piece of buttered bread. As he reached blindly for his water glass and poured the liquid down his throat, ice and all, Josey just laughed. "Oh, Nate, come on. Cut it out.''

Nate gave a few more hacking coughs, drawing a few concerned glances from other outdoor diners at the small bistro. "Excuse me," he said, testing his throat. His voice sounded strangled and hoarse. He took another sip of water, then wiped his lips calmly with a cloth napkin. "Excuse me," he repeated, his dignified voice restored. Then he looked across the table, straight into Josey's dark, dark eyes. "Now," he began, as smoothly as he could manage, "what did you just say?"

"You heard me. I'm going to have a baby." She must have correctly deciphered the incredulity on his face at last, because she amended hastily, "Not right now. I mean, I'm not going to have one *now*. I'm not *pregnant*. Is that what you thought I meant?"

"No," Nate lied.

Josey fixed him with a shrewd look. "Yes, you did. Lovely thing to think, Nate. I'm not even seriously dating anyone. Did you really think—?"

"I really thought nothing," he insisted. "I had no time to think it through at all. You surprised me, the way you said it, all right? I was just surprised. I still am. Because where is this baby idea coming from, anyhow?"

"I…" Josey reached to the middle of the table and broke off a piece of the honey-wheat loaf. But she didn't put it into her mouth. She just held it, staring off over his shoulder. She sat there in silence, squinting against what must have been a spectacular sunset behind Nate, if the lights and shadows that passed across her face were any indication. But rather than turning to admire the view, Nate watched her, shocked by her revelation and anxious to hear her reasoning.

"I can't explain it, really," she said after what seemed like ages. "It just dawned on me. It just came to me like a dream. That this should *be* my dream. Having a baby. Starting a family."

Nate leaned back in his chair and studied her dreamy

expression. "So basically, it's the old biological clock kicking in."

Josey made a face. "No. I mean, I guess so, but that isn't really the best way of putting it. It's not just the biological clock. It's more than that. It was like a vision or something." She put the bread into her mouth and chewed for a moment, then said, "Like a *calling*."

Nate was beginning to feel a little uneasy. He was accustomed to a laughing, kidding Josey, and this new intense, rather spiritual talk was unnerving. "A calling? Out of nowhere? Just like that?"

"Yeah, I don't know. It was the strangest thing. One minute I was in the classroom just going about my business and the next minute—" She broke off again to take a ladylike sip of her diet cola. "I guess it's just that I want to teach my own child. Everything, not just math and reading. I can't really put into words how I feel. Just trust me that this is very real."

Nate didn't really know the correct response to all this, but Josey appeared to be waiting for some kind of reaction. All he could think of to say was, "Are you going to a sperm bank?"

"Am I going…?" Josey finally focused on his face. She wrinkled her forehead, almost as if she didn't understand the question. "No, I'm not going to a sperm bank. There's nothing wrong with that, of course, but that's not what I want." She leaned forward, and her long gold medallion dangled dangerously close to her soda glass. "You haven't heard a word I said."

"I heard every word you said," Nate countered, reaching over and pushing her glass a safe distance away. "I just don't get what you're saying. Call me stupid, but…"

"I want the whole thing, Nate. I want a family. I want kids—and a husband. The whole package. A family."

He leaned in also, so that they were nearly nose to nose. When he spoke again, it was with a lowered voice so the neighboring diners, at tables crowded close together on the patio, couldn't hear. "Since when, Josey? You love being single. How many times have we gone out to dinner and you waxed philosophical about how impossible it must be to find the right man and so you weren't going to bend over backward to do it? I'll tell you. A hundred times. At least."

"So what?" Her voice turned stubborn, almost rebellious. "So what, Nate? I can't change my mind?"

"You can change your mind, sure you can, but this is a complete about-face. It's weird."

"Oh, I'm so glad you think my dreams are weird."

Just as Nate opened his mouth the waitress arrived with their dinners on a tray. When she placed the huge colorful salad down, Josey grabbed her fork and dug in. This great revelation of hers certainly didn't affect her appetite any, Nate was relieved to see. *The real Josey is still in there somewhere.*

But just as that thought crossed his mind, he felt a prickling in his chest. He wasn't being fair. He wasn't a woman. And he wasn't Josey. Even if *he* couldn't understand ever wanting to have children, it wasn't right to belittle what she wanted. Maybe this new desire of hers was just as confusing to her as it was to him. It seemed to come from nowhere, and she definitely was taking it seriously. He was her friend—her best friend. He owed it to her to be supportive.

He took a bite of steak, chewed it slowly and swallowed, all the while looking at her. She appeared to be concentrating hard on the task of spearing a tomato.

"Josey."

She glanced up at him, her face a picture of embarrassment, and Nate was ashamed for possibly having been the one to cause it. He never wanted her to think she couldn't tell him things, personal things.

"I'm sorry. Listen," he said, grabbing her hand so she couldn't ignore him by taking another forkful of lettuce. "It's just surprising, that's all. Kids, husband... I think...I think it's wonderful. I really do. I wish you luck."

"You do?" she asked, her voice catching before she asked again. "You really do?"

Nate wondered why she was getting so emotional. Although he would prefer her not to be angry with him, she certainly didn't need his approval. But he granted it anyway. "You know I do. You're my friend, and I'll do anything I can to make sure you're happy."

Josey dropped her fork onto the glass table and turned her hand over to clasp his. A huge grin spread across her face, bright under the darkening sky. "I'm so glad you said that! You have no idea."

"I meant it."

She smiled even wider. "Good, good," she said, bouncing a little in her seat. Nate grinned, too, at Josey's old, enthusiastic, bubbly self.

"Okay, Nate," she stated, letting go of his hand and settling back in her seat. "Now I can get to what I really wanted to ask you tonight. I need your help."

"Sure, with what?"

"With my plan, of course. You are the perfect one to help me get this plan off the ground. I need you."

Nate had been nodding, but he suddenly stopped.

I need you....

She couldn't be saying...no. No.

She needed him? For—for starting a family, she needed his help? That meant— No, it couldn't be.

Panic was starting to swell in his chest.

And here was Josey, staring at him with a dangerous gleam in her eye.

Okay, he admitted silently, in all the time he and Josey had been friends, there were possibly two times he had looked at Josey's beautiful face and let his gaze roam over her sexy body and thought about what she'd be like, look like, feel like in bed. He furrowed his brow. Maybe it was more like three times. And now, right this minute, she was probably thinking that very same thing about *him*. Thinking about making love. Having his baby.

Nate glanced around the patio, but the other diners continued with their own meals and their own conversations, unaware that his best friend in the world was going to ask him to do the very thing he had sworn never to do as long as he lived. Become a father.

And she wanted a husband. Did that mean she was going to ask him to—?

Nate had to end this discussion right now. He couldn't let her get around to asking the question that was obviously in her mind. Because he didn't want to be forced to turn her down, and break her heart. "Josey," he began, "I don't think, um…"

"I know this is sudden," Josey said earnestly, picking a garlic crouton out of the salad with two fingers and crunching down on it. "But I can't do this alone. I need a neutral party to screen my dates."

Nate stared at her. "Screen?"

"Yes. I want to find the right man and start a family, but what if I pick the wrong man just because I'm in a rush? I don't think I'm that kind of person, but I still want someone sort of monitoring the situation so I don't get carried away."

"Monitor?" Nate's relief washed over him, replacing a

quick twinge of disappointment. It wasn't him. It wasn't
him, after all. He was still her buddy, her pal. "Why me?"

"You're perfect, Nate. You're sweet and responsible and
dependable. Plus, you're a good judge of character. You're
friends with me, after all." She grinned. "You've got all
the qualifications to help me find Dream Man. So I can
have Dream Family. Will you help me?"

Nate was still getting over the fact that Josey was not
going to ask him to impregnate her. Not that getting there
wouldn't have been half the fun—all right, *all* the fun—
but…well, it was moot now, he supposed. Thank God she
had been so wrapped up in her own plans; he didn't want
her to guess he had thought she wanted him to marry her.
"What do I have to do?"

"Well," Josey replied thoughtfully, "my dates will be
far more significant now. I'm going to be much more dis-
cerning. I mean, after all, I'm searching for a husband now.
I'm not going to agree to dinner and a movie with a friend
of a friend just for kicks." She spun her ice around in her
glass with the tip of her straw. "So I think, I'll check the
man out on the first date. And if he makes the cut, I'll
invite him to do something with you and me as our second
excursion. That way, you can check him out and tell me
afterward if he's someone to pursue further, or a complete
waste of my time."

"I would like to take this opportunity to bring up a couple of points here," Nate interrupted, sounding even to
himself too much like an attorney. "First of all, I'm quite
sure that on a second date, if the man likes you in the
slightest way, he will be a little confused at my presence.
I mean, another man hanging around?"

Josey opened her mouth immediately to answer, but Nate
held up his hand. "Wait, let me finish. Because the thing
is, you and I know quite well the platonic nature of our

relationship. But will a man understand this? And will a man want to share you in any way, friendship included, with another man?''

"That's easy," she replied promptly, with the same satisfied expression he was sure her students wore when they answered a tough question in class. "One very important husband-to-be trait is being so comfortable with himself that knowing I'm best friends with a handsome man wouldn't faze him in the slightest. If he feels threatened, he's no good for me. Because after I'm married, you'll still be my best friend. He'd have to get used to it right away. And we don't have to hang out with you the whole night, either," she added. "We can just have drinks with you and go out to dinner later, or meet you after dinner, or whatever. Just so we're with you long enough for a decent conversation so you can evaluate him."

"Handsome, huh?"

Josey wadded up her napkin and threw it at him. "It figures you'd fixate on that subtle compliment. Pay attention, will you?"

Nate retrieved the napkin off his lap and put it next to his plate. "I'm just kidding. The other thing is that I can't tell you if a man is right for you. Don't you think your feelings are the most important thing to go on? If you think a man is nice, and you bring him to me for approval, and I say, sure he's nice, go for it, you'd better make certain your feelings for him are genuine before you buy a wedding gown. There are plenty of responsible, dependable men in the world, believe it or not. But you can't fall in love with all of them."

"Thank you, Dr. Bennington, for the lecture on love and romance."

Nate frowned at her. "I'm serious, Josey."

"For crying out loud, I'm not a two-year-old. Being in

love is the most important thing. Because without love, everything else—all the things I want—won't mean anything." She signaled for the waitress and ordered decaffeinated coffee for Nate and an herbal tea for herself. Nate felt a wave of affection for this woman who knew him so well.

They stayed silent for the few minutes it took the waitress to return with two steaming mugs. As Nate lifted his for a sip, Josey said matter-of-factly, "I just want someone sensible looking out for me, so I'm not blinded by my quest."

"I always look out for you, Jose. Whether you want me to or not."

Josey reached over and squeezed his hand again. "I know. And guess what? I always count on that, whether I admit it or not." Her eyes, sizzling with excitement, burned into his.

At that moment, something happened to Nate. His heart did a sudden, very deliberate, slow-motion somersault, landing somewhere near the bottom of his gut. It startled him, but he didn't have a chance to ponder it for more than a split second because Josey prompted, "Well?"

Nate tilted his head back and drained his almost empty water glass to moisten his suddenly dry mouth. "Well what?" he finally replied.

"Can I count on you to help me? If you don't want to, I suppose that's all right. I can manage."

"No," Nate said. "No, don't do that. Bring on the candidates. I'll do my best."

"Thank you, Nate." And his heart might have flipped again if Josey hadn't followed up her expression of gratitude by saying, "And if you tell my parents a thing when we go to the Cape for my dad's book reading in a couple of weeks, I will smack you upside the head. I don't want them knowing about this. My mom will never leave me alone about it. And my father—forget about it.''

''You just got finished telling me how trustworthy and dependable I am. Now you think I'm going to—''

''I don't think. I know. You always gang up on me, you and my parents. All three of you, trying to outdo each other, telling me what's good for me.'' Her voice was still fierce, but her lips hinted at a smile.

The waitress casually dropped the check on the table next to Nate's plate.

''You love it, admit it,'' Nate said, pulling out his credit card as Josey offered him several bills. He pushed her hand back. ''I've got it this time.''

''Thanks. I'm serious, now. Don't tell my parents anything.'' Then she really did smile widely, and leaned down to retrieve her handbag off the concrete next to her feet before leaning over Nate's shoulder and putting her lips close to his ear.

''Anyway,'' she whispered, and her sudden warm breath in his ear startled him, ''keeping your mouth shut is for your own good. You know they're both nuts about you. If I did tell them my whole plan, they'd just try to make me marry *you*.''

Chapter Three

Josey's mother was talking her ear off. As usual. Josey held the phone slightly away from her head, angling the receiver toward the ceiling, but her mom's voice carried so far she may as well have been sitting in Josey's living room. It wasn't that her mother was loud or nagging or annoying. She was just—exuberant. About everything.

"I swear, I put this slipcover on the sofa—this slipcover that I bought for $12.99, Josey—and the sofa looks like an entirely different piece of furniture. I'll buy you one, too, honey. Just name the color—"

"Mom." Josey interrupted. "You don't have to do that for me."

"Oh, honey, your sofa is so—so…" Josey knew her mother wanted to say "ugly" or "disgusting" but was tactfully choosing her words, not wanting to insult her daughter. "So young-looking. Like you bought it at a garage sale your first year out of college."

"That *is* where I bought it."

"My point exactly, Josey-Posy. So I'll pick one up for you, and when you come to the reading, I can give it to you then. Is there anything else you need for your place? They had dish towels on sale, too...."

Josey marveled at the way her mother prattled on. To listen to her, any stranger would think she was a crazy old lady, with nothing else to do in her life but take on her daughter's interior decorating. But she was a young woman, only fifty, with many priorities, including her work at a travel agency.

"Mom," Josey interrupted again. "How's the wide world of travel? Any hot destinations I should look into?"

"Aruba's always hot. Hawaii."

"I meant hot as in popular, not hot as in ninety-five degrees. Where are the available men flocking to this year?" As soon as the words were out of her mouth, Josey regretted them.

"Actively looking, are we?" her mother asked, the teasing not quite fully masking the parental interest.

"Mother," Josey said sternly. "No. Forget I said anything. What's Dad up to?"

"Oh, you know your father." Her mom sighed with a resignation Josey knew was completely exaggerated. "It's a beautiful day outside. Just gorgeous. The Cape tourists are swarming the streets and cafés. And your father is sitting in the study, piddling around on the computer."

Josey smiled. "Piddling around" meant working on his next book, and her mother was fully aware of this fact. Josey saw her mother in her mind's eye, rolling her aquamarine eyes and shaking her yellow-blond head at her father, hunched over his desk, amid forty books filled with equations and theorems.

"So I guess he can't come to the phone."

"Do you need to talk to him? I'd be happy to make him come out of that cave into the sunshine. Do you know when he'll emerge? At dinnertime. At *sunset*."

"Well, that's only about a half hour or so from now."

"That's it. I'm getting him."

"No, don't, Mom. You used to work all day Saturday, too, don't forget, until you hired a few agents. And that wasn't all that long ago."

There was a triple rap at Josey's door, and as she called, "Yeah!" Nate walked in.

"How many times do I have to remind you to keep your door locked?" he demanded, ignoring the phone in her hand. "Any freak could just walk in here and—"

"Threaten me with a baseball bat?"

Nate grimaced. Josey chuckled, then put her mouth to the receiver again. "Sorry, Mom. Company."

"Company by the name of Nathan?"

"Yup."

"Put him on. I haven't talked to him in ages."

"We're going out, Mom. To get some food and a movie."

"Just for two minutes."

"Okay, but I'm hungry. Don't be long." Josey shrugged and handed Nate the phone. "It's Mom."

Nate cradled the phone on his shoulder and focused on her ASPCA wall calendar while he talked. Or, rather, answered questions. "Margaret!... Fine. And you?...Work's fine.... Oh, not too bad.... Derek's great.... He started classes at Emerson.... Yeah, he wants to go into TV...."

Josey flopped onto the sofa and relaxed. He'd be on the phone forever. He liked her mother and wouldn't want to be rude. So she'd talk and talk and he'd let her.

"She's fine.... She is taking care of herself, working hard with her kids...."

Nate and her mother certainly had one thing in common—concern for Josey's own welfare.

It was only her mother on the line, but he looked like he was on a business call, nodding and concentrating on the conversation. He didn't pace around the room, stretching the cord out, the way Josey did. He just leaned against the wall next to her crammed bookcase, and he didn't fidget. She imagined his manner must be a comfort to the victims and victims' families he worked with daily. His empathy showed in his face—in his crinkled brow, his tight lips.

But his seriousness made his smile, when it appeared, all the more startling, Josey thought now. Startling, but very contagious—and handsome.

"Neil, how are you doing?" Nate said into the phone, and Josey sat up straight.

"You have Dad now? Mom made him stop working to talk to you?" she said in a stage whisper, and Nate shrugged at her. *Unbelievable,* Josey thought. They both adored this man.

Not that she blamed them, of course. Nate was…well, *Nate.* Worried and concerned and intelligent and even funny, when he put his mind to it. He wasn't like any man—or any person, for that matter—that she had ever met. He willingly took on more responsibility than anyone would want to handle—his job, which probably had its rewarding moments but which Josey imagined an often depressing and sad line of work; his brother's education and general well-being, which was ironic, since Nate was the younger of the two; and Josey herself, though she fought his protective meddling every step of the way.

Interesting that she and Nate hadn't killed each other yet, Josey thought, tuning out his conversation with her father. They both often accused each other of being stubborn and strong-willed—she in her noisy, defiant way, he in his quiet, controlling one. But between them there was an un-spoken agreement of acceptance—probably because they were so alike under the surface.

And *on* the surface, Josey had to admit to herself, Nate was looking pretty good. She studied him critically. His jeans and navy-blue sweatshirt looked right on him—as right as his lawyer suits. His running shoes were beat-up—possibly the one thing he owned that wasn't in mint con-dition. He wore one piece of jewelry, his class ring. Josey had always thought a man who still wore his school ring was the sort who just couldn't let go of his carefree college years, but Nate's was a symbol of accomplishment. He never talked much about it, but she knew enough about him to gather that life had been hard for him and his brother. Their parents were dead, and the brothers had lived on their own for many years, practically broke.

His dark brown hair was still damp from a shower, since it was a two-second trip to her apartment from his. He smelled like soap and his familiar aftershave. Josey didn't know the brand, but was sure that at any time in the future, no matter where she was, she'd be able to recognize it and connect it to this man.

Why was she getting so mushy all of a sudden? She jumped up off the couch, a sudden movement that earned her a reproachful look from Nate. She pointed to her watch. ''Hey you, time's a-wastin'. Give me the phone.''

Nate hastily formed some kind of closing remarks before Josey snatched the receiver back from him. ''Dad?''

''Hi, Josey.'' He sounded distracted, but Josey wasn't insulted. It wasn't unusual for him to have many thoughts going around in his head at once. The mistake would be to take offense and ask him what he was thinking, so that he'd bombard her with mathematical problems he was trying to solve.

"Dad, you'd better quit for the day and take Mom out to dinner."

"Why, is she angry at me?"

Josey sighed. If her father wasn't the classic absent-minded professor, she didn't know who was. She was positive her mother had been pestering him all day to leave his desk, but he was so wrapped up in what he was doing that he didn't give her imploring much thought. Luckily, her mother loved him so much it would never really matter.

"Believe me. Just go, Dad."

"I will. And you have fun, too, Josey. We'll see you for the reading."

"Can't wait, Dad. I love you. Tell Mom I love her, too. I would have told her myself but she just had to talk to Nate."

"I hope he's keeping you out of trouble."

"Who's ever been able to keep me out of trouble?"

"Nobody," her father answered with a laugh. "But I'm hoping he can keep an eye on my wildest girl."

"I'm your *only* girl."

They said their goodbyes and Josey hung up the phone with a dramatic sigh. "Ah, my parents. Sorry about that, Nate."

"Don't apologize. They're great."

"If that's how you feel, I'm just going to give them your phone number. Then my mother can call *you* at all hours of the day. Maybe she'll buy you some new dish towels." Josey giant-stepped across the living room and grabbed her bomber jacket—worn out enough to give the impression that it *had* gone through a war—off the lopsided rack in the corner. "You're to keep an eye on me. Keep me out of trouble."

"So I'm told. By both your parents. What have you ever

done in your life that would make them think you need me?''

"Absolutely nothing.'' Josey pushed her arms into her jacket sleeves. "Whatever you've heard, it's a big fat rumor.'' She stood in the middle of the room and tried to compose her face into an innocent, good-girl expression.

Nate reached over her head and, with both hands, adjusted an imaginary halo.

"Yes, that's perfect,'' he said. "An angel in leather.''

He stared straight into her face, from very *close* to her face, a half smile playing on his mouth. The skin on Josey's upper lip grew moist. Then she shook her head quickly.

"In your dreams, Bennington,'' she retorted. She crossed the room, flung open the door and made a grand, sweeping gesture with her arm. "After you, sir.''

The video store was a mob scene. Customers were wandering the aisles in search of the perfect viewing experience. Couples were arguing and bargaining, trying to choose between action films and romantic comedies. Nate had pushed into the store ahead of Josey, and as he made his way to the New Releases section—saying "excuse me'' over and over—he turned and rolled his eyes at Josey.

She grinned back. "The Saturday night scene,'' she said. "Hey, pick something fast. We still have to get the Chinese food.''

"No problem. Give me sixty seconds,'' Nate replied, reaching the section. Josey always let him choose the movie. Usually he selected exactly what she would have chosen, anyhow. And if the flick turned out to be a real stinker, she still had a blast with Nate, making fun of it the whole way through, sometimes even muting the sound so they could create their own hilarious and racy dialogue. Movie nights with Nate were never disappointing.

While he scanned the shelves, Josey scanned the clientele. It was mostly date night in here, but she figured it wouldn't hurt to check people out. And just as she was thinking this, she spied a man in Foreign Films, reading the back of a video box.

His trench coat gaped open to reveal a smoke-gray suit. His trouser legs were slightly rumpled, as if he'd been sitting at a desk all day. He was leaning on the shelf comfortably, seeming in no rush to make up his mind. Josey craned her neck to see his left hand under the box he was reading.

No wedding ring.

"I made a decision."

Josey whirled at the sound of Nate's voice close to her ear. "You scared me!"

"I'm sorry, but you…" His eyes traveled to where she had been staring. "Ah, I was picking a movie, but you were busy checking out the merchandise yourself."

Josey poked him in the arm. "I was just looking, that's all." The man glanced up then, catching her watching him, and she felt stupid for about two seconds while he held her gaze. Then he smiled amicably. But when he glanced behind her, his smile dissolved into a slight frown and he went back to his video.

Josey turned and saw Nate glaring in the man's direction. She pushed him behind a big Disney display.

"What is wrong with you, Nate? You're going to ruin things for me." If she peeked over Minnie Mouse's head, she could check the man out without him seeing her.

"What things? You don't have any 'things' with that guy. You don't even know who the hell he is. Or do you?"

"No, I don't. Why are you being so negative? Don't you remember my plan? Well, I may have my first candidate."

"That guy?" Nate scowled. "You look at him for twenty seconds and you've decided he's perfect?"

"He has potential, that's all I'm saying."

"*What* potential, for crying out loud?"

Josey felt herself getting defensive. She *would* be uncomfortable going up to a total stranger and starting a conversation—and trying to make a date—in a video store. Most of her dates were men she already knew via friends or relatives, or had met previously at gatherings of some kind. But there was this urgency in her she couldn't explain…and here it was, one week after telling Nate her plan, and she had no date. No life-changing possibilities. She had to take some kind of step here.

"He's in the foreign films section," she stated, her gaze darting from Nate's wry face to the man and back again. "Which is frequented by the more intelligent, educated person, I'd say."

"The only thing it means," Nate replied dryly, "is that he can read subtitles. That would require, maybe, a third-grade education at the most."

Josey was determined to make Nate agree with her. "Look at him. He's dressed like a—like a *lawyer*."

"Or a used-car salesman. Or a porn mag publisher. Or a mobster."

"Why are you making this difficult for me?"

"Because of the way you're going about this, Josey. You're checking him out mechanically. Scientifically. You haven't even said he's cute or handsome."

Josey peered back at the man. He put the video box back, behind the long white band of elastic that stretched from one end of the shelf to the other, holding the videos in place. He moved one long finger along the row of titles, selected another, pulled it out from behind the elastic and examined it. His blond hair was cropped short, almost in a military style. His face was all-American boy-next-door, but otherwise nondescript. She wasn't about to admit that to Nate, however. After all, the man wasn't ugly. "He's perfectly nice looking," she finally said.

"Perfectly nice looking. That's strong. Why don't you just go up to him and ask him to marry you right now? Obviously, from what we've seen, he's the man for you. Maybe you can catch a justice of the peace at this hour. I'll go along, be a witness—"

"Oh, will you stop it? When did you become so sarcastic?" Exasperated, Josey continued, "Go pay for that. Go stand somewhere else. I don't want him to think I'm *with* you."

Nate's mouth dropped open. "Are you kidding me? I—"

"Nate!" Josey's words sounded to her own ears a lot like whining. "You promised you'd help me."

"I didn't promise this."

"Okay, this is an extenuating circumstance. I didn't come here looking for a date. Please just don't mess this up."

They stared at each other with an obstinate clash of wills. Nate never let her win. He shouldn't let her win now, he thought. He couldn't understand why he was so against this—walking away so Josey could make a date with a decent-looking, probably perfectly nice guy. But something in the back of his mind nagged him, pushing and pulling at him, telling him it was a bad idea and he should stop her. *Dammit,* he thought, *she can do whatever she wants.*

"Fine, Josey." Nate started to back off, but Josey grabbed his hand and shoved him in the other direction, where he wouldn't have to pass Foreign Films.

"Nate…"

"*You're* paying for the Chinese food," he said, pointing

a finger at her, close to her nose, "and don't give me any 'teacher's salary' crap."

Josey's smile lit up her face so brightly, he half expected all the customers to reach into their pockets and purses and pull out their sunglasses. "Thank you, Nate." She ran both hands through her golden hair, then blew him a kiss. Nate stubbornly turned toward the cash register before the airborne affection could touch him.

The line was about six miles long, but for the entire time Nate stood there, he refused to glance toward Foreign Films. He wasn't sure how Josey was doing, but he couldn't imagine it was too badly. He figured that whoever the man was, he'd have the good sense to be flattered. Nate knew that if he was out alone on a weekend, browsing through movies, and Josey walked up to him, he'd be amazed at his luck.

Again he resisted the urge to glance over to see how she was faring. She'd tell him when they got outside. She kept no secrets from him.

"Next?" the girl at the register snapped, and Nate realized she'd probably had to say it more than once. He dropped the video box on the counter, but just as he went to pay the girl, an enormous clattering sound at the back of the store caused everyone to turn around, including Nate.

There stood Josey, red-faced, sheepish. At her feet was a huge pile of videos, and more were landing on the floor from the now nearly empty shelf beside her hip. As each one dropped, Josey flinched. The elastic that had held the videos in place had somehow caught on her purse strap and snapped, releasing all the boxes. It was still dangling there, next to her elbow.

Nate clapped a hand to his forehead and shook his head slowly. Josey caught his gaze, her own eyes desperate.

Then she knelt on the floor and began frantically scooping up boxes.

Nate left his rental on the counter and started to her rescue, but the trench-coated man was suddenly kneeling beside her. Nate stopped in his tracks as the man whispered something in Josey's ear, and she threw her head back and laughed. Then the two of them began picking up the videos and stacking them.

Nate grabbed the video and his change, turned on his heel and stalked out of the store, ignoring the indignant "Hey!" of the person behind him when he neglected to hold the door open. He leaned against the brick wall and inhaled the fishy smell of the spring breeze, carried from Boston Harbor.

Josey and her new friend seemed to be bonding quite nicely. He'd just wait for her here.

Chapter Four

Nate didn't see Josey once the next day, but spent the whole day annoyed at her, anyway.

And he had no idea why.

On the way to the Chinese take-out place, Josey had told him about the man in the video store—Mike or Mark or something. As they ripped open cartons of lo mein at her apartment, she'd informed him the guy lived only a few blocks away from them, on Columbus Avenue. And as Nate popped the movie in the VCR and fast-forwarded the previews, she mentioned that Mike or Mark had given her his phone number and they might go out next week.

And with each new casual revelation, Nate had vigorously nodded his head with an enthusiasm that wasn't genuine.

When he went home, he'd brushed his teeth, hard. Then he'd stripped, dropping clothes all over the spotless bathroom floor. In two strides he was in his bedroom, where he flopped into bed and turned out the light. He'd squinched his eyes shut and forced himself to fall asleep, without any thinking.

But he'd gotten up with the Sunday dawn, a pink-and-gold vision he'd passed up in favor of sleep for many years. He tried to ignore it this time, too, but it rushed through the window underneath the blinds he had forgotten to pull down, and heated his face. He'd sworn under his breath and swung his legs over the side of the bed.

A lousy beginning to a lousy day.

He attempted to concentrate on television, on work, on practicing his golf swing in the living room. On anything but Josey's voice in his head, sounding pleased about her first prospect.

First *victim* was probably more like it. That man had no idea what had hit him. A commitment-crazed, biologically ticking lunatic, that's what, Nate told himself every hour.

And forty times during each hour he asked himself what his problem was. Each time, he didn't answer, but rather swung the club with a bit more intensity than he ordinarily would have so close to his stereo equipment.

He didn't feel like talking to anyone, so when the phone rang twice he didn't pick it up, and both times the caller hung up before the answering machine clicked on. By the time evening came he'd successfully spent the entire day moping. He still had no grasp on what had caused his day-long aggravation, but by now it was out of his system.

Or so he thought.

Monday was just as bad. He arrived at the office an hour earlier than anyone else, but got nothing accomplished.

Okay, he told himself, it doesn't take a genius to figure out that I'm upset about Josey and her new video store pal. But why? Who cares who she meets and talks to? Who cares who she has a laugh with? She's free to do whatever she pleases.

Maybe that was his problem. She *was* free to do whatever she pleased, and he—because of reasons he could never control—wasn't free. And he would never be free to start the same search she had.

He didn't want to be thinking like this. He didn't want to remember anything, and he didn't want to be preoccupied with it next time he saw her for fear he'd blurt out things he'd hidden from her, from everyone.

He was somewhat relieved when Derek called and suggested meeting at the Common for lunch. If anyone in this world was grounded in reality, it was his older brother.

And Nate wouldn't have to fear breaking down and telling his story—because Derek knew the story. He had been there.

Nate had been waiting on the bench for only about three minutes when his brother jogged up, carrying a few battered books in one hand and stuffing a hot dog into his mouth with the other.

As he approached, Nate marveled at how his thirty-three-year-old brother could look so much like a twenty-something college student. He wore an Emerson College T-shirt and battered jeans, and the long laces on his basketball sneakers flopped up and down with each step. His hair was the same shade of brown as Nate's, but Derek wore his a bit longer on top and was always pushing it back with his hand.

"Hi," Derek said around bites. "I'm sorry. I was sitting in my ethics class for an hour and a half, fantasizing about a hot dog." He gulped down the last bit. "Don't worry, I'm still hungry for real lunch."

"Real lunch" meant their favorite greasy-spoon coffee shop up the street where Nate always got his salad, but he suddenly wasn't in the mood for sitting indoors. He was agitated, itchy to walk.

"No, let's get a few more hot dogs and just wander around. It's nice out."

"I thought you hated hot dogs," Derek commented as they headed across the grass toward the vendor in the middle of the Common. The old man lifted up the metal lid on his cart, sending a stream of steam into the air.

Nate pulled out his wallet and picked out several singles. "No, I just normally refuse to eat them because I know what's in them. But I don't hate them."

"Oh, that makes sense," Derek said, tucking his books under his arm so he could balance two more hot dogs and a soda can as he headed to the nearest bench. Nate followed with his own lunch.

"Nobody's making any sense these days. Why should I?" Nate asked belligerently, taking a huge bite of his hot dog. It *was* good.

"As a matter of fact, you are acting weird. You haven't even asked me how class was or if you're getting your money's worth of tuition, the way I used to always ask you. And you haven't reminded me that Thursday is three days away, so not to piss away my money until you come by to give me a check. And you haven't mocked me on my choice of food. You haven't gotten on my case about anything for five whole minutes. It's a record for you. And to top it off, you, the original creature of habit, didn't want to go to our usual restaurant." Derek paused, seemingly lost in thought. Then he looked closely at Nate. "Okay, mister. Who are you and what have you done with Nathan Bennington?"

Nate couldn't even laugh. "*I'm* fine. There's nothing wrong with me. It's the rest of the world that's gone crazy."

"Define 'the rest of the world.' Who, for example, is going crazy?"

"Josey, for a start."

"She's always crazy, isn't she? That's what we all like about her. What's she been up to? Last time she—"

"I'll tell you how she is," Nate interrupted. "She's gone off the deep end. She's like a damn cat in heat. Sorry that sounds crude."

Derek threw back his head and laughed. "I encourage crude. Cat in heat? Why?" He lowered his voice. "Are you saying she made some kind of move on you? Because if she did, I say it's about ti—"

"Me? Not me. This has nothing to do with me. We're friends." Nate's agitation level moved up still another notch. "She's on this mission."

"Mission?" Derek took a long swig of soda.

"Yeah, she's on a mission to find the man of her dreams."

"So what? She's single. She's a babe, in case you haven't noticed. She's got every right to find the man of her dreams."

Nate hastily filled Derek in on the details of Josey's perfect-man, perfect-family plan, feeling more and more aggravated with each additional word. When he got to his date-screening assignment, he was even more peeved by Derek's loud burst of laughter.

"Nate, she's got you figured out, that's for sure. It's kind of funny, actually."

"No, it's not funny. It's really not funny when I'm standing at the other end of the video store, pretending not to know her while some slob she's hitting on is drooling all over her in the foreign films section."

His brother studied his face. "Don't you think you're getting a little too worked up about this? It's probably some kind of phase. She'll slow down. She's a smart lady. She knows she can't find a husband in a month, especially when she's actively searching one out. Just go along with her for a while until she tires of this.''

''I *am* going along with her insane little crusade. It's enough to make you sick. You're right. She is a very intelligent woman. So when I see her looking at men like they're meat in a butcher shop, it's—it's embarrassing. And disgusting.''

''I think you're making a big thing out of nothing.''

Nate turned to watch a police horse clop by, its head bobbing with pride. ''Maybe I am. It was driving me nuts all day yesterday. But why should I be so upset? It's her life, after all.''

''That's right.'' Derek crumpled up the two pieces of wax paper that came with his hot dogs. ''In fact,'' he said slowly, ''maybe instead of criticizing Josey's idea, you should take a cue from her.''

Nate's head snapped around to catch a glimpse of Derek's boyish, troublemaker's grin. ''And what's that supposed to mean, oh older-and-always-wiser brother of mine?''

''Simple. Maybe you should start looking for someone to make *you* happy.''

''Who says I'm not happy?''

Derek shrugged. ''Well, I just think—''

''Besides,'' Nate interrupted, ''I'm busy.'' He stood, an abrupt movement that shook the bench. He waited a second for Derek to get up, too, then turned and started down the longer path to the station, where he could catch the T back to his downtown office. Derek fell into step beside him, the rubber soles of his sneakers silencing his footfalls, while Nate's loafer heels announced his.

''Yeah, you're busy, all right,'' Derek said in a mocking

tone. ''Busy taking care of everybody. Protecting the world from bad guys, not to mention trying to protect me from malnutrition and burnout. You're trying like hell to take care of Josey, too, and you're annoyed she doesn't listen to your wisdom. You're so busy taking care of everyone else on this planet you have no time for *you*. Or for a girlfriend. Is that it?''

''I'd say that's pretty close, yeah. Girlfriends are a lot of work.''

''You love work.''

''No, Derek. What I mean is, every thirty-year-old woman out there is looking for a commitment. Now Josey is part of that group, too. I don't want to get involved in that mess. I don't want all that.''

''Is that true?''

''Yes, it is true. I don't want a family. I don't want children. I refuse to have children. And what's more, you of all people ought to understand the reason for that.''

Derek moved off the path then, to where some fraternity-type guys were playing baseball on a fenced-in Little League field. Nate followed, and leaned on the fence next to his brother. He kept his eyes on the game but directed his comments to Nate. ''Can't you let it go? It's over, Nate. It's been over for years. Dad can't hurt us now.''

''You're wrong. Dad's not here, but we're still his blood. And deep down, we're like him, dammit. We think we're not, but we are. It's inborn.''

''No, Nate. We're different from him. We chose to leave. I went through it all, too. He was wrong, he was a horrible person. But he was him. I'm me, and I can choose to be a good person. So can you. Don't deny yourself a life because you think you're like him. You can have a wife, a family—''

''I'm through talking about this, Derek. Maybe you

should study psychology and other forms of brain scrambling instead of news reporting.''

Derek faced him then, and his voice became a little sharper, a little harder. "You're not like him," he repeated. "And look what you're doing to yourself. You're letting this get in the way of you and Josey."

Nate found it difficult to stare into the only pair of eyes that had seen what he had. He sighed and moved to the path again. They walked in silence for a few minutes before he said, "You're right. Maybe that's it. To be honest, I thought of that earlier today. I'm jealous of Josey chasing this dream of hers. It's a normal dream, a normal goal everyone has, and I'm jealous because it's something I can't have."

"That's not really what I mean."

They arrived at the Green Line T stop, and Nate fished in his pocket for change. "What do you mean?"

"I meant, you and Josey..." Derek shook his head. "Never mind. Just try not to give her a hard time. Like you said, it's only natural for her to want to start a family. She doesn't need crap from you."

"The kind of crap I give you?"

"I'm your brother. I have to take it."

Nate yanked open the subway entrance door. "I'll drop by your place Thursday."

"I know." Derek walked away, but Nate heard him mutter. "Creature of habit."

Josey was sitting at her desk, her head bent over math papers, when she heard footsteps in the hallway approaching her room, which was at the very end. All the female teachers' heels had that authoritative sound, but these steps were slower and harder. A man's dress shoes, Josey guessed, not taking her eyes off the current paper. She stopped pondering the topic when she realized she had marked seven out of ten answers as wrong. She glanced at the name on top. *Jason,* she thought, *what is the matter with you? You came for extra help last week....*

The "Hi" from the doorway startled her. She turned with a gasp and saw Nate standing there. She let all her breath out in an audible whoosh and bent to the floor, groping around with her fingers for the red pen she'd dropped.

"Nate!" she gasped. "Way to scare a person. Sneaking up on me."

"Sorry, teach," Nate said in a sheepish student's voice.

"That's just not enough," Josey replied haughtily. "Go stand in the corner."

He pretended to head to a corner, then stopped. "Do you really make kids stand in the corner?"

"I'm usually a little bit more creative than that," Josey said, retrieving her pen from where it had landed near her foot.

"What do you do?"

"Oh, if I catch you passing a note, I tack it up to the bulletin board behind me here, so everyone in the class can read it at their leisure."

"Harsh."

"If I catch you chewing gum, I make you stick it on your nose."

"Gross."

"And if I catch you cheating, I make you write an essay about how brilliant the student is that you were trying to cheat off of."

"Wow. You would have been my most hated teacher. I did all those things. Except the cheating, of course."

"I'll bet."

"But come to think of it, all my teachers were old hags."

"Nate!"

"They were. I probably would have had a big crush on you, though."

An unexpected flush of embarrassment swept over Josey. "Nate, all your teachers were probably my age. They just seemed like old hags to you at age eight."

"Untrue. I caught my second-grade teacher cleaning her dentures once."

"You did not!"

"I swear it." He pushed a student's chair out from a tiny desk and tentatively sat down in it. Apparently deciding the short metal legs would hold him, he relaxed.

"You're finished with work awfully early today, aren't you?" Josey asked.

"I was feeling pretty lousy, so I went in early and knocked off early."

"Oh. Were you not feeling well yesterday, either? I called you a couple of times but I thought you were out."

"No," Nate answered, stretching one long leg out in front of him and inspecting his pants leg. *For lint, probably,* Josey thought. "I just didn't feel like talking to anyone."

That was unlike him, but before she could start in about it, a small scuffling noise drew her attention to the door, where a little girl with a blond ponytail stood, hesitant to enter, glancing uncomfortably at Nate. She brushed a pink sneaker back and forth on the floor.

"Sara! What are you doing here so late?"

"I was playing on the swings with Joan and Courtney, and I remembered I forgot my spelling book."

"Well, then, you're lucky I'm still here. Run and get it."

Sara didn't make a move. She just stared at Nate.

"That's a friend of mine. Mr. Bennington." Josey waited for Nate to introduce himself or say something to put her student at ease, but for some strange reason—he looked as nervous as the child did. They just watched each other in a wary game of size-up.

It was Sara who broke the silence. "That's my desk," she said, her words turning forceful. "You're sitting in my *seat.*"

Nate jumped up with a guilty look on his face, muttering, "I'm sorry." He put his hands behind his back. His masculine frame towered over all the desks and chairs, making it seem like he had just stumbled into a dollhouse. Sara walked past him to her desk, knelt down and pushed her arm into it, fumbling. She slid her spelling book out of the mess, bending the soft cover back as she did so. She smoothed it out with a flat palm and then, as an afterthought, pulled out a thick round pen. She held it toward Nate. "Look at my pen."

Nate wordlessly put out his large hand and Sara dropped the pink item into it. "It writes in a million different colors," she began. "Well, actually, only about ten colors. It's on blue now, see?" She pulled out a scrap of paper from her desk, quickly surveyed it to judge its importance, then turned it over to the clean side. She grabbed the pen back and scribbled something on the paper. "There. Blue. But if you want to change colors, you just press one of these buttons down until it clicks, see?" She waited.

Josey saw Nate swallow before clearing his throat. "Um. How about green?"

"Okay." She pushed the pen back into Nate's hand. "Press the green button. All the way down. Yup. Now write your name." She shoved the paper over.

Nate had to crouch to reach the surface of the desk, and Josey saw him carefully write something. Then he pressed another button and wrote again, then switched colors and wrote again, and again.

Sara leaned over and smiled triumphantly. She held up

the paper for Josey to see. Nate had written "I like this pen" in red, purple, orange and green. "Cool! Right, Ms. St. John?"

"Very cool, Sara," Josey said, now as uncomfortable with witnessing the scene before her as Nate seemed to be. What was wrong with him? Why did the presence of this friendly little girl elicit the same response in Nate that Josey would have expected if twenty-five poisonous snakes had slithered into the classroom?

Sara shoved her wonder pen in her pocket and skipped out, waving at both Josey and Nate. "See you tomorrow, Sara," Josey called, but Nate only smiled tightly, as if it would hurt his facial muscles to go any wider.

"Are you almost ready?" he asked then, and Josey assumed he was talking to her and not the empty doorway he was staring at.

"Yes, I can go now, actually. I only have about eight papers left and I can do them in the morning before class starts. Just let me pack up."

Nate nodded and began to wander around the room, examining the children's work on the far wall.

Josey studied the back of her friend's head as she locked the stack of papers in her top drawer. Nate had grown up with only one brother. Maybe he just didn't know how to act with a little girl because he had no experience being with young females. But, she realized, she'd never seen him with a little boy, so it was impossible to make a mental comparison.

She stopped shuffling things on her desk and sat still for a fraction of a minute. She'd never seen him playing or talking to any kids. Ever.

In all the time they'd been friends, he'd never been to school to see her when children were on the grounds. She hadn't given it much consideration before today, but the scene she'd just witnessed made the wheels in her mind spin relentlessly. Had he deliberately *avoided* coming when there were students around? Was Nate Bennington that shy and strange with all kids?

But that wouldn't be such a terrible thing, would it? Josey wondered, dragging herself out of her reverie and dropping a few teacher's edition texts and a lesson planner into her big tapestry bag. Lots of people weren't good with kids.

No big deal, she told herself as she zipped up her bag and slung it over one shoulder. But for a reason she couldn't quite put her finger on, she was disappointed.

Something told her to leave it alone, but the words were out of her mouth before she could think better of it. "Nate, don't you like kids?"

Nate, now about ten feet from her, swiveled to meet her even gaze. But he didn't answer.

"It doesn't matter," she added hastily. "It really doesn't. I just thought…"

"Sure I do," he said, the forcefulness behind his words making it sound as if he couldn't convince even himself. "Of course I like kids."

"Okay," she replied in a near whisper.

"Let's go," Nate said, moving toward the door. He got there before Josey did and went out. She followed him, clasping the doorknob to shut the door behind her. But halfway through the motion, she looked up and saw that Nate wasn't waiting for her in his usual polite way. He was already ten paces down the hall ahead of her. Her hand froze on the knob as she watched him shuffling away, his head down, scrutinizing his polished loafers the same way a kid would stare at his sneakers on the way to the principal's office.

He didn't glance back once at Josey. Didn't notice she wasn't beside him.

His abrupt mood change, his weird behavior was because of…Sara?

Because of a child?

Why?

Nate rounded the corner toward the parking lot exit, and Josey yanked the door shut and jogged to catch up with him, the click-clicking of her heels echoing in the after-school silence of the hall, her long floral skirt twisting around her legs.

She would never have imagined there was something she didn't know about her best friend.

Somehow, she was going to find out what it was.

Chapter Five

"Nate! Nate, wait up!" Josey slid down the hall, cursing her shoes and the janitor for his excellent floor-waxing job. "Nate!" Her bag banged against her calf with every other step. She rounded the corner, only to catch a glimpse of the heavy door swinging shut.

"Geez," she muttered, reaching the door and pushing it outward with a mighty shove. Stepping out into the still-warm spring afternoon, she glared at Nate, who'd finally stopped, looking as if he'd just remembered her existence.

"No," Josey said, her words dripping with sarcasm. "Please. Don't hold open the door. Even though I'm carrying a ton of stuff here, I can handle it."

"I'm sorry, Jose." In one fluid motion, he moved forward and took her tapestry bag, swinging its heavy weight over his own shoulder. "It was…kind of hot in there and I'm in this suit and everything…."

"It's okay," Josey replied, instantly regretting her flippant remarks. She wanted to pry, to find out what was wrong with him.

But just as she was trying to form a polite but probing question in her head, Nate spoke again. "We should stop for ice cream on the way home. It's your turn to pick the flavor. Not the cookie dough, though."

He started to walk, his gait easy despite balancing her bag in one hand and his hefty briefcase in the other hand. They crossed the parking lot to the sidewalk, heading for the T station.

"If it's my turn to pick," Josey answered tartly, "I get to pick what I want. And I like cookie dough the best." She stretched her empty hands over her head and inhaled and exhaled deeply with each stride, savoring the faint scent of fresh new leaves mixed with the city street smells.

"I'm going to have to give you all the dough gobs then."

"Why do you think I pick it? Why would I pick a flavor *you* like? So you can hog the whole thing?" This conversation had not gone in the direction Josey wanted, she realized. But she'd been suckered in because she hated it when Nate won. And he knew she never backed down, so he'd probably changed the subject on purpose. Josey squinted at him sideways, studying his profile. Never mind. She'd find some other time to pry, when his guard was down. She wasn't likely to forget that odd scene in her classroom.

"...saw Derek today," Nate was saying.

Josey struggled to get her mind back to the present. "Derek! Oh, I miss him. I haven't seen him in—"

"That's exactly what he said about you. But we never manage to get together because you both always have homework." They clattered down the underground stairs to the station, bought two tokens and hopped on board the train that screeched to a stop at the platform.

Clutching the overhead bar, Josey continued their talk as if they hadn't been interrupted at all. "Oh, right, Nate, blame us. As if you never take work home with you. Plan something with Derek and I'll be there. Seriously. Anytime."

"Actually, I was thinking on the way over to the school that tomorrow night we could all have dinner. I'll cook. You guys can fight over who brings wine and who brings dessert. Though I vote for you bringing the dessert. You always find the good bakeries."

Josey bit her lip. "Darn, that won't work. I have a, uh…" Date, she finished in her head. Why was it weird to tell Nate this fact? It wasn't as if she'd never had a date that he didn't know about; in fact, he usually got the play-by-plays, boring as they generally were. But maybe she was a little embarrassed because now he was privy to her new mission. It was pretty pathetic-sounding to be on a husband hunt.

But he understood her situation, she told herself. He knew the whole story. There was no reason to stammer. She forced a smile. "I have a date."

Nate made a living out of anticipating what people were going to say on the witness stand, and still he didn't expect Josey to say that. He tried to recover. "A date? With who?" As the words left his mouth, he realized he knew the answer.

Josey smiled as if she thought he was kidding. "With Matt."

"Matt *who?*"

She started to look a little annoyed. "*Matt.* Video store? Foreign films?"

Nate stared at her a moment. "I thought that was Mike."

"No. It's Matt."

"When did this happen?"

"He called me yesterday. I would have mentioned it to you but there was no answer when I phoned your place," she reminded him.

"Oh."

"That's it? 'Oh'?"

"What do you want me to say?" He didn't ask it out of defensiveness, just out of puzzlement.

"I don't know."

She turned her face slightly away from him, stared at a crisis center billboard overhead and heaved a loud, obvious sigh. Nate was aware she was doing it just to make him feel guilty for not reacting in an appropriate manner to her news.

He took the bait, though reluctantly. "Where are you going?"

"Movies, maybe. I don't know."

"Tomorrow's a school night," he pointed out.

"I *know* that, Dad. Early curfew."

Nate flinched and hoped she didn't see it, or else attributed it to the sudden jostling of the subway car over something on the track. She was being sarcastic, but he knew she couldn't understand that she'd called him the worst name possible. A name cloaked by the shadows of his past, and a name he'd vowed to make sure no one *ever* called him in his future.

Of course, she was calling him nothing now. She seemed to be ignoring him, gazing out the window at the grimy, slimy underground tunnel walls as they rumbled along.

What was the big deal about all this, anyhow? Why did Josey suddenly have to be on this quest? They'd be laughing, having fun now if she didn't have this on her mind, in her day planner, on her new agenda for life. Maybe she'd get stood up.

And then he felt a stab of guilt as she continued her

silence. He wouldn't want anything in this world to make her unhappy, even for ten minutes. It wasn't fair to make her feel bad. It was what he had said to Derek—he was just jealous, that was all. Jealous of Josey because she had an opportunity to be normal.

That was all.

People got on and off at the first stop, and it wasn't until the train began moving again that Nate said, with all the nonchalance he could muster, "Well, have fun."

"Have fun?" Josey was confused. Since when was that any kind of Nate advice? Nate advice was "be careful" or "bring an umbrella" or something like that. Have fun? "Um, okay, I will. I'll let you know if he passes muster and has to move on to the Nate test."

She didn't get more than an acknowledging nod, so she let her mind drift to Matt. He'd seemed pleasant enough on the phone. She never would have called a man the very next day herself, so he must be interested....

Nate tugged her elbow gently, signaling their stop. She hopped off and followed him dutifully up the stairs to the street. A warm breeze blew a sheet of newspaper against her legs and she had to bend down and peel it off.

Again, Nate didn't wait for her. He kept up his pace, continuing up Massachusetts Avenue, not noticing her absence, but she caught up with him at a red light.

"How was work?" Josey asked him as they waited for the Walk sign. "Did you have a particularly tough case today?"

"None of them are real crowd-pleasers," Nate answered with a wry smile. "It was the usual criminal element. Why?"

"You seem…" Weirded-out. "…distracted."

"I'm sorry, Josey," Nate said, for the second time. The

light changed, and they surged forward. "I don't mean to ignore you. I have a lot on my mind."

"Obviously." Then she said no more, offering him an opportunity to explain.

"I'm kind of shifting jobs. Changing focus. I'm going to be concentrating on certain cases exclusively."

"What kind of cases?"

"Domestic violence cases."

"Ouch," Josey said with sympathy. "That's rough stuff."

"That's just what Jeffers said."

"Well, it's true. Imagine, the only place you feel truly safe is home. But for those victims, well, home is the worst place to be. What a nightmare."

Nate fell silent for a moment. When he did speak again, all he said was "Yeah" in a hoarse voice.

Josey let a few minutes and about two blocks go by before she reached out and put her hand on his shoulder as they walked. He was stiff, staring straight ahead. Poor Nate. To be confronted with all that violence—secondhand, of course, but it was probably nearly as bad. Those wives, those children... Children! "Nate?"

"Mmm?" He still didn't turn his head to look at her.

"Is it mostly wife-beaters, people like that?"

"Yeah, and...well, I'm going to be dealing with child abuse."

Josey let out a long breath. No wonder Nate had been so upset at the sight of Sara. Who knew what terrible incidents he was seeing and hearing about and working on at the courthouse now? If she had to deal with child abuse all day long, she was sure she'd burst into tears at the mere sight of a happy, healthy child.

Poor Nate, she thought again. Always worried. She slid

her hand down the length of his arm and clasped his fingers in hers. Intending to comfort, she squeezed reassuringly.

What she wasn't prepared for was the warm way his hand wrapped around hers. Or the way his grip tightened, as if rather than him being the passive recipient, it had been his idea to grab *her* hand. His footsteps slowed, and her own steps matched his stride, so that they weren't walking each other home now, they were strolling, hand in hand.

Like lovers.

Josey's breath caught. She fixed her eyes on whatever point Nate's seemed to be glued to, and tried to get control of her thoughts. She and Nate had taken several physical liberties with each other before, such as exchanging hugs in thanks for birthday gifts, draping an arm over the other's shoulder, even slow dancing at the last New Year's party. But it was suddenly clear to Josey that she'd unwittingly stepped over a boundary—a friendship boundary.

If she dropped his hand now, it would seem to him this was a big deal to her. She didn't want him thinking *she* was thinking of him—of them—in any other way. He had to understand that she saw hand-holding as casual and normal. And wasn't it, really? Friends, holding hands? Even the children in her class held the hands of their ''buddies'' on class trips.

Nate's thumb moved then, slowly, stroking the sensitive skin on the back of her hand in a lazy caress. The hair on Josey's arms stood on end, even in the unusually warm spring air.

That wasn't the move of a buddy.

I have to let go, Josey thought, and just as she was relaxing her fingers to ease them away, Nate abruptly stopped walking and faced her. His eyes seemed strange, scrutinizing her face as if he'd never met her before and wasn't quite sure what to make of her. She considered and discarded a hasty explanation for why she'd taken his hand. She couldn't stand the likely prospect of mutual awkwardness.

Did he feel what she felt?

She kept her lips shut tight, squelching her natural tendency to inappropriately blurt out questions. She didn't really want to know what he felt. She wanted this sudden...thing to go away. But she didn't know what to say or do to make that happen.

He saved her from that decision by speaking first. "Aren't you going in?"

"What?" she asked, confused.

"To get your ice cream."

She looked around and realized they were at the door of the convenience store. "Of course." She slid her hand out of his, ashamed of her perspiring palm, and rummaged through her bag for money. "God, I really need to cool off." Her hand froze and she could feel her cheeks turning pink. Had she really said that? "All that walking," she continued, happy he couldn't see her flushed face as she bent over her bag, "made me boiling hot." Her fingers found her wallet. "I'll run in. What flavor did you want?" she asked, handing him her bag.

"You wanted cookie dough, remember?"

Josey was so flustered now she wasn't sure she could remember her own name. "Oh, right. Are you sure you don't want to choose? You had a bad day and all..." Her words trailed off. She sounded so stupid.

"Nope," Nate said, and she saw him swallow once. "It's your turn. Nate Bennington never reneges on a deal. Especially an ice-cream deal. I'll wait out here."

Josey turned and swung open the door, and the rush of cold air-conditioning shocked her overloaded senses. She scanned the three small aisles and, spying the freezer in the corner, practically ran to it. She slid open the icy glass cover and thrust her hand in, the one that Nate had been holding. She grabbed the first frozen dessert her fingers trailed over, and clutched it, without withdrawing her hand. She had to collect herself, and numbing her skin seemed like a step in the right direction.

She was going to buy the ice cream and go out there and pretend nothing had happened between them. If he tried to talk about it, she would just cut him off before he said anything he'd regret. She understood perfectly well that even if a man and a woman were friends, there could still be some underlying sexual tension. Maybe it had always been there, Josey thought now, and taking his hand had been the key to finding it. But now that she had confronted it, she didn't want to dwell on it. She remembered Ally once telling her about a friendship with a man that was destroyed because his fond feelings for her had turned into love, and she hadn't returned it.

Josey wasn't going to lose her best friend over something so foolish—an involuntary physical reaction. And for all she knew, it was just on her part. Verbally acknowledging it would put an unnecessary strain on their friendship.

She dropped the fudge pop she had been hanging on to and reached toward the ice cream. Pulling out the first pint she found, she carried it over to the counter. She wiped her cold, condensation-covered hands on her skirt before paying.

When she went back outside, Nate was about ten feet from the door, reading some colorful concert posters fixed to the pole of a streetlight. He didn't see her right away. Two women in short shorts wandered past him and both smiled brightly, but he didn't appear to notice either one of them. When they passed him, Josey tried to look at him as those women did—as a man she didn't know. A random man on the street.

A handsome, sexy random man on the street.

He glanced up at her then, and the recognition in his eyes ruined her little game. She smiled and walked over, a bounce in her step. Everything was normal. He reached out to open the paper bag in her arms and peered in, his hair brushing her shoulder as he bent his head close. "Mint chip? Josey, that's *my* favorite."

She hadn't even realized what flavor she had chosen. "Oh, well," she said, casually waving one hand in the air, "you deserve it. After a rough day and all."

"Thanks. Now we need spoons. My place or yours?"

They were only a block from their building. "Actually, this heat is pooping me out, Nate. I think I'll go home and crash. Put it in your freezer, and I'll steal some another time."

"Everything okay?"

"Sure, sure."

He looked as if he wanted to say something else, but Josey thwarted his attempt by starting to move down the street toward home. They silently made it to the lobby, where they both stopped to collect their mail from their boxes. Tucking her junk catalogs under her arm, Josey yanked open the door to the stairwell. "Well, partner, this is where we part company. I'll see you later, or probably tomorrow. Or, no, not tomorrow night, I'm busy."

"Josey."

He tapped a few envelopes against his palm, and Josey's mind shrieked, *No! Maybe it affected you, too, but don't bring up the hand-holding thing. Ignore it. It's past now. It'll just ruin everything to talk about it. We'll always be reading each other's every move, we'll lose our comfortable friendship. Don't say it—*

"You know that beige dress you have? The one you wore to my firm's party a few weeks ago?"

Huh? "Yeah…"

"Wear that on your date tomorrow. With that big gold heart necklace. You'll knock Mark dead."

Nate tapped her affectionately on the nose with one finger and disappeared down the hall. Josey's hand stayed motionless on the knob, and she stood statue-still for a few seconds. Then she let out a resigned breath and addressed the spot on the floor where Nate had just been standing. "It's *Matt,* you fool."

The case file was open and papers were scattered across Nate's desk when Jeffers called him the next day. "Nathan. How are you doing with the Stapleton case? Do you have any questions?"

Questions. Well, according to the police notes spread out before him, Mrs. Stapleton had allegedly burned her eleven-year-old daughter's arm and hand with a smoldering cigarette, locked her in her room with nothing to eat for an entire weekend as punishment for not doing a good job scrubbing the dishes, and yanked her around several times by her hair, so hard it fell out in clumps. Questions flared in Nate's head, and they all started with *why?*

But he could handle this. He would force himself to handle this, because the opportunity to throw an abuser behind bars may have been the reason he'd gone into law in the first place. And Jeffers didn't really need to know that.

"Going fine," Nate heard himself say. "I was planning on swinging by your office in a couple of hours."

"Good. I want to get together with the other three A.D.A.s on the domestic abuse team and go over our other current cases with you. See you then." He hung up with an abrupt click.

Nate dropped his face into his hands. His head was pounding and his eyes were sore from lack of sleep. He had stayed hunched over his desk, absorbed in work, for many long hours last night. The slumber he did get was interrupted. He'd wakened every hour, it seemed, waiting for footsteps over his head or water running to signify Josey's return from her much-anticipated date. But each time, he heard nothing, and closed his eyes again with a silent self-admonishment, only to enter a terrifying dream world for another hour. Finally, at 5:00 a.m., he couldn't take it anymore and had grabbed a quick shower, thrown on a suit and traveled in the eerie silence of the pre-rush-hour subway to the office.

But in all that lonely quiet—his apartment, the subway, his office—the memories that Nate had fought so long had come back to haunt him. He'd avoided them in college, he'd evaded them in law school; he'd trained himself not to dwell on his past.

He wasn't like Derek. The beatings, the violent shouting, the rage weren't things that could be put aside. It was all a part of him. His *father* was a part of him.

Now, in this office, all the old feelings were being dragged back to the surface, but maybe that could be a good thing. The anger would be useful; it would help him throw everything he had into prosecuting these lowlifes. And he could leave behind the hurt every day, locked in this room, to be confronted only during working hours.

But he hadn't counted on Sara.

The little girl had spoken to him, reached out to him as if he were normal. As if there were no monster inside waiting to get out, a monster that at her age had seen and heard and felt pain he hoped she would never fathom, even if she lived to be one hundred and three.

He was frightened of her innocence, of her smiling face.

She'd held out her prized pen and he'd been shocked at her actions, at how she'd revealed her gentle soul with absolute trust. He'd wanted to shout at her, *"No!"* He'd wanted to find her parents and grab them by the shoulders and shake them hard, and scream at them, *There are bad people in this world! Be thankful for what you have and don't ever lay a finger on her..."*

Stop! Nate's eyes popped open and he realized his whole face and his hands were tight and tense. He couldn't let this happen again. Years ago, after he and his brother had fled their only home, Derek had held him every night to erase the nightmares. "He's not chasing us," he had whispered to Nate in the dark of their dank hiding place. "He doesn't even like us. He doesn't want us back. Forget him." They'd been two teenagers, yet they'd clung to each other without any embarrassment. Just anxiety and finally, some relief.

Nate hadn't forgotten any of it, but he had deliberately stored it in the secret attic of his mind. Now it was sitting in his mental living room, looming large, and he was afraid of letting it be seen by anyone—his co-workers, Josey.

Josey.

A person had no choice but to smile around Josey. She was good for him, had been good for him since day one of their friendship. She was fun to be with, filled with laughter and exuberance, and she'd brought out all the same qualities from somewhere inside him in the time they'd been best friends. But he'd never told her the truth—not because he didn't trust her, because next to Derek, there was no one he trusted more. He didn't want her to see the imprint on his soul caused by long-ago violence. She was a good person, and he wanted to be the same in her eyes. So he'd led Josey to believe his parents were both dead.

Which was fine, because his father *was* dead to him.

The intercom buzzed next to his wrist on the desk, and Nate started. He pressed the little red button. "Yes, Lauren."

His secretary's cheerful voice scratched the air. "Line one for you, Nate. It's Josey."

Nate's hand moved to the phone receiver, then froze as he realized with weariness that he didn't want to talk to her. He didn't want to hear about her date. Maybe he should have Lauren take a message. He did have all these notes to go over in the next hour and...

Nate shook his head. He was being selfish. For all he knew, Josey really needed him. For all he knew, maybe the date had been lousy and she was feeling despondent, thinking she'd never find the man of her dreams. She needed him to soothe her and suggest ice cream at his place, where he could sit with her and try to hash out plan B.

It's all right, he'd say to her, and then he'd take her hand, the way she'd taken his yesterday. He knew she'd done it to comfort him somehow, and it had worked—though not the way she had intended, he was sure. The smooth satin skin of her hand had purged everything from his mind except—

Another loud buzz made him jump again. "Nate? Should I have her call back?"

"No," he said, clearing his throat as well as clearing his head. "No, I'll take it. Thanks, Lauren." He grabbed the receiver and pressed it against his ear. "Josey?" he said in a quiet, calming voice, ready to listen to the date from hell.

"Hey, Nate!" Josey's voice, however, sounded like the Easter Bunny and Santa Claus had both paid her a visit for afternoon tea. "Can I interrupt you for a minute?"

"Well, I..."

"I know, you're busy. I'm sorry. But I wanted to catch

you while my kids are at recess. Are you available for an after-work drink?''

"I'm not entirely sure when I'll be getting out of here. Why?'' Nate added. "Are you…upset about something?'' Why did his voice sound so hopeful? "How was your, uh…''

"My date? It was great. And I want you to meet Matt. Tonight.''

Chapter Six

The trendy downtown bar was bustling when Josey swung in. The lights hadn't yet been dimmed in anticipation for the evening crowd. The clientele was laughing and bright.

She ran her eyes over every corner of the room, then sighed. She didn't want to be the first one there, but it looked as though she had no choice. She briefly considered walking around the block and coming back in, but discarded the idea. Nate was never late and—she checked her watch—it was actually seven minutes before their appointed meeting time. Too early was not her own style, but it beat pacing the apartment in a nervous state.

Spying an empty seat at the bar, Josey pounced, and when the bartender raised questioning eyebrows at her, she shouted a gin and tonic order over the blaring music. She tapped her fingers rhythmically on the bar and stopped when her index finger encountered a bit of moisture. She was definitely anxious. *About what?* she chastised herself, accepting her glass from the bartender and slapping a few singles down. Not about Matt. She really couldn't find anything to complain about. Last night, they'd seen a hilarious movie and ate some delectable steaks at a restaurant near the theater. She would have had more fun, admittedly, if the date had been a few weeks ago, before she'd cooked up her marriage-and-family plan. Then she could have enjoyed the evening for what it was—a fairly nice time with a fairly nice guy. Instead, she'd been fluttery, a bit giggly— embarrassingly so—and too absorbed in monitoring her own behavior to really concentrate on Matt himself.

At the end of the evening, he'd been a perfect gentleman and asked if he could see her again right away—tonight. Normally, Josey would never have accepted. A date for the next day, with less than twenty-four hours lapse time? A sign of too much eagerness.

But then, Matt was suddenly suggesting a drink, and her mind had zapped to Nate. Drinks with Nate. Perfect. Matt had pretty much done nothing to fail her acceptability test. So she fibbed, telling Matt she had already made after-work drink plans with her best buddy in the world, but he was welcome to come along.

It was kind of last-minute, but thank goodness Nate came through for her.

Josey flinched. She hadn't seen Nate since that hand-holding thing, but in that time she'd thought it best to try to convince herself that she'd overreacted. The heat outside, Nate's somber, strange mood, a long day in class with spring-fevered kids—all were to blame, somehow. Probably. Besides, although she could have sworn that he was deliberately and sensuously rubbing her skin, he'd seemed completely unaffected by it. So it would be easier to carry out her original plan—to pretend nothing had been unusual if he brought it up.

And he wouldn't be bringing it up tonight—not with Matt here.

In her peripheral vision, she saw the door swing open, and Josey turned her head just in time to watch Nate stride in. She felt relieved, and realized at the same instant that it was Nate she had been watching for at the door all along, not Matt. She lifted her fingers in a subtle wave, and almost immediately, he nodded and moved through the crowd to her side.

"Hey!" Josey shouted, even though he was practically on top of her. She stuck her pinkie in her ear to dull the thumping, bass-heavy tune. Then she reached out her other hand and tugged at his ultraconservative navy tie. "Loosen up, pal. The fun's just starting."

"Yes, I can tell," Nate answered with a wry smile. "Where's Mike? Late? He's already flunked. Lacking punctuality on the second date, that's just terrible."

"For crying out loud, his name is Matt! You couldn't have been number two in your law class and have such a pathetic memory, so I think you're just full of it. And besides, we can't all be as punctuality-obsessive as you. It's one minute after six. I can forgive one minute if it means he won't be racing through traffic and getting hit just to be on time for me. How do I look, by the way?"

She hopped off her bar stool and smoothed the creases out of her short black straight skirt. She tugged the bottom of her satiny lime top, and when Nate still didn't say anything, she made a face. "Oh, please, tell me more. Don't stop. I just love these wonderful compliments." Then she added seriously, "Do I really look that bad?"

"Josey, you're beautiful. You're always beautiful. What does it really matter what I think? I'm not the one you're trying to impress."

Josey opened her mouth to tell him indignantly she

wasn't trying to impress anyone, but then Matt walked in the door. Before she could signal him, he spotted her and waved rather widely, attracting a few glances. Endearing, Josey told herself.

"Hi! Long time no see!" he teased her when he reached the stool where she had perched again.

She fervently wished they'd turn the music down, and was aware that that wish made her feel old. "Yes, I could barely remember what you looked like!" she teased back.

He leaned in and she could feel his warm breath brush her cheek, near her ear. "I certainly didn't forget what *you* looked like."

Josey hesitated, knowing she should at least say thank-you, but instead she reached her arm out behind her. "Matt, I want you to meet my friend, my…" She groped at air, then turned to see that Nate had moved a few feet away to grab a beer. "My best friend," she continued with impatience. She glared in Nate's direction, even as he returned with bottle in hand. "Ah, *here* you are. Matt, meet Nate Bennington, esquire. And Nate, meet Matt—" she narrowed her eyes dangerously "—Miller."

They shook hands hard, Matt's smile wide and genuine, Nate's tight and apprehensive. Josey's concern gave way to satisfaction. Nate never backed down on a deal. This was going to work out fine.

She spotted three people leaving a crumb-covered, napkin-strewn booth and she was over there like a shot before anyone else could sit down. She slid in on the right side and glanced up at her male company long enough to see the confusion cross Matt's face as Nate confidently slid in next to her. Josey picked up Matt's slight shrug before he seated himself across from her.

A waitress rushed over and wiped the table clean with a

wet rag. Josey rested her elbows on the damp surface and gave Nate the fakest smile she could.

"What were you drinking?" Matt asked Josey.

"Can you get the lady another gin and tonic?" Nate asked in a smooth but soft voice, so the young, dark-haired waitress had to bend nearer to hear him over the din. She flushed slightly under his charming gaze.

Matt winked at Josey, but she barely registered it. Nate flirting? What was that all about? It was baffling. But, she thought as the waitress left with Matt's beer order, she'd dwell on that later. She clapped her hands together once and took a deep breath to start the conversation rolling, but one look at Nate and she forgot to exhale. His friendly expression had transformed into a face she'd seen on him before—last year, when she'd paid a visit to Suffolk Superior Court to watch Nate argue a case. She couldn't remember the exact details of the case—several counts of some kind of assault—but then, she'd seen only a few hours of the trial before the judge broke for lunch. The defendant's face was hazy in Josey's memory but she remembered the features had been distorted by his cockiness.

After the judge made a few comments Nate had stood up. He held a manila folder, which he'd tapped against his other hand. The room was silent, except for the uncomfortable shuffling of feet. He'd pivoted around, and Josey saw his face. He wasn't looking at her. He wasn't looking at anyone. He was stone, a granite statue of a man that had seen it all and hated what he'd seen. A man without compassion or sympathy—only hard, cold determination—steeling himself for battle. Then he had turned around, approached the stand and fired question after question at the accused.

Josey couldn't remember the cross-examination word for word, but she remembered the way the defendant's gestures had faltered, how his self-confident mask had crumbled, how his sure voice had cracked and stumbled over his lies. And she remembered the moment she'd been sure he would break down into tears and how Nate had turned from him in disgust and taken his seat, shaking his head and making a note on his file. More than one juror's mouth had been agape.

And now, holding her breath, she suddenly knew Matt was in for it. Here was Nate—calm, stony. An inquisition was imminent, and Josey wasn't sure that Matt—or anyone, for that matter—could hold his own when Nate began firing questions.

"So, Matt, what do you do?" Nate asked before Josey could stop him.

"I—" Matt began.

"He's a psychologist," Josey said with her most winning smile. "Isn't that interesting? I'd listen to people's problems for free, myself."

Nate looked a bit taken aback, so Josey surged on. "His office is in Brookline, up on Beacon Street, near that little bagel shop we found about two months ago—do you remember it?"

Matt was staring at her as if she were some bizarre space creature, and she became keenly aware she was babbling. The waitress placed her drink on the table, and she drained her glass in one long swallow.

"How long have you been there?" Nate asked, and although Matt opened his mouth, Josey heard her own words come out.

"He's been there six years. He moved his practice here from New York."

"Really?" Nate continued, still watching Matt, but cocking his head toward Josey to hear her better. "Well, can't blame you. Boston's still a big city, but a bit more manageable than New York, I think. And Josey mentioned you live near us, in the South End?"

"Yes," Josey answered yet again, before hastily explaining for Matt's benefit, "Nate and I live in the same building. Different apartments. Neighbors."

Matt just nodded.

"Matt, while I have you here, maybe you could help me out with something," Nate requested.

Josey nodded enthusiastically.

"I'm an A.D.A. and I'm now working with domestic violence victims. I'd like a little help in dealing with them. I've heard of post-traumatic stress disorder. Could you just outline the symptoms for me and explain them in detail? If you don't mind."

Josey opened her mouth and stopped. Post-traumatic stress disorder? Symptoms? She had no idea. Then she noticed the two men were both laughing. At her.

"Stumped you there, didn't he, Josey?" Matt asked.

"I don't know about that. For a minute there, I thought she'd just make something up," Nate added, still chuckling as he raised his beer bottle to his lips. His eyes caught Josey's, and she fought the urge to hang her head. Instead, she waved the waitress over and ordered mozzarella sticks. Nate excused himself to visit the rest room, and Josey, almost forgetting Matt was there, muttered, "I'll give *him* post-traumatic stress disorder."

Matt laughed again. "Josey, I know what's going on here. You wanted Nate to meet me. And you want me to have all the right answers, because obviously, Nate's opinion of someone you date is important to you. To be honest, I'm flattered. But I'll be fine. I think he'll approve of me."

Josey was mortified at his brief analysis. As her face grew hot, she wondered how she'd been so foolish as to think a smart psychologist wouldn't have figured out the reason behind this little gathering.

Nate slid back next to her, his thigh brushing hers, and the brief contact made her already-nervous pulse rate quicken. And Josey had one more thought before the conversation commenced again: If she made an appointment with Dr. Matt Miller, could he explain to her why she had a hard time forgetting the way Nate had held her hand?

"How was bachelor number one?" Derek asked around a mouthful of chocolate bar.

"Hmm?" Nate mumbled, touching the tip of his tongue to his upper lip as he wrote Derek's name across the next check in his checkbook.

"I said, how was Josey's new man?"

Josey's name prompted Nate to finally look up at his brother. He already regretted telling Derek on the phone this morning that he'd gone out with Josey and her date last night. "I'd hardly call him her new man," he said reproachfully. "They've only been out twice."

"Twice in two days, you said. He must be making quite an impression."

Nate tore the check out and handed it over. "There. Don't spend it all in one place." He pushed the lone stool back from Derek's kitchen counter and stood.

"Nope, just two places this week. Tuition payment and the supermarket." Derek waved the slip of paper. "I still can't get used to taking handouts from my little brother."

"It's hardly a handout. You did the same for me when I was in college and law school. Call it payback."

Derek popped the rest of the candy in his mouth and crumpled up the wrapper. "Yeah, but you had a lot of it paid for by scholarship."

"Stop it. You paid for my books, my food, my rent and

everything else under the sun. You worked so many jobs it's a wonder you remembered my name when you saw me. I promised I'd pay you back. So here it is.'' Nate glanced around the cramped kitchenette with distaste, then headed over to the sink, rolling up his sleeves. ''Forgot to do the dishes?''

''Yeah, for the past six days, approximately. Don't do that.'' But his protest fell on deaf ears as Nate turned on the faucet. ''Nate, you neat-freak, leave it alone.''

''So I can look at the same dishes when I come back next Thursday? No thank you.'' He poked around among the slimy pots and found a dingy pink sponge. ''Why can't you eat off paper plates?''

''Why can't you give it a rest?''

Nate tackled the disgusting dishes with gusto. To his left, Derek dragged out his stool and sat. ''I noticed you deftly changed the subject. That might work for your witnesses, but not with me.''

Nate knew that tone—Derek's tell-your-older-brother-the-truth-and-I-won't-kick-your-butt tone. It had been years since Derek had actually enforced it, but somehow Nate felt trapped, anyway. He let out a long-suffering sigh and rolled his eyes. ''If you're going to sit there and make small talk, at least dry.''

Derek grabbed a blue dish towel and snatched the first clean dish out of the drainboard. ''We were discussing Josey and her new man. She's my friend, too, you know. Give me the dirt.''

''For crying out loud, Derek. This is like being in junior high. There's no dirt.''

''You were supposed to administer the pass-or-fail test, right?'' Derek persisted, holding out his hand for the next dish.

''He's okay. He has a decent job. He seems to have

respect for her. He doesn't show any immediately recognizable signs of being a psychopath.''

''So you gave her permission to spend the rest of her life with him, bear his children and all that?''

''No, Derek, I did not.'' But in the white dish he was scrubbing he suddenly saw Josey, her face alive and bright with happiness as Matt slipped an enormous diamond solitaire on her third finger. The plate slipped out of Nate's hands into the soapy water.

''So what did you tell her? Or did you not talk to her yet?''

''I talked to her.''

She had called him at work early this morning before her kids began their school day. Nate had thought the first thing out of her mouth would be an impatient, ''Well?'' Instead, she'd berated him for making her look foolish, and then demanded to know why he was suddenly flirting with waitresses. It wasn't until he'd had a smile on his face at what sounded suspiciously like jealousy that she'd hit him with, ''How did I do? Did you like him?''

Nate hadn't known what to say except that Matt seemed like a nice guy. Which was the truth. Then, before he could say anything else, the school bell sounded in the background and Josey had said she had to go.

But he'd wished they could have had just a few more minutes on the phone. He had to say something other than Matt was nice. Matt was nice, *but…* But what? But lots of things.…

''What did you tell her?''

''Derek. I told her he was okay.''

''So he got the stamp of approval.''

Nate winced. Derek's persistence, though an admirable trait in the journalism career he was pursuing, could get on a brother's nerves. He handed him the dish. "Only Josey can give the final stamp of approval. It's her life, after all."

"But—" Derek forged ahead, working the towel around and around the dish until it squeaked "—if you had said you didn't like him, she would have dumped him. Am I right?"

Nate's hands ceased scrubbing for a moment. "I guess so."

"So your opinion does hold clout. Otherwise she wouldn't have asked you to be her date-screener in the first place."

"Uh-huh…" Nate stared at the closed cabinet door directly in front of his face. Then he returned his attention to the dishes. "But even if I said I didn't like him, she's certainly free to ignore me, if she really likes the guy."

"Sure, if she really likes him, you're right," Derek conceded. "And that means if she's quick to drop a man on nothing more than your say-so, then she probably doesn't really like him to begin with."

"What's your point?"

"No point." Derek carefully laid the dish on the small stack he was creating on the counter. He was silent for a few minutes, and Nate didn't bother to ask what he was thinking. He knew his brother too well to assume he'd keep his thoughts to himself.

"Maybe this whole thing is a ruse."

Nate tossed the sponge into the sink and turned to look directly at his brother. "What are you talking about, a ruse?"

"A ruse. A setup."

"By Josey?"

"Yup."

Derek's know-it-all grin infuriated Nate. "You'd better

explain right now why you think Josey, my own best friend, would be trying to…to—''

"Manipulate you? Yup. Think about it. Maybe she secretly *wants* you to reject these guys. Maybe it's all a little test to see how you feel about her."

"Why?"

"Because maybe she likes you. Did that ever occur to you?"

Nate couldn't answer. Instead he waited a beat, then said, "Josey's too straightforward to pull a stunt like that."

"I don't know, people do crazy things when they're in love."

"And how would you know that?"

"Hey, I've got women falling over my feet, calling here at all hours of the night, begging me to talk dirty to them. I tell them to back off on Thursdays, though. I don't want to embarrass you."

Nate couldn't laugh. His mind was stuck on Josey, the wheels of his brain spinning. She wasn't in love with him. She couldn't be. "And what do you suggest I do, wise guru? I can't start playing games with her about this. This is really important to her. You should've seen her last night. I was asking Miller questions and Josey was answering for him so he wouldn't say anything I could criticize later. That doesn't sound like someone who's dying for me to reject her boyfriends so she can—" he stumbled slightly over the words "—so she can have me."

"I'm not saying you should play games." That damn annoying grin was back on Derek's face. "I just thought if she did like you…well, it's just something to think about, that's all."

Nate went back to soaping up a greasy pan. "Thanks, Derek. I don't have enough on my mind already without something else making me crazy."

But what Nate wasn't about to tell Derek was that Josey's manhunt was already driving him crazy. He wanted the old Josey back, the Josey whose first priority was being with him.

Chapter Seven

"*R-O-C-K in the U.S.A.!*" Josey bellowed, horribly off-key, and bobbed her head to the beat until the next line, when she started singing along again.

The guitar took over and her goofy smile and rhythmic body-bouncing were too much for Nate, who had one hand on the steering wheel and the other arm out the driver's-side window. They were speeding along south on Route 3 toward the elder St. Johns'. He flinched at her awful intonation, and then hoped she thought he was just squinting at the bright sunshine.

"Josey," he said. "I thought you hated John Mellencamp."

"I do, I do," she agreed, reaching over and turning the radio down the tiniest bit. "But well, you know, good driving music is good driving music. That's how they should classify music in the record stores, I think. Not classical, rock, country or whatever. They should have sections like driving music, beach music, maybe elevator music, make-out music...."

"Make-out music," Nate repeated reflectively, and turned the radio down almost to silence. "Is that, by any chance, a section you'd be hired to work in as an expert?"

"Ha-ha. *No.*"

"So you're not an expert?"

"Not exactly. I know what I like when I hear it, is all," she teased.

"Well, what do you like?"

"Let's put it this way—it's been quite a long time since I heard that category of music in the right context," Josey said pointedly.

This was too irresistible for Nate to drop. "All right, what *would* you like?"

"I would like you to change the subject." She looked purposefully out her window. "Oh, what a lovely day," she said with false sweetness.

Nate would have been inclined to tease her a little more if his brain hadn't begun constructing mental images of Josey half lying on a sofa, humming along with some kind of appropriate melody, her fingers sifting through strands of hair, her breath warm on a cheek, her lips brushing against an ear....

His ear, *his* cheek, *his* hair. Nate almost slammed on the brakes in the middle of the highway that he only just remembered they were driving on. He glanced at his passenger, but she was staring out the window, lost in thought, totally oblivious to him. One thin strap on her light-blue sundress had slipped off her shoulder onto her smooth-looking upper arm. He shifted slightly, as it was getting a little uncomfortable to sit in his khakis. Josey seemed oblivious to that, too.

Was she imagining a similar scenario? They often

thought of things simultaneously and interrupted each other, and he wondered now if she wanted the make-out subject dropped because she was feeling…warm. And nervous.

Or maybe, Nate thought, tearing his eyes from her flawless face and staring at the yellow line on the road, she was thinking about Matt what's-his-name, remembering a tender moment, reliving some kind of magic touch.

Nate opened his mouth, knowing before words even came out that he was perhaps starting something he shouldn't. He never began a line of questioning without thinking it over thoroughly: his inflection, his tone, his gestures, his pauses, the possible surprise responses and his appropriate actions. He never went in cold. But now he plunged ahead anyway, with dubious confidence.

"Josey?"

"Hmm?" She didn't bother to make eye contact.

"How, uh, how are things going with Matt?"

"Oh." Josey sounded a little taken aback, then said, "Well, okay, I guess. He's a…nice guy. That's what you said to me the next day on the phone, remember?"

"Yeah, I know I said that. But I was kind of wondering, if things are going fine after a couple of dates and you two like each other, why didn't you bring him today?"

"Well, I…" Nate glanced at her again and she was looking back at him now, her face contorted slightly, her teeth working her lower lip. "I just didn't ask him," she answered finally. "This is something you and I were planning to do together, and I didn't ask him."

"I see." Nate drove quietly for a few seconds, then murmured, "I just thought, since he's your boyfriend now…"

He stole another glance at Josey and damn if she didn't wince at the term. Her reactions had been lukewarm until now, but that fleeting pained look… He was inspired. "No big deal," he added. "I thought it was… Nothing, forget it."

"What?" Josey demanded. "What did you think? There *was* something about him you didn't like. I knew it, I could tell. I know you."

Nate felt a twinge of creepiness and almost shut up for good, but Derek's voice popped into his head, his superior-older-brother tone incredulous: *"Maybe she likes you. Did that ever occur to you? People do crazy things when they're in love."*

That was all it took.

"I was thinking that you possibly didn't want to bring Matt because of that…" he paused for a brief moment, just enough to make it sound as though he was reluctant to reveal his opinion "…condescending way he has of talking, and your parents—your mom, really—would be annoyed with that."

"Condescending?"

"Maybe it's because he was nervous meeting me or nervous because he was trying to make a good impression on you, but throughout our entire conversation, he was a bit…a bit—"

"Kind of a know-it-all?" she interrupted. "Like when he talks to you, he studies you, like a psychological experiment he's trying to solve?"

She said it, Nate assured himself, *not me.* "Yeah. You thought so, too, huh?"

She caught herself then, Nate noticed with some amusement. "Oh, he's not that bad. I mean, it was somewhat…unnerving, but it wasn't that terrible. Maybe just slightly…annoying. But just barely."

Spurred on by her hesitation, Nate moved in for the kill. "Like I said, it could have been he was feeling uncomfortable, and maybe he'll drop that condescending way of talking. But when he did it with his mouth full, I really couldn't stand it.''

''He *did* do that! I saw that, too.... Of course, it was only that one time. Or twice, at the very most.''

''Come on. It was a few more than that. Every time the guy took a bite, he realized he had to immediately add something to the conversation.''

Josey fell silent, and Nate decided to wrap this up. ''Josey, I'm not being fair. You know that I'm overly polite and really into manners, so this kind of thing would drive me nuts. But hey, if it didn't bother you, that's the important thing here.'' He glanced in the rearview mirror. ''After all, I'm not the one who would have to live with the guy and eat every meal with him and talk to him for the rest of my life. You are. And if you like him enough, you probably won't even notice after a few years. If it's true love.''

''Right.'' But her agreement was less than convincing, and she tapped her fingers a few times on her thigh before turning to look out the window again.

Nothing further, Your Honor, Nate thought with relish, congratulating himself on a job well done. But when his conscience demanded to know why it had been necessary to do this job in the first place, he just turned the radio up again.

Readings weren't exactly Nate's thing, but he supposed it went well, if the hearty applause in the bookstore was any indication. The little reception following was filled with academic types, who took turns shaking Neil St. John's hand and sipping drinks. Neil looked both pleased and embarrassed by the attention.

''You did a great job,'' Nate said when it was his turn. He hoped that was the right thing to say to someone who had just finished a reading. He added, "Everyone seems…impressed."

"Thank you, thank you," Neil replied, almost automatically. "And thank you for escorting my two best girls here. They are here, aren't they?" His eyes squinted behind his gold wire-rim glasses as he scanned the faces behind Nate.

"Of course, they're here, they're—" Nate began. He was cut off by a loud "Dad!" and then Josey appeared out of nowhere, throwing herself into her father's arms. "Hey, Dad," she said again, her voice muffled in her father's lapel. "I wanted to wait and let all the important people get to you first."

"No one is more important than you," her father answered, patting his daughter's back.

Nate wondered, with a twinge somewhere in the vicinity of his heart, what it felt like to hear those words from your father while he hugged you.

Josey broke away from her dad and smiled at her mother. The youthful-appearing Margaret stood at her husband's side, looking as though she'd never once complained about his inattention, as if she wouldn't trade this moment for anything.

Josey turned to Nate. "Hey you. Let's go browse the books until Dad and Mom are ready to split."

"Sure." He offered his arm gallantly. *"Mademoiselle?"*

Josey reached over to take it, but before she could touch him, she changed her mind and rushed over to child-size shelves full of picture books. Nate watched as she knelt to read the titles. He glanced at a tiny red plastic chair, but decided not to chance it. Instead, he bent down and put a hand on the floor to steady himself as he folded up uncomfortably on the rug. He watched Josey frown as she scanned the books, pulling out an occasional title, glancing at the cover and pushing it back in. "Josey," he called. "Grab any one. What's the difference?"

"I want to find one perfect for you," she answered without hesitation, not even looking up. "Give me a minute."

That was Josey, Nate thought, watching her tuck a pale gold lock of hair behind one small ear. Doing the perfect thing for him. Finding the perfect book, going to the perfect restaurant, thinking of the perfect joke to make him laugh. And now, Nate realized, she was looking for something perfect for herself. The perfect man, the perfect family. She'd never asked Nate for anything before. But this time, she had turned to him for help. So it was his turn to deliver.

She drew a thin oversize book out of the case, ran her hand lovingly over the colorful cover, opened it and flipped through a few pages. Lifting her head, she caught his eyes and smiled, with a hint of a secret she was going to share with him.

Me, Nate thought. *Me. I can give you me.*

And just like that, as if the first two decades of his life had been erased, he was thinking of a future, a future that wasn't out of his reach, a future that included Josey and happiness and love.

Nate! the rational part of his mind screamed. *What are you thinking of, you fool?*

"I found it," Josey said. "This is a good book. Mom used to read this one to me all the time." She peered into his face, blinking for a second in confusion. "Hello? Are you there? Do you need some water or something? There's some over by Dad. It's kind of hot in here."

Nate shook his head. She was so near him, and he was so near telling her, *I want, I want…you. I want you.*

"Well, come back to Earth then." She reached out and gave his shoulder a little shake, then opened the book, which had an alligator on the cover. She hadn't even read the title yet when she glanced up again and said, "Mom!"

Margaret walked over to the pair on the floor, and Nate took a deep breath to mentally steady himself.

"Mom, you're not going to believe what book I found. I didn't even know it was still in print." She held the book up for her mother to see, and Margaret broke into a wide grin.

"Oh, Posy! That takes me back more than twenty years, my goodness!" She snatched the book out of her daughter's hands for a closer look. "You wanted me to read this to you over and over again, even after you'd learned to read yourself. How you drove me nuts!"

"Stop! You loved it!" Josey teased.

"Oh, you know I did. I would tell you it was time for bed but I always secretly hoped you'd beg for the story again so I could spend a few more minutes with you. And you always did."

"Let's read it now." Josey popped up so her mother wouldn't have to get down on the floor. Nate rose to his feet, too, his ankle bones cracking loudly. He looked from mother to daughter and noticed their faces, so alike, reflecting the same joy at a nostalgic moment. He turned away. He had to.

"Where are you going?" It took a second for Josey's voice to penetrate.

"I think I need some water, after all," he said over his shoulder, "and I want to see how your father's doing. I'll be right back."

He walked away, and kept walking, past the shelves, past Neil and his cohorts and fans, past the cashier, all the way out into the mall, where he sat on a bench. Then he allowed himself to look back at Josey and her pretty blond mother, huddled together, smiling. From this distance, they looked like sisters. No, they looked like the same person in two stages of life, side by side. You could see the exuberant, beautiful young woman Margaret had been and the lovely mature woman Josey would become.

Nate pounded his fists on his knees once. There was no denying who Josey was: a woman destined to become a mother, a wonderful mother. And there was no question about who he was. A man incapable of raising a family.

He couldn't believe his selfishness, even thinking he and Josey might share a future. He couldn't ask her to give up her dreams for him. Then she would always feel unfulfilled. He couldn't live with himself if he was ever responsible for her unhappiness.

But damn her stupid plan. Because the problem was, he wasn't sure if he could live with himself if he helped her find love with anyone else.

Chapter Eight

Although the next month and a half flew by, Josey wished almost daily that she could grab hold of the days and keep them close. Instead, in late June, her children were again no longer her children, and as she watched them run out of the classroom for the last time—some stopping to say a private goodbye, some rushing out the door in exuberance—her feeling of loss cut deep.

She surveyed the room and sighed. Scribbled papers were scattered on the floor, left from this morning's desk cleanup. A lone navy-blue sweater hung from a peg where it had remained unclaimed since March. Instead of the buoyant hope that she might remain a significant influence in some student's memory, Josey felt left behind, rejected.

Easing herself into her chair, she dropped her head into her hands and massaged her temples with her forefingers. Summer vacation. She didn't even know how she was going to make it through the day, much less the next few months. If only she had a distraction tonight.

But that arena was empty, too, the last week or so. She'd broken things off with Matt a day after the reading, and although he'd expressed disappointment, Josey couldn't help but notice his voice was tinged with relief. She supposed he felt it between them, too—the big nothing.

And that nothing feeling was becoming a familiar one. Even though she'd tried to increase her odds by going on a few dates with a few different men in the month that followed—one a friend of a friend of Ally's, one a man she'd met on the T on the commute home one afternoon, one she'd met at a party at a neighbor's—all that came out of them was nothing. Nate had met all three, and though he never criticized them outright, he casually mentioned some insignificant flaw and gave that *look*. The Nate look of vague disapproval. He didn't call any of them a complete bastard, but somehow she came away from each conversation with a deeper conviction of how she had felt already in her heart—that it wasn't the right guy.

Now that she thought about it, she realized it was pretty easy for her to scamper away from all her prospective men. So easy that none of them lasted long enough to be considered prospective anything. It was disconcerting to discover that even before Nate gave his lame assessments, she had already decided no to each one.

If any of them *had* found her favor, would she have dropped him on Nate's say-so?

On the other hand, using Nate as her yardstick, had any of them had an honest chance at finding favor with her? Could any in the future?

A frightening conclusion fought to emerge from her weary mind, but luckily, Ally's appearance at the door stopped it cold.

"Hey!" Her friend made a big show of looking to the right, then to the left. "Are they gone?"

"Completely," Josey said, a little wistfully. Then, more strongly, to convince herself she was fine with it, she stated, "Just us grown-ups."

"That's great." Ally perched on the small desk nearest to Josey. "I love these kids— I mean it, they're my life. But I plan to have adult conversation only for the next two months. I need that." She peered into Josey's face. "Hey, what's wrong, hon?"

"Oh…" Josey's voice trailed off. She forced a smile. "Just trying to figure out what to do tonight to celebrate."

"No hot date? You've got a date every weekend, it seems. Every time I ask you to do something, you already have plans."

"Not tonight," Josey said, her smile more genuine. "It's you and me, kid. And if the hunkiest man on the planet begs me to change plans with you tonight, I refuse. We'll go anywhere you want to go."

"That sounds wonderful. I was beginning to think you were ducking me." She pretended to pout, then laughed.

"No, no, Ally, don't even say that in a fooling-around way. I've…well, I've been kind of on a quest," she admitted. "Don't say anything to anyone?"

"Like who?"

"Good point. I've kind of been actively shopping around for a man."

"As in, a permanent man?"

"Yeah," Josey said, reddening. "Not very PC, is it?"

"Wait, shh…" Ally whispered, cupping one hand to her ear. "Listen." She was silent for a couple of seconds. "Hear it? Kind of a tick-tock, tick-tock…"

"I know, I know," Josey whined. "Nate's already given me a hard time about that."

"You told Nate?"

"Why not? He's my, well…"

"I get it. He's your A-list top pick."

"No!" Josey shook her head vehemently. "I was going to say, he's my friend."

"Girlfriend, he *should* be on your A-list. He is *fine*."

"He happens to be my date-screener."

"Your what?" Ally fell into a fit of giggles, doubling over on the desk. "Are you kidding me?"

"It doesn't matter, anyway," Josey said when Ally's mirth had dissolved. "I'm giving up this stupid quest."

"Why? Not going well? There *are* a lot of duds out there."

"It's not that they were duds as much as…" Josey worked her teeth against her lower lip for a moment "…they just didn't have it."

"And you've got Nate encouraging you to go for it with these gentlemen?"

"That's the other thing. He didn't like any of them. Though…he didn't really dislike them. He just pointed out a few obvious idiosyncrasies they had."

"So he thought all of them had obvious problems?"

"*All* is a big word—it was only four. And the thing is, I agreed with him on each of them. But he was getting sort of picky. That's not like him. He's good about people in general. He gives them a chance. He's not so quick to judge."

"Uh-huh." Ally leaned in closer, studying her. "So you think…"

"So I think it may be crap," Josey said, startling herself. Then she realized she was only now about to say aloud what her heart had been telling her. "I think he's finding stupid little things wrong with everyone I've dated, and I'm willing to bet anyone in the future would get the same criticisms.''

"And why would he do that? Because he's…''

"Protective,'' Josey said automatically. "Very protective of me and the people he cares about, like his brother, Derek. Or—'' Josey stopped abruptly. Dangerous ground ahead.

"Or?'' Ally prompted.

"Or he's jealous.''

Ally made a sound resembling a squeal. "Oh, Josey! How do you feel about that?''

"I could be wrong,'' Josey added hastily. "I could be dead wrong.''

"Josey, does he have a girlfriend?''

"No. He hasn't had a girlfriend the entire time we've been friends.''

"I wonder why?'' Ally's response was sardonic.

Josey stared at her friend, who looked excited. Her own heart was pounding, she realized, and she chose her words carefully. "The thing is, Ally, when he's in the room I'm always trying to impress him. Whatever man I'm with, when I lead him over to Nate, it's only Nate I'm looking at. It's only Nate's opinion I care about. And it's only Nate I think about. The idea that he may be jealous makes me want to go and find him and…''

The two women stared at each other. After a minute, Ally touched Josey's wrist lightly. "Now what?''

"We're friends. He's so special to me. I don't want to wreck that. I don't want to lose him.''

"The best kind of lovers are friends, I think.''

"Weren't you the one who told me about that friend of yours who fell in love with you and you didn't care about him that way and the friendship went to hell?''

"People are all different, Jose. Relationships are different. And this will be different if he feels the same way you do. And you have plenty of clues, right?''

"Oh, Ally, what if I'm wrong? He hasn't said anything, after all.''

"I don't know. It would hurt. But, my God, Josey, what if you're right and neither of you ever says it?''

Nate dropped his pencil on the desk blotter and rubbed his eyes. It was 10:00 p.m. He'd been at work for hours on the Stapleton case and there were hours more to be filled. His secretary had fetched him a submarine sandwich from the coffee shop downstairs before she left for the evening, and he'd eaten it ages ago. His weary body was getting hungry again. But the shop would be closed at this hour, and Nate couldn't work up any excitement for more take-out. Besides, the details of this case—including the emergency room doctor's report to the police—made his stomach turn. The child had since been turned over to foster parents, and Nate trusted that was a better situation than remaining at home, scared out of her mind, and even worse, not having a sibling with whom to hide and plot escape.

The jury had been selected today to decide Mrs. Stapleton's fate with regard to the charges against her—multiple counts of assault and battery and neglect. How far this had gone before anyone caught on! Nate thought with a pang, clenching his hands into fists. There was so much evidence.... But what hadn't the child told the psychologist assigned to the case? What had she left out? How much?

"Monday," he said out loud. Monday he would begin his case. He would tell the jury what life felt like for this girl.

It almost wasn't worth going home at midnight, only to return to the office first thing in the morning. He might as well camp out on the sofa here. Maybe he could call Josey, ask her to run over a change of clothes and his toothbrush or something. She did have a key to his place.

He put his hand on the receiver and then withdrew it. No, it was late and he didn't want her traveling across town alone at night. He'd offer to pay for a cab, and he knew she'd agree and then stubbornly hop on the T, anyway, just to save a few bucks. And he didn't want her to do that.

Too bad, because if she came all the way over here, she'd want to stay for a little while. And that would be nice, to have her company. He could tell her to bring a book, and she could sit on the couch, just be in the room with him while he worked. She could even bring her pajamas if she wanted to.

Nate's mouth curled and his body warmed at the mere thought. No, she couldn't. He'd never get any work done. Even if he could hold himself back from jumping onto the couch and taking her in his arms and running his hands all over her body, he'd never be able to concentrate on work for thinking about it, and willing his eyes not to turn in her direction, and forcing his hands to stay on his desk.

And she'd probably just go on turning pages, oblivious. Every few minutes, glancing up and smiling at him....

No way. No. He didn't need her to come over here. He could work a few more hours, go home, get a little sleep, shower, change and come back in. No problem. And he didn't need the company, really. Jeffers was around here somewhere, still. He was on the Stapleton case, too, but Nate was the lead prosecutor for the trial, as he'd spent far more time with the witnesses and interviews. He'd wanted to know everything. He'd made it his mission to make sure Mrs. Stapleton would be looking at striped sunlight for a good long time. And he couldn't wait for the relief it was bound to bring his psyche.

"Nathan," said a disembodied voice, "this is your conscience."

Nate was startled, but only for a moment. At least his psyche was intact enough to make him realize his conscience sounded an awful lot like Jeffers. He pressed the Speak button on the intercom. "Yeah?"

"Go home," Jeffers said from his own office.

"I still need to—"

"Go *home,* I said. The case will still be here tomorrow. This is a terrible case, but don't try to be a hero. I'd rather just have someone conscious. Don't argue. Just go."

Nate didn't bother to respond. He reached under his desk, pulled out his briefcase and began neatly placing papers and folders inside. When he was done, he stood up, closed the case, snapped the lock shut and put both hands on the desk, leaning forward, his head drooping. From that position he could just see his leather loafers.

He remembered buying them, remembered the shock of the price tag. He had just landed his job here and knew he could afford them, but he wasn't accustomed to handing over that kind of money for something he was going to wear. He took great care of them, even though he could buy another pair tomorrow if necessary. He brought them to a shoemaker's for reheeling and polishing, but even so, he could see the wear on the tips of the toes. He unknotted his tie quickly, almost strangling himself in the process, and slid it out from under his collar. He then sat and proceeded to shine his shoes with the navy blue silk. He'd finished one shoe and recrossed his legs to buff up his other shoe when he realized what he was doing. The tie was crumpled up like a dishrag in his hand. He threw it across the room into the wastebasket, which had been emptied hours before by the building cleaning crew.

He really was stressing out. He had to relax. Jeffers was right, wasn't he? Time to leave.

No, even Jeffers had no idea what Nate's job really entailed. His job was to exorcise his memory, to cleanse his past, to heal the sickness he carried in his blood. His life's task was to work against his genetic nature. To see Mrs. Stapleton pay, and ensure that as many like her as he could get his hands on would pay. Pay for what his own father had done to him and to Derek.

Because Nate was far away from his father now, and would never be able to make him pay.

Jonathan Simmons looked out the grimy window of his new, cheap, dusty apartment. He lifted a cigarette to his mouth, inhaled greedily to the point of choking, then blew out a hard stream of gray smoke. He flicked the ash out over the windowsill. Plenty of people walked by on the street two stories below him, and he was close enough to the ground, even in the nighttime darkness, to scrutinize faces. Almost half-consciously, he looked at all the males that passed by, young and old.

He didn't know if he would recognize either one of his sons if he saw them, it had been so long. He didn't really care. This wasn't nostalgia.

The damn firm had let him go last week. Let go. What a sweet, sensitive way to put it. Let go. Downsizing. Screwed over.

Fired.

Even now, the word was like a punch in the gut—so far from the dreams he'd always had of money and prestige and success. He had brains, and when he was unleashed on the working world after college, he'd been ready for anything. He got a decent job in Connecticut, planned to settle in for a while before moving on up.

Then he got married.

Then he had kids.

Kids, Jonathan thought, were the worst thing that could happen to a man with dreams. From the moment a kid was born, he sucked you dry—clothes, diapers, toys, formula, doctors. Every penny you made vanished. After Derek was born, Jonathan wasn't able to buy himself so much as a new shirt for what seemed like years. Then Nate made his appearance, and it had started all over again, with twice the expenses, twice the burden, twice the headaches.

Angelica couldn't understand, but then, she wasn't working her ass off all day, only to see her wages get flushed down the toilet. Derek was Jonathan's mistake. Angelica had wanted a baby, and Jonathan gave her one. But he didn't want another one. Angelica had been on the pill, and said it didn't work. Jonathan suspected she'd just stopped taking it. But either way, it was clear that Nate was Angelica's mistake.

Jonathan pushed Angelica out of his brain, as he had for years. Her name was enough to make his body ache, his heart feel sick. He didn't know why; they certainly hadn't gotten along those last few years, and he knew she'd hated him. She was gone now.

This wasn't the first time he'd gotten laid off, downsized, screwed over. The first time, after Angelica was gone, it was out of left field; he hadn't been prepared. He had driven home knowing he had nowhere to go the next day, for the first time since his career began. Somehow, he'd gone from wanting the world to having nothing.

And then, those stupid college catalogs Derek had collected. When Jonathan came home and saw them spread out on the kitchen table, he'd almost lost his mind. There were two-parent families in higher tax brackets who couldn't afford to send their kid to college, and seventeen-year-old Derek had hauled those goddam things home from school that day to look at. Jonathan had rolled one up and smacked him in the head with it. *"You idiot!"* he'd yelled. *"College? Are you a friggin' idiot? Do you have any idea how much that will cost me?"*

And the kid had dared to mouth off to him. *"I have good grades,"* he'd bragged. *"Scholarships…"*

Rage had bubbled up inside Jonathan until he'd thought his head would burst. His blood burned through his veins, heating up the arm he'd lifted to hit the kid again. *"Do you have any idea what happened to me today? I lost my job! I got laid off! Do you friggin' understand me?"*

"I have a job… I can help out…." Derek had insisted.

"You're going to do more than that from now on. You're going to work full time. And you're not going to just help out. Every cent you make is going to me."

"But I need money—"

"I need money. Or you don't eat. I don't want to hear any more crap from you. Not a word. In June, I expect you to get permanent full-time hours at that grocery store, and if you don't, or if you say one more word to me, I'm hauling your dumb-shit brother's ass out of school for good and he'll work day and night. I don't care how old he is. He's old enough to work to support me now. You both are. I'm sick of you both. I've busted my ass for you for years, and I haven't gotten anything in return. It's your turn now, pal."

A few weeks later, Derek had graduated from high school. A few days later, he'd turned eighteen. And that morning, Jonathan had woken up and found both sons gone.

His financial burden was lifted. It was a relief. He didn't care where they went. The main thing was they were through sucking him dry. He didn't even bother to report them missing. He couldn't have cared less where they ended up, as long as they didn't call him and ask for money.

They didn't. They never called.

He'd found more work, and lived in the big house alone all this time. Peace and quiet. Until last week.

He was getting older. Who'd hire him now? He arranged to sell the house—but not without bitterness. He thought about selling some of Angelica's old jewelry. He was eligible for unemployment, but the idea of standing in that line was so repulsive, so against his work ethic that he couldn't bring himself to go, to fill out any paperwork.

Then he'd remembered. His two ingrate sons had skipped out without repaying their old man for everything he'd sacrificed for them. Years had passed, but a debt was a debt.

It was easy enough to find them. He could've found them years ago, if he'd cared to look. He stopped in the library, where a nice young college girl with a firm body leaned close to him for half an hour, showing him the wonders of the Internet. He told her he was trying to find his long-lost children, who'd run away from him many years before. Her eyes had filled up with tears. Moron. Soon he had all the information he needed.

Those two fools had dropped their last name, and legally changed it to the middle name they shared, their mother's maiden name. Bennington.

He couldn't locate Derek, but he found Nate. His little hot-shit kid was a lawyer now, an assistant district attorney in the city of Boston. Jonathan found his name in a few news articles, which praised him for throwing some criminal or another behind bars.

Didn't matter what Derek did. Lawyers made plenty of money.

Jonathan had hopped a bus north to Boston's South Station, taken the T to a cheap hotel, and within a few days, found this rat-trap apartment in Allston, in a building occupied by dirt-poor students and English-deficient immigrants. It didn't matter, really, because he wouldn't be here long. Just long enough to catch up with his son and strong-arm him for a little cash.

The little bastard owed him big time. He was family, after all.

Chapter Nine

Rain was pattering on the living room windowsill when Josey finished with her tutoring session. She was almost as distracted today as her small towheaded charge, Brandon, glancing up as often as he did to stare a bit wistfully through the droplet-covered glass. When her apartment buzzer went off, a startling sound, she was as relieved as Brandon, happily handing him over to his mother and collecting her hour's pay.

Josey often took on summer students, mostly kids in danger of being left back, or children for whom English was not a first language who needed to get up to speed. She usually enjoyed it. But today she vowed to give Brandon a few extra free-of-charge minutes next week, because she was so preoccupied.

It seemed strange to be preoccupied with something—or someone—she hadn't seen in ages. Or maybe that was why he was on her mind. It certainly felt like ages.

A week ago, while out with Ally, Josey had promised to tell Nate how she was feeling. It would be taking a great risk to admit that she was beginning to recognize her feelings for him ran deeper than friendship. But Ally had convinced her—and the more Josey drank, the more logical it had all seemed—that telling him was the only honest, real, correct approach. And it wouldn't hurt to test the waters, see if her suspicions were correct. See if he felt the same way about her...

The next day, a little hungover and a lot scared, she had knocked on his door, and had gotten no answer.

Sunday, same thing.

Then she'd called him at the office Monday, and Lauren told her, "He's in court, Josey. Can I have him call you back?"

"No, I'll try him later. Is he in trial?"

"That's right."

"Well, no message. I'll catch him at home."

And she'd listened well into the evening, through her open window, for sounds of Nate entering or moving around in his apartment. Nothing. She'd also tried his home phone right before she went to bed, hearing the machine ring in stereo—both in her ear and out her window. No answer. What was he doing? *Sleeping* at the office?

Workaholic Nate. That was possible.

But now it was Friday, and still no word. And still no sounds from his place. Maybe he was angry at her for some reason, though she couldn't imagine why. There had been many, many times in their friendship she thought he would be perfectly justified in being angry at her, and he'd been patient as a saint.

She glanced at the clock, though it didn't really matter what time it was. Summer meant Josey was able to set her own hours. It was nearly five, and she felt she should do something productive, so she grabbed the copy of the *Boston Herald* she had picked up this morning with her bagels, and flopped onto the sofa, vowing to read every word in the news section, now that she had the time to leisurely peruse. It was twenty minutes later that she saw the article tucked away inside.

"Jury mulls mom's fate in abuse case," the headline read, and Josey breathed, "God," as she read on:

"A jury began deliberating yesterday on the future of a Boston mother accused of twenty-nine counts of abuse and neglect, including allegedly burning her young daughter with a cigarette.

"In his closing argument, Assistant District Attorney Nathan Bennington told the jury, 'This little girl has been beaten repeatedly, locked in a closet without food, and emotionally battered. No matter what happens she will have to live with the consequences of that treatment for the rest of her natural life. Gayle Stapleton, the woman who gave birth to her and who was supposed to protect and love her, did this to her. Why should *her* future be any easier?'

"The defense argued that Stapleton, 32, was falsely accused. They claim the child was rigorously questioned and made up the abuse stories to appease the prosecution...."

Josey let the newspaper fall limply into her lap. What a nightmare. And what a case. No wonder she hadn't seen hide nor hair of Nate in days. He probably *was* sleeping at the office. Poor guy. A rough case to deal with, win or lose.

But why hadn't he talked to her about it?

If their situations were reversed, she knew she would have sought him out to talk to him about how the case made her feel, or for advice, or just someone to act as a sounding board. She was aware that he was bound not to discuss the specifics of any case with her, but that didn't mean he couldn't let her be there for him.

And just as she was thinking that, she heard what sounded like a door slam below her.

She grew still and listened. He must have kept his windows open, because the thump of his briefcase landing on the kitchen table was quite clear.

Josey stood and raked the tips of her fingers through her rumpled hair, futilely smoothing the strands. She looked down at herself and dashed into her bedroom. She yanked open a dresser drawer and pulled out a short-sleeved, thin white cotton cardigan. She pulled off the ratty black T-shirt she had on and undid the top two pearl-like buttons of the sweater before pulling it over her head. She glanced in the mirror and decided not to redo the buttons. Her collarbones seemed bare, somehow, so she slipped on a silver chain with a small silver heart that rested in the hollow of her throat. She unbuttoned the fly of her old jeans with the knee material worn thin, and then stopped.

What the hell was she doing? Josey almost laughed out loud. First of all, it wasn't as if Nate had never seen her looking like crap before. He'd probably seen her looking less-than-presentable more often than he'd seen her looking good. Second of all, what was she going to do? Go down there and seduce him? Put her arms around his sexy neck, lock her legs around his lean waist and incline her head toward the bedroom before lowering her lips onto his, tasting him for the first time as he carried her to the bedroom where he'd…

Hmm.

No, you fool, she said to herself sternly as she rebuttoned her jeans and slipped her bare feet into a pair of black ballet flats. You're going to go down there and offer yourself…purely as a friend.

She picked up her keys, slammed out of her apartment and skipped down the stairs. She raised her hand, and saw it trembling slightly. *Stop it. Stop it.* She knocked.

The door swung open, and Nate stood before her.

How many times had he stood in front of her, near her, so close? Many times. And he'd even touched her—a few times, anyway. Her hand, her hair… Those few times made her long for more. And she'd never been so close to reaching out, taking more, as she was now.

His suit was only slightly rumpled from a day's wear. He hadn't yet removed his jacket; his tie wasn't even loosened. One of his shoes was unlaced, as if he'd just started to allow himself to relax when she'd knocked. On the surface, he looked ready to work another eight or twelve hours straight if necessary.

Except for his eyes. His eyes showed his exhaustion.… He blinked a few times, but each time was slow to open his eyelids again, as if he was ready to drop. His shoulders remained square, though, and he took a deep breath before flashing a smile she suspected was forced. "Hey, Jose," he said, but his voice was so weary.

"Nate," she replied. Josey took a step nearer to him, tilting her head back a little to hold his gaze. "Are you…are you all right?"

"Sure," he said, and then again, with more emphasis. "Sure. Why do you ask?"

"Well, maybe because I haven't seen you in days."

"Sorry," he said vaguely. He kept looking at her, but his mind was clearly elsewhere, working hard wherever it was.

Probably in court.

He remained blocking the doorway, though, and Josey wondered why he seemed to be shutting her out.

"Can I come in?"

"I...Josey," he said, looking at her with a little more comprehension, "I'm not very good company right now."

She nodded slowly. "I read about the case in the paper. The jury's still out?"

Nate nodded.

"Is that why you're still dressed? In case they come back with a verdict tonight?"

He nodded again. "Yeah. It's a Friday and the jury doesn't want to miss another day of work Monday, so they're going into overdrive tonight. They could be at it for a few more hours."

"But even then there's no guarantee."

"No."

"Can I come in, anyway? I can keep you company while you wait. We can play cards or something. Or if you're hungry, I could run to the corner for take-out really quick for you." She felt like an overeager rock-star groupie, but his sad eyes said he needed something, and she was just trying to guess what it was she could give him.

"It's okay, Josey," he said then, as if he were reading her mind. "I don't need anything. I'm fine. You can stay if you want, but I'm not in the best of moods."

He stood aside to let her walk past him into his living room, but Josey hesitated. She didn't want him to accommodate *her*. She wanted him to say he *wanted* her to come in. That he needed her friendship, needed her around. What was with him? Why was he keeping her at arm's length?

Josey stepped into the living room, brushing her arm against Nate's as she did so. That slight contact tempted him out of his preoccupation, but the moment was quickly over. Josey walked to the sofa, but didn't sit down, just waited for him as he closed the door and followed her in. He stopped in the middle of the room, surveyed the dust-free floor, the bright white walls, everything but her. It was as if he didn't know what to do with this woman, now that she was here. He wet his lips with the tip of his tongue and sighed, then felt his tired eyes shut in a long, deliberate blink.

Josey was scrutinizing him, he realized when he opened his eyes again. Peering worriedly into his face, she moved closer, and Nate suddenly remembered when he'd held her hand on Massachusetts Avenue. Their palms had melted into each other, and his heart had flamed with the heat of letting her in.

But that had been a risk on his part, a careless risk. He couldn't let her in again, couldn't possibly invite her to a place where she didn't belong. She could get hurt—by him—and he couldn't bear it.

"Nate?" Josey said, and took one last step to him and wrapped her arms around his waist. He stiffened, but she persisted, tightening her hold. She smelled like cinnamon perfume and hot summer air. She trailed one hand up and down the thin cotton covering his back, as if soothing a child. Her breasts pressed into his shirt.

He didn't put his arms around her. But he released his breath and relaxed his weight against her body, just for one moment. A moment of sweet, quiet peace.

Then it was over.

He drew away from her embrace with a small, subtle step back. Josey let her arms fall to her sides and sighed.

"You've done this before, dozens of times," she reasoned. "I've never seen you worry so much while a jury's out."

"This," he said, and he had to struggle to keep his voice from shaking, "this is different. It's different."

Josey studied him for a long minute before she spoke again. "I know it's different," she began tentatively. "It's tougher than before. It's a child."

The irony of the moment was inexplicable, Nate thought. Josey understood the case was what was tormenting him, because it involved a child. What she was not even close to understanding was the real truth—that this wasn't tougher than before. That nothing was tougher than what had come before, in his life. His problem was not examining this abuse but reliving it. Reliving the nightmare on the outside chance that this time, he could wake up and forget it.

So he could be normal.

Josey was waiting for an answer. But he could only whisper his next words. "You don't know."

It was the closest thing to the truth that he'd told her about his past. But when she raised her eyebrows in a silent entreaty for him to repeat himself, he realized he'd likely been speaking too softly for her to hear. And lacking the courage to repeat it, he merely shrugged.

Then he turned away from her to aim his blank stare toward the wall, forcing his best friend to address the back of his head.

"Are you going to beat yourself up this way every time?" Her own voice was suddenly hard with anxiety, but he heard her swallow, and her next words were more gentle. "You can't make everyone's problems your own. I know that in this case you have to protect a child, but don't heave her terrible problems up onto your own shoulders. There are a lot of people out there now who'll help her, now that it's all out in the open." Josey laid her hand on his upper arm. "It's not your problem, Nate. It's not your life."

"You sound like Jeffers," Nate said then, tonelessly, still not looking at her. "You sound like everyone, actually."

"Something wrong with that?"

"No," he answered, "something's right with that. I wish…I wish I could—"

A sharp ringing sound pierced the room, and Nate's head damn near hit the ceiling. There was another full ring before he comprehended it was the telephone. It rang one more time before he snapped out of his haze and snatched the receiver from the cradle. "Yeah?"

He turned away from Josey for privacy, but the conversation was over almost before it had begun. He slammed the phone down and sat on the nearest chair. Josey plopped herself on the floor by his feet and poked him in the knee.

"Jury's back?"

"Oh," he said, his mind now on what came next, what papers to bring, who he had to phone… "Yeah. I have to call a cab."

He picked up the receiver, and as he gave the dispatcher their building's address, Josey tied his shoelace. He hung up, stood and was across the room in one step to grab his briefcase off the table. Then he focused on Josey's face, the first time he'd done so since she'd walked through his door.

"Go," she said simply. "Do what you have to do. You know where I'll be."

He was out the door before she finished her last sentence.

Nate stared hard at the glazed wood tabletop in an effort to conceal and control his emotions and memories. Consequently, he heard the jury enter before he saw them. Feet shuffled on the polished floor as they slid into the narrow space between their two benches. Papers rustled, one person coughed. When the bustling ceased, Nate tore his gaze from the table and scrutinized the jurors' faces, searching for clues to the verdict. These men and women were no longer strangers to him—they had become a kind of purgatory committee, handing down his future in the small, folded white scrap of paper that the young forewoman grasped in her manicured fingers. She held it now, for an extra-long moment, before giving it to the bailiff, who in turn, passed it to the judge on the bench.

To Nate's right, Jeffers stood silently waiting, but he showed no anxiety. His hands were crossed calmly in front of him, his body still. Nate hoped his own outward appearance didn't reveal his inner turmoil. He was itchy and antsy and sick at the prospect of letting him escape.

No, he told himself, darting a glance at the defendant's table, where Gayle Stapleton swayed unsteadily, listening to her lawyer's low whisper. No, *her.* Letting *her* escape.

He tried to mentally morph his father's face onto the spot below her hairline, but he couldn't do it. Not because he felt any remorse over it, but because his father's face was a detail pushed so far back into the depths of his mind that Nate had difficulty dredging it up.

The judge shifted in his rustling robes on the bench, and Nate forgot all about Gayle Stapleton.

Josey pushed against the heavy door, worried that the action would attract attention to the back of the courtroom. She slipped in as soundlessly as possible, grateful for her soft ballerina shoes. She slid into the nearest bench on the right, flinching as she banged her spine while straightening up against the very erect seat back. Rubbing her tailbone with her left hand, she made a perfunctory survey of the crowded room before settling her gaze on a pair of suited shoulders visible over many heads. Even if she hadn't known Nate was wearing his navy jacket, she thought she'd be able to pick him out from the shoulders alone if required.

She had told him she'd be at home, but on the way up to her place, she'd been overcome by the urge to witness this verdict. Partly so that when he came back home, she'd know what to expect. But also partly because there was something different about his case. *Different* was the exact word *he'd* used, without elaborating. And if he wasn't going to tell her himself what was the matter, she was ready to find out.

She was just being a good friend.

Which was what she told herself while she'd waited quietly in the hall outside her door until she figured his cab had left. And what she'd told herself as she studied the second hand on her watch and gave him a three-minute head start before sprinting to the Mass. Ave. T station and heading downtown to the Suffolk County Courthouse, a hulking building housing truth, justice and something she couldn't quite put her finger on yet.

The jury entered the room, and Nate turned his head to watch them take their seats. Gazing at his profile, Josey saw his jaw tighten as he clenched his teeth together. The jurors didn't seem to pay much mind to him, but if they did, they might have seen what Josey was seeing.

That Nate was looking at them as if they held the key—not to the defendant's immediate future, but his own.

"Has the jury reached a verdict?"

"Yes, Your Honor," the forewoman said.

It was hot. These old rooms were in violent need of central air. Nate's perspiration crawled down his scalp, streamed down his neck under his collar, ran down his back and pooled somewhere near his belt.

The judge half stood and leaned way down, passing the refolded paper scrap to the clerk, a skinny bespectacled man who opened the sheet, scanned its contents and then called out, "In the case of the Commonwealth of Massachusetts vs. Gayle Stapleton—" he read off the docket number "—we, the jury, find the defendant…"

Nate tensed, his whole being waiting for the release that redemption could bring.

"…guilty."

The verdict hung there in the air in front of all present for a moment, almost a living, breathing entity whose arrival was not entirely unexpected, but sudden all the same.

Then the room was a flurry of action.

Gayle Stapleton burst into loud, soul-wracking sobs, her family members cried out from the back of the room in outrage, reporters scratched on small pads and camera bulbs flashed relentlessly as the clerk continued reading each of twenty-eight more counts of assault and neglect.

"Guilty."

"Guilty."

"Guilty."

It went on and on, until even the spectators stopped listening and began to leave the room. Jeffers clapped a hard hand on Nate's shoulder, nearly causing him to leap out of his suit. When he turned his head, his friend and colleague was smiling, relief etched across his features. "You can relax now, Nate," he said in a normal tone of voice, since he couldn't be heard over the din, anyhow. "Take a vacation or something for a few days. You need to get away."

Nate threw a desperate look at the jury, at the clerk, at the forewoman, at the defendant being led from the courtroom, dragging her feet and moaning like an animal. This was the moment he'd been dreaming of with each answer he'd scrawled on his law school exams, with each textbook

Derek had paid for, with every rung on the ladder of his career. This moment was all he'd worked for—a chance to erase memories, to punish and banish his past, to be free to pursue the future.

And it didn't happen.

He made no move to pack up his papers and leave. He remained there, looking through the invisible bars of his own prison cell.

He'd never get away.

Chapter Ten

The T was jammed with loud college students on their way out to parties and exhausted nine-to-after-fivers on their way home. Josey wedged herself into a corner and contemplated the potential of the hours before her. If Nate decided not to go out with colleagues, she could take him out somewhere and buy him dinner. That is, after he spilled his terrific news. All those guilty counts—Josey had stayed to hear every one of them and had watched Nate efficiently pack up and leave the courtroom before her. It was strange to see him in action, as usual. She felt like the only one in the courthouse who knew what the handsome man in the suit was really like—how if you pried and pried, you could get him to crack a smile. She used to have to pry, but now she generally got those smiles without any intensive goading.

There was really no reason not to tell Nate she'd been in the courtroom today; he might even appreciate it. But she vowed not to, anyhow—that way, Nate could have the joy of telling her about his success, and she could be surprised.

Maybe even so surprised she could throw her arms around him, and…well, who knew what could happen next?

She glanced at the commuters surrounding her on all sides, hoping no one noticed her suddenly-flushed face. When she was finally expelled onto the platform at the Mass. Ave. station, she gulped in a lungful of warm and sticky, but cleaner air before continuing home on foot.

Her key stuck in the vestibule door for some reason, and she patiently jiggled it and jiggled it until the lock gave way. She stopped to pick up her mail, went up one flight and passed through the hallway without looking in front of her. Which was why she didn't see Nate—the Nate she was sure was still out backslapping congrats with his colleagues—slumped on the floor outside her door until she almost fell over him.

At first she didn't think it was Nate, but rather someone who was simply a dead-ringer for him, since it wasn't possible Nate could be curled up next to her door, his briefcase abandoned beside him, his hands cupping his face and covering his ears. Nor could Nate look so helpless and disconsolate after the trial's multiple victory, which Josey had witnessed with her own eyes.

But it *was* Nate, and she knew it for sure when he slowly turned his face up to her and said, "Josey."

She fell to her knees beside him on the thinning hallway carpet. "Nate, my God, are you all right? What's wrong? Did something happen to you on the way home?" She raised her hand and passed her palm over his face, his hair, his hand without really touching him. She didn't know what he needed. "Did you…get mugged or something? Did something happen to Jeffers or someone else? Did something happen back at the office?''

Nate looked at her as if she was the one making no sense. Josey was taken aback, and waited a few moments before saying, "How was the trial?" She still didn't know what had happened, but at least it would get him talking about something.

"Trial," Nate echoed. "The trial." And he gave a shrug, accompanied by a strange little mirthless laugh. "It was...it was, well..." His voice trailed off and then he squared his shoulders and said with more confidence, "Can I come in?"

"Oh!" Josey scrambled back to her feet and fumbled with her key ring. "Of course you can come in, of course...." She jammed the key into the lock and turned it, practically falling into the room as the door swung open. She dropped the mail from her arms and it slid all over the hardwood floor. She chucked her key ring and purse into a corner, and when she turned, Nate was pushing the door closed, and then he locked it with a deliberate flick of his wrist.

"I know I never lock it, I should be better with that. You're always and forever telling me to be careful," Josey babbled into the uncomfortable, unsettled air between them. And she would have gone on and on about nothing if Nate hadn't walked over to her with no hesitation and put his arms around her.

His heart pounded against her chest through her thin sweater, and his forearms were tight. One hand was splayed across the small of her back and one hand cradled her neck. He bowed his head and laid his cheek on her shoulder, and his ragged breathing warmed her skin.

Unsure of his actions, and even more unsure of the reactions he might be wanting or expecting, Josey returned his embrace.

Her blood swirled hot throughout her body, especially in every spot where their skin made a connection—especially between her legs, where she suddenly felt coiled up and tight and damp. Instinctively, she pressed a little closer to Nate. Some kind of sound emerged from the back of her throat, and she wondered if he had heard it and interpreted it for what it was—overwhelming magnetic attraction.

"Josey," she heard him say into her neck, and his voice sounded broken. She inclined her head slightly to try and get a look at him. His facial features were contorted with what seemed like pain and some kind of attempt to hold back—tears?

"Oh, Nate," Josey whispered, and his weight sagged against her. She couldn't hold him up alone, so she bent her knees and as softly as she could manage, guided them both to the floor. She landed cross-legged, and drew him in. "Oh, Nate," she whispered again. "Ah, baby."

His arms tightened around her even more, and she rocked him back and forth with gentle, soothing motions for a long, long time.

Over his shoulder, she watched the late summer sunlight coming in through the window fade to a dusky haze, and still she held him. She thought if she could hold him until the light vanished altogether and then reappeared, that would be fine. His breaths lengthened and calmed eventually, but she kept rocking him, and he made no move to pull away. At some point, she stopped wondering what was wrong, and could somehow only think of what was suddenly so right—being in Nate's arms as he clung to her.

Their sweet silence was broken by an abrupt rumbling of a stomach. Their bodies were pressed so close together, Josey couldn't tell whose it was, but she thought maybe it was Nate's. Fifteen seconds later, a weirder rumbling followed, and Josey knew for sure that one was hers. A giggle threatened to emerge from her throat. Nate stirred. Josey tried to stifle her laugh, but another rumble from someone drew a chuckle out of Nate, and suddenly the two of them were clutching each other in dual hysterics, tears streaming down Josey's cheeks, Nate's head thrown back, both laughing and laughing until it hurt.

When their glee dissolved a little bit, they looked at each other, grinning, their faces so close. "We forgot about dinner, huh?" Josey asked. "Leave it to our bodies to remind us of the important things."

As she said it, she realized her body was giving her a few other messages—very clear, easy-to-interpret messages. She shook her head and tried to ignore them. "That felt really good," she said, and her words somehow seemed to pass from her lips directly to his, so slight was the distance between them.

And without pausing to savor the novelty of that fact, she closed the distance altogether.

Josey was like some beautiful, extravagant, divine gift he felt he had no right to accept, but Nate couldn't bring himself to deny her. Not now, when her lips were suddenly on his, melting, yielding, searching and taking. She was not his, she could never be his, but for at least this moment, he just couldn't give her up. The protests of his conscience weakened and finally vanished as he drank her in—the powdery smell of her soft skin, the rich velvet of her lips. He clasped the back of her neck to draw her in deeper.

He heard a faint moan emanate from the back of her throat and he ran the tip of his tongue across and around her lips, tracing them, urging her to open to him, and when she did, and her tongue slid around his own, his eyes flew open to affirm that this was real.

It was, and she was.

He raised his other hand to caress the smooth skin of her face, and his thumb slid down to the corner of her mouth, still moving so sensuously against his, pulling away only for an instant to capture his thumb and run her tongue down the length of it before returning with even more hunger to his lips. He brought his hand away from her face, reached under the edge of her thin sweater, traveled up an expanse of perfect, flawless skin, slipped underneath the flimsy material of her bra and stroked one hard nipple with his kiss-dampened thumb.

Josey gasped and Nate stilled completely. She opened her eyes and looked questioningly straight into his. Her mouth was rosy, swollen and still parted. Her face was flushed a flattering pink. Her gaze focused first on his right eye, then his left, then alternated every couple of seconds as she, he supposed, waited for him to make some kind of next move.

He wanted to scoop her up in his arms, feel her lips on his neck while carrying her to her bed, and lay her tenderly among her blankets, ready to make love to him. His whole body ached and pulsed with need. His hand itched to reach out to her skin again.

Instead, he raised himself to a standing position—not easy with both feet and legs having fallen asleep. He flinched once, and as soon as he felt as if he could stand on his own, he glanced down at Josey, her legs tangled up underneath her, her arms hugging her small torso. He couldn't stand the way she looked up at him from down there, so he put out a hand to help her up. She stood, also a little unsteady, and dragged her fingers through her hair. Every blond strand fell into its perfect natural place.

She blinked, and Nate couldn't read her expression in the dusk-darkened room. He took two steps to the wall switch, snapped on a light and led her to her kitchen, turning on more lights as they went, like a miner with a torch striding through a black cave. He opened a cabinet with one hand and surveyed its contents—or pretended to survey. He was really trying to change the subject in a nonverbal manner.

Josey took the hint without any more prodding, but she didn't seem to mind; she produced no girlish pout at the abrupt end to their physical activity. She pulled a few dishes out of a cupboard, laid them on the counter, then opened the refrigerator door to take stock of what edibles were available.

They prepared dinner in silence—spaghetti and meat sauce and salad. They eased their bodies around one another in the small kitchen in a self-aware, but not completely self-conscious, way. Nate was grateful for the lapse of conversation, and although he knew his next words to her would have to take the form of some sort of explanation, he was also somehow fairly sure Josey would understand whatever it was he was going to say.

Josey attacked a loaf of French bread, warm from the oven, with a large knife, and arranged the slices in a little wicker basket while Nate set the table. It occurred to him to put a couple of candles on the table, but he discarded the idea as soon as he'd had it.

Things were different enough already.

Josey dished up the pasta and seated herself across from him. When he finally looked directly at her, she smiled a comfortable smile. It gave him the courage he needed to finally open his mouth—and not to put food into it.

"Listen, Jose," he began, and she laid her filled fork on her plate. She clasped her hands together under her chin and leaned forward. Her anticipatory look made Nate nervous again, as if she expected words more pithy than he was prepared to deliver. He went on, anyway.

"I won my case."

Not exactly Shakespeare, but Josey's face lit up. "That's wonderful! That's really great. I know it was important to you. And I know it was a...difficult case for you to handle." She squinted at him then, and leaned in even closer. "Aren't you happy? You certainly should be. But you...definitely aren't. Talk to me."

He could. He could tell her everything. The dinner could get cold and they could get cramps from sitting at the table in the time it would take him to tell her everything. His father, the beatings, his and Derek's escape, his reasons for becoming a lawyer and what he'd learned today—that he could really never escape. He could tell her, because she'd understand. He could tell her, because she might feel so strongly about him, she'd love him regardless of his faults. Maybe she already did.

But he couldn't tell her, because he refused to deny her the family she wanted just because he himself was doomed.

Yet he couldn't just lie right to her trusting face. There was no way he could actually bring himself to say he didn't want her.

"In the last hour, I've felt every emotion a human is capable of," he choked out. He cleared his throat and went on. "Even though we won, I'm drained. I'm worn-out. My insides are so...so *raw*. Do you know what I mean?"

"It's okay to have conflicting emotions, to feel sad when things are happy, to feel relieved when you're sad, whatever," Josey said. "You don't have to explain that. Or...I mean, explain it if you want to. I didn't mean don't talk, I meant—"

"It's all right. I want to tell you I'm not really myself. That's all."

Nate watched Josey's expression, trying to discern how she was interpreting that comment, so he could go from there. But Josey's face, usually an elastic caricature of her emotions, remained unreadable. Then her mouth curved up in one corner and she reached for her fork. "You'd better eat. All that work, and it's getting cold." She shoved food into her mouth lustily, and Nate dragged his eyes back to his own plate, not sure what was going on between them. He took a bite and realized he was starving.

They made quiet but short work of their dinner, both of them smearing slices of bread over their plates to get every last drop of sauce. A blob of it landed on Josey's sweater, and instead of getting annoyed, she laughed. The sound made Nate's heart ache. He craned his neck to glance at the watch on her tiny wrist, even though he was wearing his own. "It's late. I really should go to bed. Sleep," he added. "I have to get some sleep."

"You don't have to go in tomorrow, do you? I mean, now that your case is finished."

"I think everyone will cut me a break if I take a normal weekend for once."

"That's wonderful. Sleep as late as you can. Sleep until the afternoon. It's an incredibly liberating thing. And I'll…" Her voice trailed off.

"You'll what?" Nate prompted after a few moments.

"I'll…be around."

Nate was already worried about how he was going to control himself, his body, next time they were together. He pushed his chair back and stood. "I'll help you clean up."

"No way. All these dishes are going straight into the dishwasher and then I'm going to bed myself." She stood, too, and piled a couple of dishes together before saying,

"Do you, well, do you need me to come with you? I could sit with you or...something."

She was something. Being in her presence here was breaking him. "I'm fine. I mean, I'm feeling much better now. I'll be okay." Nate almost ran to the door and Josey followed at a slower pace. He waited there for her, to let her open it. She did, and then stretched her arms up high over her head, groaning with satisfaction from their meal. The hem of her sweater lifted to expose the creamy skin of her abdomen, and Nate stayed fixated on it until she dropped her arms and caught him staring. He stepped out into the safe territory of the hallway. "Um, well...bye, Josey."

"I'll catch you tomorrow sometime. If you need me, you always know where I am."

Josey waited a moment, but Nate made no move to leave, so she very gently closed the door while he was still standing there. Then she pressed her ear hard against the door and held her breath. She stood there listening to his silent presence for what must have been three whole minutes. Then she heard a noise resembling a sigh, but it was cut off halfway through, and she heard his footsteps retreat to the stairwell.

Josey caught her lower lip between her teeth and nodded once, then shook her head. She sat on the floor right where she was, drew her knees up to her chest, wrapped her arms around her legs and rested her chin on top.

She believed Nate was going through some conflicting emotions. She believed this case had been extra rough on his psyche and she believed his job's intense stress had finally gotten to him, causing him to seek her out here at her apartment tonight.

It was best to let him go and sort out his mind overnight

before she did anything else. Because there was one last thing she believed was certain—so certain, she'd stake her life on it.

He had definitely been on the other side of that kiss.

Chapter Eleven

Nate walked up to his front door, the same door he had walked out of so long ago with relief and fear and total reliance on his big brother. Now, he didn't knock. Years of his past were shut up inside the white, black-shuttered home, and it was his right to just walk in. He didn't feel the rough rope welcome mat under his feet, but he knew that was because he was dreaming, and you could never feel the ground when you walked in a dream.

The hall he proceeded down was empty. He passed by the louvered doors to the den, where neglected plants probably still lined the windowsill and a path was worn in the carpet from the door to the cracked leather reclining chair where his father, when he returned from work on his good-mood days, would sit and ignore everyone until it was time to retire for the evening. Nate passed the kitchen, where dishes from some distant meal not worth remembering were piled up, and he walked past the bathroom, where he used to read while the rest of the house was asleep.

Derek's room was left untouched—with colorful pennants on the walls, jeans in a heap in the middle of the floor, a huge television set he'd inherited from some friend or another.

Nate continued walking, not climbing or descending any stairs, because in this dream the rooms were spread all around him like a maze he had to wind his way through. He found his room and slowly opened the door, the familiar shape of the knob melting into his palm.

Josey was sitting cross-legged on his bed, smiling. She patted the thin blue bedspread next to her and said, "Come here!" without opening her mouth, as if her heart were calling to his.

He sat, and she wound her dream arms around his back and kissed him. Her mouth was sweet and soft, at once offering and taking, and Nate suddenly felt secure and strong. For the first time in this house, he was safe.

"I love you," he murmured against the pillow of her lips. She drew away from him in a strange kind of slow motion, and pulled back slightly to display an enormous, rounded stomach. Nate struggled with logic—had it been there before?

"Nate," she whispered, "I'm pregnant. Isn't it wonderful? Us, a family…"

"No!" he shouted, but her happy expression never wavered. She reached out a hand to him as he stumbled off the bed and tried to stand. "No, I can't. We can't. No. Oh, no…"

"Nate!" His father's voice. His father's footsteps ascending stairs—were they upstairs? "Nate!" His voice was anger, power; he was coming to get him for something again.

"Nate!" Josey's plea and his father's roar melded, twisted in the air together, and Nate covered his ears and eyes and backed up until he hit a wall.

"No, no, no, no..."

He jerked awake, his skin coated with a layer of sweat.

"God, it's hot," Josey complained, removing her blue cap and wiping her brow with her forearm before replacing the hat on her flattened blond hair.

The sun *was* beating down with a vengeance on the bleacher seats at Fenway Park. Josey's sky-blue cotton T-shirt had been rather damp since before the national anthem was performed, and now, with the Sox down 4-3 in the fifth, things were beginning to feel a little hellish. She was glad to be there, though, baking with Nate, a result of a sudden ticket windfall from Ally, who couldn't use the seats today and had called this morning to offer them to Josey. Josey had been reluctant to disturb Nate even as late as 11:30 that morning, but his eyes had lit up with her gift, and all the time they'd spent together since seemed...back to normal.

Which wasn't bad, Josey reflected as she sipped her warming soft drink. At least he wasn't so sad anymore. Now the trick was to get him to realize how wonderful last night had been—for them, for their relationship. That kiss had been...well, if it had been any kind of foreshadowing of what they'd be like as a couple, she was ready to press fast-forward and get to the even more wonderful stuff. All hesitation she'd harbored about carrying their relationship further had melted in last night's intense heat.

Speaking of heat, Josey pressed her face against her cup, the condensation cooling but a little bit gross. A bat connected with a ball with a loud pop, and everyone in their section jumped to their feet, screaming. Runners rounded bases, there was a throw to home plate…and the call: out.

"Out?" Josey cried. She turned to Nate. "Out? Did you see that?"

"That call was bull. He was safe by at least half a mile," Nate answered in his regular voice volume, while the fans around them freaked, yelling and cursing.

"Damn right. Hey!" she yelled in the umpire's direction, and after glancing around to make sure no children were seated anywhere near her, followed it up with a few choice phrases she couldn't even remember learning.

A guy in front of them turned around, a college-age kid in a ripped-up muscle shirt. "That's right, you tell that loser," he exclaimed.

Josey moaned with revulsion again before sitting back down with Nate. "Unbelievable," she said, and Nate shook his head, amused, she realized, at her. "What's so funny?"

"You." He chuckled, taking a long swig of his soda. "You take everything so personally. It was one lousy call. Just chill out."

"Hey, pal," Josey retorted, "I *paid* Ally for these tickets. I want my money's worth. It's only worth it if they win."

"Well, that's a healthy competitive attitude you've got going there."

"Oh, shut up," she retorted.

"I'll be right back," Nate said, getting up to squeeze past the four people on his side of the row. "Don't let any other man take my seat."

"I just might." She wrinkled her nose at him and he made an even sillier face back at her, cracking her up. "If he's cute enough."

Josey watched out of the corner of her eye as Nate worked his way to the aisle, turning her head completely to watch his blue-jeaned butt slide against the smooth seats of the row in front of them. She followed his dark head as he descended the concrete steps until she couldn't see him anymore.

Then she turned her eyes back to the field, but her mind didn't follow.

She was on instant replay, but not on any of the plays in this game—rather, on the events of last night, the way his lips had responded to hers, his hand on her skin, on her... She shivered in spite of the humidity. She longed for him to return and casually drape his arm around her shoulders as if it belonged there. She wanted him to brush her cheek with a kiss every few minutes, as if he did it all the time. She desired the intimacy of resting her head on his shoulder, his fingers winding through her hair, tilting her head closer to his and...

Her reverie was interrupted by Nate's return—a clumsy affair, as he was balancing a cardboard tray with hot dogs. She looked at the scoreboard and saw that the fifth inning had ended and the sixth was already half-over. She hoped Nate wouldn't ask her for a play-by-play update. He seated himself, his hard thigh brushing her bare one. "Hot dog?"

Josey considered a lewd joke, but thought subtlety would be more to her advantage. She pulled a hot dog out of the tray, holding it high to crane her neck under it before theatrically darting out her tongue and slowly licking a drop of mustard off the tip. She threw a surreptitious glance in his direction to gauge any reaction. He was looking, but pretending not to. Maybe not *quite* subtle, but she was doing fine.

She waited until the next batter took his turn, hitting a double, then when Nate turned her way again as if to say something, she took a huge bite, pursing her lips around the hot dog a bit more than she would have under ordinary circumstances. She met his gaze with what she hoped was an innocent expression, and the next thing she knew, he was asking, "How's the manhunt coming along?"

Well, she couldn't have heard him right. Or maybe he was referring to something else. "Huh?"

"Your search for the perfect man. How's it going?"

"Oh," she said, staring into his eyes. "It's over." Way over. *Especially when perfect is staring right back at me.*

"That's just as well. You can't force that kind of thing, after all."

Josey felt lost in this conversation. What was he trying here? Was he leading up to the something that she really wanted to hear? Nate polished off his first hot dog and started on his second. If he was getting to some point, he ought to be quicker about it.

The center fielder stepped up to the plate as the announcer blared his name across the stadium. Fans cheered, since he was a power hitter and had yet to smack one home in this game. Josey cleared her throat.

"You're exactly right," she began, not quite sure yet where she was heading. "I mean, I had nothing in common with any of those men, and even when I did have something in common, that wasn't enough. I just didn't...*click* with anyone, do you know what I mean?"

The batter swung hard, missing the pitch by inches.

"I think so, yeah," Nate answered, his eyes on the game.

The umpire thrust one finger out to his right. "Strike one!" he called.

"You didn't like any of them, either."

"No."

"Why? My not clicking with them had nothing to do with you. Why didn't you like any of them, really?"

Another ambitious hard swing, and a miss.

"None of them was right for you."

Two fingers. "Strike two!"

"So, if you know so much about me, so much you'd know who isn't right for me, then let me ask you this. Who *would* be right for me?"

That got his attention. Nate looked straight at her with some confusion. She plunged ahead.

"Maybe this is what I should have done all along. Just have you set me up with someone. You know plenty of men you work with, see every day. Somebody's got to be right for me."

Josey tried to keep her voice light so he would comprehend her teasing. All she wanted him to say was "me." All she wanted him to do was kiss her again.

Nate turned back to the game with a casual shrug. She couldn't tell if he was joining her game or not, but he said, "Sure, I know someone. Of course I do. I could set you up if that's what you really want."

"Okay." She grinned. "Who is this mystery man, perfect for me?"

"Derek."

The pitcher caught the batter looking. "Strike three!"

Josey blinked. "D-Derek?" Then she burst out laughing. "Ha-ha, funny. No, come on, be serious."

"Are *you* actually telling *me* to be serious? That's a first."

Josey's laughter petered out and fell flat. "Huh?"

"You like him, right?"

"Sure I do, he's great, it's just…"

"Great. I'll tell him to call you."

Josey waited for the punch line. She waited and waited. It never came.

She waited through the end of the sixth inning and half of the seventh. Nate sat quietly beside her the entire time, intent on the game. The organ blared out the first familiar notes of "Take Me Out To The Ball Game" as the fans stood and participated in the traditional leg stretching.

Did last night mean nothing? Had she dreamed the whole thing? Nate was never anything but straightforward with her, always. Suddenly, here he was, playing games, or…regretting what had happened. Why? And could it have been possible for it to have meant so much to her and nothing to him? No, it had been too strong.

She felt about three feet tall, like a little girl who had a big crush on someone and had to learn the hard way that he didn't like her back when he walked away from her in the sandbox. She felt like making a big mud pie and flinging it at him.

Of course, maybe that was the answer.

"Sure," Josey said.

"Sure what?" Nate asked, since their last words to each other had been spoken twenty minutes or so prior, and he hadn't been following the discussion in her head.

"Sure I'll go out with Derek. What woman wouldn't? Set it up."

Nate said, "All right." But there was a moment before he said it, a long moment. Maybe he was regretting his suggestion? Feeling a twinge of regret at his stupidity?

Josey told herself silently over and over that she didn't care. She wondered how long she'd have to keep it up until she believed it.

"You did *what?*"

Did Derek *try* to make everything harder? Or was it a natural gift he was born with? Nate remembered how his brother used to wait until he was almost done building a Lego masterpiece before pointing out something pretend in the room to make Nate look, and then Derek would "accidentally" yank off a little piece vital to the tower and innocently watch it break apart. He must have been born with it.

"You heard me. You're not deaf." Nate ran a feather duster through the uncluttered spaces on Derek's coffee table for about the eleventh time, even though it was dust-free after his first swipe. He hadn't been anticipating this little chat, but since Saturday, Josey had caught him a few times in the lobby, in the hall, in the laundry room, wanting to know if he'd spoken with Derek about her yet. Nate couldn't bear to do it, but by Thursday, his regular visit day, he didn't see how he could put it off any longer.

"I must be, or else I'm going slightly insane, because I thought I heard you just say you'd set me up on a date with Josey. A date."

"Yes." Swipe swipe swipe.

"St. John."

"Yes, the very one." Swipe.

"Cut it out with the damn table already."

Nate straightened his back and opened his mouth, but his brother had adopted his older-and-wiser-and-you'd-better-listen-when-I-talk stance.

"Why are you doing this?"

"Your apartment is filthy, as usual."

"That's not what I meant, and don't pretend you thought it was. Why are you doing this?"

"Because," Nate said, and tried to make his voice sound exasperated, "I thought I'd do you a favor. Most men would—"

"Most men would never let her get away. You know it and I know it. What gives here?"

Nate fell onto the couch, already weary with the verbal gymnastics. "She's on a manhunt. I told you that."

"So, she got it into her head that I'm the one to sweep her off her feet? That's incredibly flattering, but…"

"Not exactly."

"Don't tell me this was your idea."

Nate kept silent. Derek flopped onto the rug next to the coffee table and shoved the book he'd been holding into a milk crate stuffed with texts. "Why in the world? Nate, I'm not an idiot. I've known you almost all my life." He smiled. "And I was too young to remember the time I didn't know you. So don't you realize I know you love her?"

Nate held up his hand as if to interject, but Derek ignored him. "Don't bother bullshitting me, okay? I know it and you know it. What I don't get is how come you're shoving her into my arms and not pulling her into yours?"

"I kissed her."

Derek's eyes widened.

"I kissed her, but that's not right."

"What's wrong about it?"

"I can't have her. I can't give her what she wants."

"Did she kiss you back?"

Nate let out a long breath, maybe a breath he'd been holding since that night, because it almost hurt. "Yes."

"Then she wants you. Don't you have that to give her?"

"No. Derek, you know I can't give her a future, a family, children."

"Really," Derek said in a sardonic tone. "And why's that, again?"

"My past, Derek. It's in my blood. I can't—" Nate cut himself off midsentence. Derek was the only one he could talk about this with because he'd been there, but even they discussed it so infrequently that it was difficult to decide which words to use and then even more difficult to say them aloud.

"Then tell me, my oh-so-brilliant and always rational brother. If you can't give Josey a future because of your past, what the hell makes you think I can? I have the same exact past you have, in case you've forgotten. What logic are you applying here?''

The thought of Derek giving Josey anything more than the time of day made Nate's insides twist. ''I don't know. She asked me to suggest someone who could be right for her....''

''I'll assume she thought you'd say you.''

Nate was well aware of that. Josey's word game had been transparent and he'd known the answer she was looking for. It had just about killed him not to supply her with it. ''I opened my mouth and your name just popped out. I don't know why.''

''Let me take a crack at it.''

''Fine.''

''You picked me because you can't trust anyone else with her. She's fantastic, and any man with half a brain would fall in love with her given the chance. But I'm safe, right? I won't touch her because I'm your brother and I know how you feel about her. That's it, isn't it?''

''I'm not in love with her.''

''Yeah, okay.'' Derek got up, grabbed the TV listings and flipped through to the appropriate day.

''I'm not.''

Derek clicked the TV set on. ''No?''

''No. I can't make it any clearer. I don't want to lead her on.''

''Well, in that case, I'm glad to hear it.'' Derek stretched his legs out and propped his battered sneakers on the very shiny coffee table. ''Because the truth is, from the first night I met her, I was interested. She's hot. I kept my distance only because I thought you were going to make a move.''

"We're just friends." If Nate had been on a jury listening to himself, even he'd think he was lying.

"Good. I don't have her number so give it to me, will you? I'm not going to bust you about this anymore. You've made yourself clear. I believe you." He settled on some movie channel and tossed the remote control onto the table next to his feet. "I haven't taken a woman out since at least midterms last semester. I'm due to get back in the game. Fork it over."

Nate got to his feet and walked into the bathroom. "I'll give it to you before I leave," he said, and closed the door.

Derek was bluffing.

But what if he wasn't?

Seized with the urge to put his fist through the mirror, Nate forced himself to confront it instead, staring for several minutes at his own face, so like his father's—at least as he recalled it.

"Hey, Nate! What's up in there? This is a great movie, did you ever see it? Get out here!"

Nate turned the faucet and cupped the cold water in both hands, then bent over to splash his face. Josey had turned his head, made him wish he was different, more like the rest of the world. But he wasn't, and she was going to have to find happiness elsewhere.

Even if he had to show her out the door.

Chapter Twelve

Standing on the chipped slate steps, Jonathan imagined the glass door a barrier between him and his miserable past. Between him and the kids who had ensured that his entire adulthood had been miserable.

Funny, he decided, looking into the nondescript lobby, he'd expected better. The street was rich with bright green, lush-leafed trees, a suburban touch. But the building Nate lived in was tucked into a corner of a dead-end street, and there was nothing particularly special about the beige brick, the rounded bay windows. It looked like every other structure on the street—better-looking than most of the stuff in the city, granted, but nothing outstanding. Jonathan had expected better. Nate had never been pretentious, but then, he'd had nothing to be pretentious about as a snot-nosed, wiseass kid. Being a hotshot lawyer had to have drawn out big-money snootiness in him.

But then, you usually got less bang for your buck in the

big city. These could be $3,000-a-month apartments, for all Jonathan knew.

Hell, maybe when he got what was owed him, he'd move in right next door. Be neighbors with his do-gooder, cash cow son. That way, he could always knock on the door for a cup of sugar, or a cup of money.

He'd followed Nate home today, after sitting on the steps of the county courthouse nearly all day, waiting for him to emerge. Jonathan had been expecting to have to come back several days in a row, not knowing which days Nate made court appearances. But his first afternoon, he'd seen Nate stroll out of the building, and after one look at his profile, he'd dropped his own head to make himself inconspicuous. He knew he'd hit pay dirt, as long as the kid didn't see him.

But Nate hadn't even glanced in his direction, and Jonathan was able to follow ten paces behind him as he walked eight or so blocks to what must have been his office building.

Jonathan hung around the lobby, bustling with fast-moving people with very important things to do. He waited nearly two hours before the elevator dinged. Nate walked out of it with the same purposeful stride as everyone around him, and left the building.

There was no pang in Jonathan's heart at seeing his son again after so many years. He felt only a twist of envy. He wanted that well-cut, well-fitted suit, those shiny black shoes, the smooth leather briefcase. He wanted to look the way his son looked, walk the way his son walked. He'd wanted that his whole life, and now Nate had it. *Nate had it.* That little jerk.

If he'd never before suspected fate was laughing at him, Jonathan knew it for sure as he followed his son home. He tailed Nate on foot, on the T and on foot again, then pretended to keep going straight as Nate hung a right onto a dead-end street. Jonathan jogged back to the corner just in time to see which door Nate had entered. The same door he was staring at now.

Realizing that anyone coming into the lobby could see him looking in made him descend the two steps and move to the side. He didn't want Nate to spot him yet. It was possible the next tenant to come by would let him in; Jonathan could claim he'd forgotten his key. But he needed a better plan than just knocking on his son's door. It would be slammed in his face the split second he was recognized.

He needed a way to get to Nate, to make him listen.

Jonathan made a quick mental note of the building number and ambled back down the street, back to the nearest subway station.

It would be easier if Nate had a wife, or at least a girlfriend. He swung open the silver metal T station door, paid for a token and started down the stairs to wait on the platform. He could come back here on Friday night, hang around as long as it took, see if some woman came by for Nate.

That would be the ticket, if he got lucky. Women were suckers for a sob story, and he could tell a good one.

It was weird enough that Derek had called Josey and asked her out to dinner—without Nate. A date.

But it was even weirder a few hours later, when she found herself struggling to keep her butt off the floor, holding her middle up while her splayed feet threatened to give way and her crisscrossed hands clutched at the multicolored mat, which seemed ready to slide out from under her body on the living room floor.

"Derek, dammit, hurry up. I can't keep this up much longer."

Derek reached out a finger on his one free hand and tickled her in the ribs. Josey shrieked with laughter. "You cheater! Quit it, quit it!" Her body started to lean against his and she tried to right herself with muscles she didn't know she had, much less could use.

Derek's solid frame shook with barely contained mirth. "Okay, okay. Left foot on green."

"What? On green? Oh, oh…no, all right, I can do this. Watch." She gingerly lifted her left foot and moved it inch by inch toward the nearest green circle. She was almost there when she knocked Derek on the bridge of his nose with her knee. "Oh, God, I'm sorry." She cracked up at his pained expression. "Well, Twister was your dumb idea!"

"Yeah, but it was in your apartment. This is what you do, huh? Strategically place Twister on an obvious shelf, and bring all your dates home after Mexican dinner, and they say, hey look, Twister, and you say, oh, my, I haven't played for years.…"

"I *haven't* played for years! My mom brought that the last time she visited. She was getting rid of some old toys in the attic and thought maybe I should have some of them for nostalgic reasons."

"Sure. I bet you bought it today. You were thinking, how can I get Derek, that manly man, that sexy stud, to literally throw himself all over me?" he accused. "I'll bet if I look, I can find a toystore receipt around here with today's date on it."

"Just shut up, will you? I want to win." She successfully got her foot to green, but as soon as her toe touched it, her right elbow gave way and she collapsed on her behind in an unladylike heap.

"Woo-hoo! He wins it!" Derek called, but Josey stuck out one foot and shoved it into his shoulder, knocking him down, as well. There was a thud as he hit the floor, and both of them laughed so hard Josey thought she'd wet her pants.

When they'd caught their breaths, Derek said, "So, you have anything to drink?"

Josey jumped up, wiping her hands on her thighs. "Of course. Iced tea? Lemonade? Coffee?"

"Iced tea's perfect."

Josey scrambled around the kitchen looking for a clean glass as Derek gathered up the Twister mat and folded it into its ancient, dilapidated box. She came back into the living room and handed Derek his drink. He glanced at the glass. "Oh, how cute. Cinderella. What a classy hostess you are."

She swatted him with a sofa pillow before sitting cross-legged on the floor. "Hey. That's part of the rare gas station collection from a road trip with my parents when I was a kid. My mom hates them. She practically begged me to take them when I moved out. I like them."

"Me, too. I was just teasing you." He took a long swig and sat next to her on the floor. "I—well, we, Nate and I—don't really have any souvenirs like that from when we were kids. I get a kick out of other people's nostalgia." He gestured toward the game box. "You were a happy kid."

Josey nodded, even though Derek hadn't really asked a question. He leaned against the sofa and dropped his head back on the cushions. She saw him lift his eyes toward the ceiling, and he held that pensive gaze for a few seconds.

"Didn't you?"

"Didn't I what?" he answered, grabbing a throw pillow to place under his back.

"Didn't you have a happy childhood? I mean, I know your parents died, and it was very rough for you after that, but before that, didn't you…"

"What did you say?" His head jerked up, his expression filled with confusion.

"I said, I know your mother and father died, but didn't you have a happy childhood?"

"Nate told you that?"

Josey blinked. "Well, yes, he did. Nate and I are very close…friends. He's told me some things. I'm sorry, maybe it's hard for you to talk about your parents. Let's drop it."

"No, I'm just wondering why he told you that."

"He and I have known each other for a while. There aren't really any secrets between us. I hope you don't think he betrayed a confidence with you." Josey was starting to babble, but she couldn't for the life of her imagine what was worrying him. She tried to gentle her voice. "Derek, it isn't wrong to tell people your parents are deceased, is it? It was a long time ago."

"No, it isn't wrong if it's true. Nate's just a big fool, if you ask me."

"For trusting me?"

"No, for not trusting you."

"I don't understand."

Derek heaved an exasperated sigh and studied her. He stared at her so hard and for so long it made Josey uncomfortable. Finally he spoke.

"You're a wonderful person, you know that? You're sweet, understanding, intelligent and as pretty as anyone I've ever seen."

She couldn't think of any response to this unexpected praise except a deadpan, "Oh, no. Are you dumping me?"

Derek threw back his head and laughed out loud. "Oh, I forgot, and a great sense of humor. What I'm trying to say is, Nate's much closer to you, and I'm sure that he knows even more things about you that are just as special. And that's why he's an idiot."

"Sorry, I still don't get it."

Derek sat forward and took her hand, but it was the gesture of a friend. He squeezed it and said, "I'm willing to bet if we sneak downstairs and open Nate's door really, really quietly, we'll find him standing on his sofa with his head stretching toward the ceiling, trying to hear what's going on up here."

"Oh, he couldn't care less."

"You think so, huh? Then tell me, what's been on your mind all night tonight? Don't say, 'You, Derek.' You don't need to worry about hurting my feelings. I know I'm a stud. I don't need constant reassurance from a pretty girl."

Josey grinned.

"Go on, tell me."

She looked into his eyes for a moment before glancing away, toward the window, where the outside blackness served as a mirror for the lamplight inside. It hurt her eyes, but she couldn't look back at Derek as she said, "I've been thinking how nice it is to spend time with you, but I keep thinking, maybe we should call Nate and invite him over for Twister. Let's see if he wants Mexican food, too, since I know it's one of his favorites. I've been gazing at you and thinking you look so much like Nate, except for this little detail and that little detail. I've been talking to you and I've been thinking you're so nice, but Nate wouldn't have said that, or he wouldn't have made that joke, he would have taken it too seriously, and I'd have to be trying harder to get laughter out of him than out of you." She dragged her eyes back to Derek, and cringed. "Oh, God, I can't believe I'm saying any of this. I—"

Derek put a restraining hand against her mouth. "You don't know how happy I am that you did. I was afraid my brother had already made a mess out of things and drove you away for good with his foolish idea that you and I should go out. I don't know what's been going on between you two up until now, but I've gotten the impression that he cares for you more than he will ever allow himself to let on. To you, to me, to anyone.''

She grabbed Derek's wrist and pulled his hand away from her mouth. ''But why? Is he so afraid of me and what we could be? I admit I was afraid myself at the prospect of losing our friendship, but the more I think about it, the more I realize I can't be just friends with him, anyway, feeling the way I do. Is that what he's afraid of, too? Or has he been hurt before?''

''Nate *has* been hurt. Just not in the way you might be thinking.''

''Please, tell me. Please tell me how to get through to him.''

''I can't.'' Derek raked his hands through his hair the way Nate so often did out of frustration. Her aching for Nate intensified just seeing him do it. ''If I tell you about Nate, about things that have made him the way he is, I'll be betraying him. I just can't do that, not even for you. Just let me say that it's worth it for you to keep trying.''

''Why? It's useless. I have too much pride to continue throwing myself at a man who doesn't want me.''

''He loves you.''

Josey went still, her whole body absorbing the power punch of his statement. When she could make sentences again, she said, ''How do you know?''

''Nate's had some girlfriends before, but when they started saying they wanted more, he's always bailed. Since meeting you, he's different. He always talked about you and his voice seemed bursting with happiness every time. He's smiled more in the past year and a half than in his entire three decades of life, and it was usually when you were around or when the conversation was about you.

When you announced you were going on this husband-hunt—''

''He told you about that?''

''Yeah, he did. You know why? He said, 'What's the matter with her? She's crazy, insane.' When the fact was, *he* was crazy and insane over the very thought of having to share you with someone else.''

''He rejected every date I had. I knew something was up.''

''Of course you knew. He wants you.''

''Well, what is he waiting for?''

''He's not waiting for anything. He doesn't think he can have you.''

''What?'' She remembered their searing kiss, his hands on her breasts, her gasping for breath in his ear. How could he doubt he could have her?

''I can't tell you why. I can't. I want to. I want you to be happy, and I want my brother to be happy. But I just can't. Please trust me on this.''

Josey shook her head, dazed.

''Don't give up on my idiot little brother. He's got his reasons for putting you both through this. Just be there for him. He'll come around. Or I'll make him come around.'' Derek abruptly stood with a grin and ran into her bedroom. She dashed after him just in time to see him pull her bed frame a few inches from the wall. He banged it back into place against the wall with his knee. Then he pulled it away and banged it back again, and again, until he had a steady rhythm going. Then he started moaning dramatically, angling his head toward her bedroom window. ''Join in. This will kill him.''

Josey laughed and yanked him away from the bed. ''Stop, he's going to think we're—''

''That's the idea!'' His eyes sparkled with sibling mischief. "What's that saying—drastic times call for drastic measures? He'll come right up here, kick my ass—which I'm willing to tolerate for a good cause—and sweep you away forever. Oh, Josey! Oh, oh, baby!"

"Stop! All the neighbors are going to think I'm running a brothel in here. *Geez*." She collapsed on the bed and smiled at him. "You're mentally disturbed, you know that?"

"I prefer to think of it as being a good brother."

"You are." She reached out and took his hand. "And a good friend."

"I hope so." He gave a mock satisfied sigh and looked around. "Well, the important thing is I got you into bed. Another successful date for Derek Bennington."

"That's good. I wouldn't have wanted to be the one to break your perfect record."

"Yup. Now I can leave without unfinished business. Walk me out?"

They left the warm apartment and ambled down the hall to the front door. When they emerged into the night, the refreshing, salty breeze surrounded Josey, soothing her. They strolled slowly past the other building on the short street to the corner, and upon reaching the streetlight, Josey said, "Thank you for a great evening. I mean it. We'll have to do this again."

"I'd like nothing better than to spend another evening with you, anytime," Derek replied, "but I hope you and Nate are both inviting me next time. Hey, hey," he said, touching her chin, "don't get all wistful. He's closer than you think. Keep trying. I would never tell you to waste your time if I didn't think you were perfect for him, for each other."

Josey reached up impulsively and wrapped her arms around his shoulders. He hugged her back and said, "At least, do it for me. I would love a sister. I'm tired of teasing Nate. I need a new victim.''

"I warn you," Josey said into his neck before pulling back and gazing fondly at his smiling face, "I give as good as I get."

"That's what I hear."

He couldn't hear them, but seeing them was enough.

He had to hand it to his eldest son, he could certainly pick a looker. Great legs.

Nate was the one he'd hoped to see out and about with some girlfriend. Jonathan hung around the apartment building Friday night, Saturday night and Sunday morning. He'd almost given up the idea that Nate had any woman, but he'd come back tonight just in case. The last person he'd thought he'd see was his other son. Jonathan hadn't even known Derek lived in Boston, also. But there he was, and Jonathan had almost swallowed his cigarette at the sight of the kid who'd brazenly bolted years ago.

The two of them were all over each other. Well, hardly all over each other, but they were in public, after all. And they had just come out of the apartment, so maybe his kid had at least gotten lucky. Or else they had been visiting Nate, or…whatever. It hardly mattered. What was important was he'd located both sons, and quite accidentally.

But Derek was moving away from the girl now, turning the corner, walking up the street. Which meant he didn't live in the same building as Nate. And—Jonathan pressed himself even thinner against the alleyway wall he had been leaning against, even though she didn't know who the hell he was—the girl was going back to the building, letting herself in with a key.

Perfect. Derek's girlfriend and Nate lived in the same

building, which meant they were probably friendly. It was all so convenient.

Jonathan had brought pictures from the old family albums Angelica had kept until she didn't care to anymore. Cute little adorable pictures and a story that would turn even the most skeptical girl into a believer of miracles—of a father back from the dead to discover the sons he'd thought he'd lost forever, of forgiveness and of love.

Of bullshit.

But women bought that stuff every time. And surely she could make her boyfriend and his brother see the light.

Jonathan was running out of money. He was forced to smoke his cigarettes longer and with more time in between. He was sick of his rat-hole apartment already.

He'd have to move fast.

A fast mover. That's what Derek had always bragged about being. It's tough being me, he said on his mock ego trips. Women are constantly tripping over themselves to get to me. Nate knew it was all garbage.

But that self-proclaimed stud was out there now, in the golden haze of the streetlight, with Josey in his arms.

That bastard.

Nate had heard his brother's little acting job upstairs earlier. As if he was listening to their date. He'd just happened to hear the two of them come home—only because the walls were so thin—and he'd happened to decide not to watch any TV that night and instead try to get some work done, so it was quiet. And his windows just happened to be open because it just happened to be summer.

And so Derek's little game—his moaning and groaning and banging around—was just for Nate's benefit. Which he knew because he also heard Josey admonish him.

And that was fine. Derek wanted to play games? Teach his little brother a lesson? Whatever.

But now that backstabbing bastard was out there with Josey in his arms.

Also for his benefit?

No, look at them, Nate said to himself, grinding his teeth as he held the curtain open and strained his eyes to see them at the end of the street. Smiling and laughing and having a swell old time. Next he'll lean in for the big kiss.

And Nate suddenly felt completely nauseated. He turned away from the window, unable to bear witness should that happen. But when he peeked out again a few moments later, they were no longer embracing in the halo of light. Derek was gone, and Josey was walking back to the front door.

Without thinking about it long enough to stop himself, Nate dropped the curtain and left through his own door.

Chapter Thirteen

Nate banged on Josey's door a little too hard, causing someone in the neighboring apartment to stir. His toe tapped violently but noiselessly on the carpet. She'd just got in; what was taking her so long? More than likely the door was open, anyway, even though he was forever telling her to keep it locked. He grabbed hold of the knob, turned it and pushed the door open, nearly tripping as Josey swung the door open from her own side. "Nate? What the heck's the matter with you? I was in my room changing."

Indeed she had been. The cropped white T-shirt left her midriff exposed, a creamy swatch of skin with a tiny indentation of a navel. The thin cotton boxers covered practically nothing of her legs, which were smooth and perfect and ended in clean white crew socks. She held a small portable fan in one hand, the cord dangling nearly to the floor. "You couldn't wait two seconds?"

''What did I say about locking this door? Don't you ever listen?''

Josey's eyes narrowed and her head cocked to one side. ''Right. I think you have some kind of serious attitude problem that needs a little altering, my friend. I just got in and I'm tired. You've got something to say that's so important you had to barge in here after my *date?* Make it quick. I have to plug in this stupid fan and then I'm going to bed.''

Her words were tough but her expression was nervous. She seemed to be checking his face for clues, but coming up empty.

He had to control his broken breathing. It was scaring her, and it was making it hard for him to ask what he needed to ask. He tried to slow down his thoughts, his heart rate, but it was impossible, and five seconds later he was even more frustrated for trying. With no plan, with no idea what his reaction would be if she confirmed his fear, he blurted out, ''Do you have feelings for him?''

''Who?'' Josey said without hesitation, the middle of her forehead creasing.

Nate didn't ask the question again because that response was too close to what he'd been wanting. Instead, he cupped the back of her head with one hand, bunching the short strands of blond hair between his fingers, stared into her somewhat bewildered eyes for a moment, and when that moment threatened to linger a fraction too long, he crushed his lips to hers.

He felt her arms twine around his neck, the fan cord tickling the small of his back. He felt her tongue inflame his. Her silky legs skimmed against the long length of his own legs. His thigh nudged hers apart and pressed between them. He could feel her heat there, could hear her breath catch in a sigh that sounded like his name.

Josey dropped the fan to the floor with a startling clunk, then brought her hands up to his face, smoothing his jawline, warming the skin on his cheeks, his chin. Her fingers traveled into his hair, combed through the strands. She placed her hands on each side of his face and drew her lips away from his slowly. Then she looked into his eyes.

And Nate realized it was the closest and most rapturous view of heaven he'd ever had. Not a heaven in the far-off distance, across the horizon. An obtainable heaven. Josey…

His body throbbed with the sweet painful need to be inside hers, to be the same body, to breathe her breath and be underneath her skin, pump her blood and pulse the same heart.

Then Josey pulled his face back to hers, feasting like a starving person on his lips. He lost control of his thoughts as he pushed her slowly backward into her living room, kicking the door shut behind him. Her fingers were working the top buttons of his polo shirt before he heard the door click closed. She yanked the hem out of his waistband and impatiently pushed the material up his chest. He reached behind his neck and pulled it off, letting it drop to the floor behind his ankles. While her eyes drank in his torso, he brought his hands down to encircle the soft bare skin at her waist.

And just then, God help him, Josey pulled her own T-shirt over her head.

Her body was bare underneath it.

Nate couldn't help staring. He looked and looked, and Josey stood like a kind of goddess, letting him, and he could feel her watching his face. Her breasts were full and firm and rising and falling with each sensual breath she drew and released. The nipples were tight and pointed, and he wanted to wet them with his tongue. He smoothed one palm from her waist over her midriff up between those lush breasts, across her delicate collarbone and around to the back of her neck, and he bent to take her mouth again, this time hard, all gentleness gone, tasting and sucking and biting.

Josey let his mouth ravage hers, grasping his shoulders when the weaknesses he unleashed in her began to buckle her knees. Her chest flattened against his, the soft hairs on his chest teasing her nipples until they ached. She tore her mouth away from his with some willpower and threw her head back, offering the expanse of skin on her neck, and Nate obliged, working his lips and tongue down the sensitive column so that her back arched. She wrapped one arm around his neck to steady herself, but he dragged his lips away long enough to half carry her to the sofa, where they both wound up in a tangle, and suddenly his lips were on her breast.

She had no idea what he was doing with his tongue, but it was amazing, leaving her throbbing when he abandoned it to lick her other nipple, still harder and even more insistent. She heard little mewing noises and realized they were emerging from the back of her own throat. Her short fingernails dug deeper and sharper into his upper arms, and she looked down at the top of his head. Nate's hair. She fought a lump of emotion inside her, while at the same time her body flamed and dampened even more. His head moved farther down her torso and his fingertips curled under the waistband of her shorts. He peeled them down and his hands touched only skin, since she wore nothing underneath them.

Then his lips were moving over that same skin, kissing her, caressing her, making her hotter and hotter. Her hips bucked and her fingers clutched the sofa cushions on either side of her as his lips and tongue worked her body into a frenzy. It was sweet agony, and she couldn't take too much of it before she began pleading with him. "Nate, please, oh please, I need you." And even as he lifted his head away, she cried out in protest.

Nate looked down at her with eyes glazed with desire, his lips swollen and damp with her, and said raggedly, from deep in his throat, "I need *you*." And as she lay there, breathing fast, he unbuckled his belt and slid off his jeans and underwear together. He dropped them to the floor and trampled over them to pin her to the sofa with his body, his beautiful, perfect, masculine body, and blinked slowly, languidly, as if awakening. And she must have read his mind in that shortest instant, because he said in a disbelieving whisper, "This isn't a dream."

And he entered her.

She threw back her head, and delirium consumed her. He was in her, she was surrounding him, and her body movements matched his, tilting up hard to meet every powerful, long, smooth thrust, her hands on either side of his face, his hands pressing into her shoulders. His skin rubbed against her, the friction so unbearably sweet, until her blood swirled into a crescendo and her fingers and toes curled and she came hard. She cried out in release at the same time Nate did, and the only reason she heard his voice over her own was because his lips were touching her ear.

She shuddered several times and closed her eyes to take a deep, openmouthed inhalation of breath. She sighed, and when she opened her eyes again, Nate was looking into her face, his own eyelids half-shut over his smoldering irises. Their skin was so molded together it didn't seem right to separate, and they lay together like that, studying one another quietly, tenderly, sleepily, for what seemed a very long time.

Nate finally rose, peeling himself off her very slowly,

and scooped her up in one easy motion, causing her to giggle just slightly.

"Something funny to you?" he asked her with a languid smile as he stepped through the doorway to her bedroom.

She shook her head. "No," she answered. "Something wonderful."

He laid her on one side of her mattress, drawing the sheet up to her chin, and she was surprised that it felt cool against her skin rather than too warm. She reached out her hand for Nate to join her and was momentarily surprised when he took a step away from the bed. She wondered if he was just trying to be polite, but what was polite at this point between lovers? "Nate?" she asked. "Will you stay?"

"I…" Nate looked as if he was struggling with something inside himself, and Josey felt a stab of disappointment. Maybe he needed to be alone, to think, and even though she wanted with all her heart for him to stay with her, what had happened between them was so fabulous, so momentous and so real that maybe he needed to deal with it in his own way. Whatever that was. She was determined to do this right. She was determined to do right by him.

"Would you be more comfortable if you didn't stay?" she asked, and though she'd meant for it to sound understanding, it came out sounding a little puzzled. "Would that make you happy?"

"I'm…" He paused before starting again. "I'm happy. I *am* happy. My God, I'm…happy here. With you."

Josey laughed out loud, and then felt bad, hoping he didn't think she was making fun of him. But suddenly he laughed, too, and his facial muscles relaxed and his shoulders went up and down, and it started her off again. They kept on cracking up for a full minute, and then Josey wiped away a tear that had mysteriously appeared for no reason.

"Well, if you're happy, by all means, please stay. I wouldn't want to toss you out on your adorably cute ass."

"*My* ass?" Nate asked, slipping underneath the sheet next to her and putting his arms around her lower back to grab her buttocks with both hands. "How can you talk about my ass when yours is twice as cute?"

She started to say, "Oh, please," but his lips covered hers, effectively shutting her up. She tangled her fingers in his hair as her own head sank into her pillow with his deep kiss.

When Nate cracked his eyelids open a few hours later, the only thing that amazed him more than the fact that he didn't have nightmares was the fact that his body was entwined around Josey. His nose was in her hair. He drew his head away from its softness and tried to lift a hand to caress her sleep-flushed cheek, but she was lying on his forearm and he couldn't feel it. Couldn't feel anything, really, except her warmth all around him.

Her breathing was heavy and she was dead to the world. But Nate was very much alive, more so than ever before. And feeling as if life was full of potential he hadn't believed existed for him. Like the possibility of being with Josey, having her, loving her, as long as she'd let him—hopefully for the rest of his presence on Earth.

His mind began furiously burning as he lay there, reconsidering his future as Josey's breath blew hot on his skin. Everything was different now. He'd not wanted this to happen—he'd not wanted to make love to her—because he'd known that it would be as wonderful as it was, and it would be a mistake, since he ultimately couldn't have her. But in her bed now, with the scent of her still clinging to him, he couldn't attach logic to this as a mistake. He even took a few minutes to try to think it was, but it wouldn't take hold.

The reality was so completely opposite. He'd never felt worthy of her before, but he was positive he'd made Josey happy tonight and that she'd wanted him. And by virtue of that alone, perhaps it meant he deserved her and the happiness she could bring him, after all. They could concentrate on loving each other and their future would just unfold. Maybe Josey would be so happy with their world that she wouldn't want children. And maybe, if she was still adamant about wanting a family…well, he could just stop obsessing about it and consider the possibilities if the time ever came.

That was the key, perhaps. Just stop thinking. It would work out all right if he could just forget his past, quit worrying about the future and keep focused on the now.

Josey stirred and rolled over into him. And as her bare breasts pressed against his chest, Nate was definitely in the now. He eased his arm out from under her and ran his hand down her side, tracing her first curve, then her second, then trailing back up to descend again. Her skin was slick with perspiration from the summer heat and from the lovemaking that had left them both spent and sated. A warm night breeze slithered in through the open window and touched her, blowing a wisp of hair across her cheek, and the sight of her there, damp, bathed in a breeze, stole Nate's breath.

He wanted…he needed… No, he told himself. No, just stop thinking.

And before his mind even finished forming that command, his hands were skimming over all that creamy skin—softly, lightly, but insistently enough to rouse her from sleep almost instantaneously. Her eyes blinked open for a second, then closed again dreamily as her hands began to mimic his movements on his own body. She regarded him from under hooded eyelids, and the sleepy smile that graced her lips almost sent Nate over the edge.

His hands moved harder, and then he followed with his mouth, tasting, sucking, nibbling until she was squirming under him and he knew she was fully awake with all senses on high alert. Her palms ran over his shoulders and down his back, and his body shook in an erotic shiver as her fingernails traveled up again. He tasted the sweet saltiness of her inner thighs, first one, then the other as his mouth blazed a hot trail to where they joined, and his tongue slid in and out of her hot center. Up and down, up and down, faster and slower. He breathed the scent of her in deeply, and he had to be inside her.

Urgently.

With one deft move he flipped Josey over, rubbing himself between her rounded but firm buttocks. He felt and heard her gasp as he snaked his hands under her torso to grab hold of both breasts, and he slid his hardness into her softness. She writhed and moaned his name, her pleasure, over and over as he thrust into her again and again. He rubbed one hand down her stomach to her thatch of curls below, and toyed with the tiny nub there with one finger until she screamed out in release. With one more powerful jerk of his body, his own release came.

He held her close through the sighs that followed, hers and his. They drifted off to sleep again.

It was highly unusual to wake up in Josey's arms on a Tuesday morning. Something Nate hoped would become usual.

But it *was* highly normal for him to wake up with the pressing obligation to go into the office. He considered calling in sick for the first time in...well, for the first time ever. And he might have reached for the phone and done just that if Josey hadn't rolled over, blinked her beautiful eyes wide at him, chirped, ''Time to get up for work!'' and bounded out of bed, naked, toward the bathroom. She paused in the doorway, turned and coyly crooked a finger at him.

Suddenly the bed was no longer the ideal place to be. He sat up, his head still dizzy from sleep, or lack of it, and he heard the shower begin to pound the bottom of the tub. She called, "I don't get much hot water in the morning, buster. But I'm willing to share if you are!"

Nate didn't need a second invitation. He got up quickly and headed into the steamy bathroom.

Josey was not only sexy, she was a liar. There was plenty of hot water, enough to last a sweet long time.

After they were thoroughly clean, Nate tugged on his jeans as Josey made coffee. He stumbled to the sofa and gratefully took the steaming mug from her. "Thanks, but I don't have time for more than three sips. I'm late already." He glanced at her wall clock and sucked in his breath. "Geez, I have to get the hell out of here." He slurped once, scalding the tip of his tongue, and gave her back the mug. She smiled and set it down, and he took both her hands.

"You know what? The hell with it. I'll call in sick. We can spend the day together. Would you rather?"

"Of course I would, but you know, I'm just thinking I have a tutoring session this morning, anyway. I'd hate to cancel. It's a kid who's supposed to come into my class this year from second grade, but he's behind and I have to try to catch him up and get to know him. Besides, his mother already canceled the last two scheduled sessions, so I want to be available. Go on. You can't get away from me even if you wanted to. I know where you live."

Nate chuckled and tipped her chin so he was looking right into her eyes. "I guarantee you, Josey, you're all I'm going to be thinking about today, no matter how much work I have. How about I try to escape early?"

"That sounds like a good compromise," Josey answered, standing up and taking his mug to pour the coffee into a portable thermos. "But if you can't, I understand. You're a true workaholic at heart. Now get going." She handed him the beverage and pointed toward the door. "Scat, scat."

He was in front of her in two strides and pressed his lips to hers in a lingering kiss. "You're wonderful," he said then. "I've been waiting a long time to tell you that. Too long." And he was out the door.

Josey shivered, but with delight, not with cold. It was already stifling in her apartment and not even 8:30 yet. She poured herself some coffee, turned on the TV and sat down to relax until her 9:30 lesson.

She flipped channels absently, not focusing on anything. Her mind's eye only saw Nate—Nate smiling, Nate without clothing, Nate staring into her eyes as he slid inside her, her name on Nate's lips. She discovered her own lips curled in a dopey smile, but who cared? She was already looking forward to his return this afternoon, and she realized she could do a lot of looking to the future where Nate was concerned.

The phone ringing made her jump, crashing into her reverie, but she grinned. It had to be Nate. Calling from work already.

"Hello?" she practically purred into the phone.

"Miss St. John?" It was a woman's voice, thin-sounding but somewhat familiar.

"Um, yes?" She struggled to sound businesslike.

"This is Mrs. Crowley. Mike's mother?"

"Oh, yes. I'm sorry, Mrs. Crowley. Do you need directions?" Josey thought she'd given them to her last time.

"No, I'm sorry, but I'm afraid we have to cancel again. I apologize, we keep doing this to you."

Josey felt annoyed. This was the third time, and she was willing to bet if she were an accountant or a hairstylist, she wouldn't get this treatment. Teachers just never got any respect. "Well, I understand. What's the problem?"

"The problem? Oh, well, Mike's got a swimming lesson. I forgot all about it."

"Well, I have a pretty free day today. Would you like to come after the lesson? Or maybe early this afternoon?"

"No, dear, I'm sorry. That won't be possible. I'll call you back to schedule another day."

Although Josey was clearly getting the brush-off, the woman's voice wasn't brisk. It was hesitant and funny sounding. But maybe that was the way she always was.

"Sure. Call anytime. I—"

"Thanks, bye." Click.

Josey stared with some contempt at the dead phone. Then she felt sorry for Mike. Any child whose parents made education such a low priority—below swimming!—was too often doomed to fail.

She wandered into her bedroom and threw on a sundress. She slipped her feet into black ballerina slippers and frowned at her mussed cap of hair in the mirror before heading out the door of her apartment. Might as well take advantage of her newly freed up time and go enjoy the sunshine. She locked her door and stopped in the lobby to look through a stack of discarded catalogs beneath the row of mailboxes. Anything left here for more than a day was a free-for-all, and Josey usually found some nice things to look at, besides getting a glimpse of her neighbors' favorite clothing and pastimes. She was flipping through a J. Crew catalog when the door opened and a workman strode in with a ladder. He smiled at her before descending the stairs to the basement.

"Excuse me."

Startled, Josey dropped the catalog at her feet. The man who had spoken to her picked it up and put it back in her hands, and when he straightened, he smiled a bit uncomfortably. Josey put him in his fifties, with salt-and-peppery hair and a nice hunter-green polo shirt and khakis. She didn't recognize him as a tenant, so he must have walked into the building with the workman.

"Are you looking for someone?" Josey asked. The weird expression on his face was making her a little nervous. But his face was familiar—similar to someone else she knew, perhaps. "Maybe I can help."

"I'm hoping you can, actually," the man said. "I'm looking for Nathan Bennington. Do you know him?"

A warning bell went off in Josey's head. Nate was a prosecutor. And when he prosecuted criminals, some people were made very unhappy—the suspect's family, business associates, partners in crime. A recent murder of a local D.A. popped into her head, and goose bumps rose along her bare arms. She was going to say no, but too late; the man had scanned the mailbox names and found Nate's apartment number. "Nate's not here right now," she said hurriedly. "Maybe you can leave your phone number with me and I can ask him to call you later. I think I have a pen...." She rummaged through her shoulder bag.

"That's okay, miss." The man put a restraining hand on her upper arm—not roughly, but kindly. She looked up at his face, and suddenly he looked very sad. "If you give him my number, he might think you were playing a mean trick on him and get angry, and I don't want to cause any trouble if you're friends."

"Why in the world would he think it was a trick?"

"He's..." The man blinked, and Josey thought it was to blink away tears. "He probably doesn't want to see me."

He turned abruptly, saying under his breath, "This was a mistake." Then, louder: "Sorry, miss. I'll be going."

"No, wait, please." She thought he wouldn't, but the man paused, not looking at her anymore. "Who are you?"

He hesitated for one second, then he spoke the next three words to his feet.

"I'm his father."

Chapter Fourteen

For several endless moments, Josey's mouth hung open, but no words emerged.

The man waited, still staring at the floor, but eventually he tilted his chin up again in her direction, and she somehow found the power of speech.

"That can't be...you can't be...you can't be Nate's father."

"Yes, miss, I am. Nathan and Derek are my only children."

Josey shook her head, torn between not wanting to be rude to a stranger and blatant disbelief. "Are you really standing there telling me you're..." She set her jaw. "Sir, you are not their father. Their father is dead. Long dead."

So that's the story they've been using. Jonathan studied the woman's pretty face, which had changed from shocked to fiercely protective. He needed to lay it on thick.

"So, I think you'd better leave," she was saying.

"You sound like," Jonathan began, making his tone pitiful, "you sound like you know them. Do you know them well? They had to have—grown up to be good men. They were—they were perfect children. And they have to be perfect now." He choked back a pretend sob and blinked hard, waiting for a reaction.

Her voice seemed to soften a little bit, but she stood her ground. "I think there's some kind of mix-up here."

"What kind of mix-up could that be? Nathan and Derek are my kids. I raised them in Connecticut with their mother, God rest her soul." He let out a phlegmy sniffle.

"She's dead?"

"She killed herself years ago. Depression, mental illness, whatever they called it. My boys blamed me. They blamed me, and left me. I guess they told everyone I was dead. But I'm not. I miss my boys so much."

He was breaking her. He could see it. She was starting to believe.

"Nate and Derek lied? To everyone…to me?" she asked, the last part almost inaudibly. "No, no…it can't be right. This can't be true. I'm sorry, but you can't be…"

Time for the pièce de résistance. "I have pictures of them. Right here in my pocket." He reached into his pants pocket. "They're old and kind of wrinkled, because I've been carrying them around for a long time, but…" He held out his hand to her. "Here they are."

Josey took the photos gingerly, not wanting to bend them any more than they already were. The first picture was of a smiling, dark-haired grade-school boy, teeth missing, big blue hippo on his T-shirt. It looked like Derek, down to the floppy lock of hair hanging over his left eye. It *did* look like Derek. But lots of children looked alike, and there was no way to be sure the sweet, laughing Derek she knew was the boy in the photo.

But then she flipped to the second picture, and her heart stopped, then began to pound painfully against her breastbone.

It was of a serious-faced little boy, with an expression older than his about-six years. Sitting at the kitchen table with a schoolbook of some kind, he was regarding the camera as an annoyance to the work he was obviously in the midst of. His little chubby fingers were wrapped around a pencil. His eyes…dear God, those eyes. Deep, knowing eyes.

The very same eyes Josey had been staring into all last night? The same eyes that swept over her when he'd told her this morning how beautiful she was?

Was it possible that Nate…had lied to her? Long ago, and still now, letting her and everyone who knew him believe his parents were *both* dead? But on the other hand, it wasn't as if he'd made up an elaborate story. He just said very little when the subject came up, and Josey had figured if your parents were dead, it wasn't something you particularly liked to discuss. She remembered Derek's strange reaction to hearing that Nate told her their parents were dead and realized the lie was Nate's alone. Her heart ached for the Bennington children whose mother had killed herself. But why had they run away from the man who could possibly comfort them and help them remain a family?

"Why would they have blamed you?" Josey blurted out without censoring herself. She bit her lip. If this was true, even if a small part of it was true, this man would be in pain, too. But that was secondary to finding the truth. These pictures looked like Nate and Derek, but she couldn't ignore that warning bell in her head—which had quieted down only slightly.

"Oh, they were kids. Teenagers. When Derek turned eighteen, he just took Nate with him."

"Didn't you look for them?"

"I did, but I'm sorry to say I just thought they'd come back on their own. They were very smart, responsible boys. I wasn't worried about Derek getting into any kind of trouble, and I really didn't have any legal hold over him at his age, anyway. I suppose I should have looked harder for Nate, but something in me knew Derek would take good care of him. Call it a father's instinct...."

But wouldn't a father's instinct have driven him to search everywhere, turn over every stone, call out in every alleyway, to find them? "Just because they could take care of themselves didn't mean they both didn't need you, and need to know you were looking for them."

"I know." A tear spilled out of his eye then, and he brushed at it with the back of his hand. In spite of her misgivings, Josey winced in sympathy. "I messed up," he admitted. "I just did the wrong thing. I lost everyone, don't you understand? But I want my family back."

This could be him, Josey thought. This really could be their father. This man who, now that she scrutinized his sorrowful face more closely, did seem to have an older version of features she knew well. "Mr. Bennington, I—"

"Bennington? Oh," he said, and his sad expression became even more so. "That was my...wife's name. They took her name. God..." He stopped, and she thought he wasn't going to speak again, but he said, "It's Simmons. Jonathan Simmons."

"They were Nate Simmons and Derek Simmons?" She paused, trying to let that sink in a moment. "But then, if you don't mind my asking, how in the world did you find them?"

"I saw mention of Nate in the paper. For some case or another—I can't remember. But I saw his name, knew it had to be him...so, I'm ashamed to admit, I found out his address and waited across the street there this morning so I could see if I would recognize him if he came out. Of course, I did. Of course, I knew my son."

"Of course." Josey had no idea what to do next. Should she tell him to wait here, and go call Nate? No, she didn't want to get him rattled while he was at work. Should she take this man's number—Jonathan Simmons, Nate's *father?*—and talk to Nate tonight, try to convince him to call? Maybe that would be best.

"The thing is," Mr. Simmons said, as though he was reading her thoughts through her eyes, "Nate and Derek won't want to talk to me. They're probably still angry, or else they would have contacted me by now. After all, they knew where I was. I have to see them. It's the only way they may be able to forgive me—if I talk to them, man to man to man. Then I know we can work it out. Please, can you help me?"

"Help you? You—you don't even know who I am."

"Is it safe to assume you know my...sons well?"

Josey hesitated again. None of this was her business, not really. Could she justify getting involved like this? And though Jonathan Simmons seemed genuinely upset, she still didn't know him at all. Her first loyalty was to Nate.

Nate.

Josey felt a stab in her heart. If Nate had run from this man, his father, and pushed him so far out of his life that it was easier to tell people he was dead, then he certainly wasn't going to agree to see him. Nate was so stubborn. Who would be able to talk him into talking to his father again—to let go and give him a chance? Nate and Derek had had their reasons, and Nate wasn't going to budge. It didn't take a crystal-ball-gazing psychic to predict that one.

But didn't she *owe* it to Nate, as his friend—as his more-than-friend—to help him see the advantages of reconciliation? She frowned. Maybe he'd be mad at her, but she'd explain how his father had practically begged for her help. Nate would forgive her. Derek, too.

Besides, she was already beginning to envision a future with Nate. It was her responsibility to aid him in healing his past so they could look forward together.

"Yes," she finally answered. "Yes, I know them both well. Nate especially."

"Nate?" The man looked confused for a moment, then seemed to shake it away. "Sorry, I just seem to recall Derek being a real lady-killer. Well, I guess girl-killer."

"But Nate was only a kid when you last saw him. He's…grown up, I assure you."

Jonathan laughed. "Did they ever tell you about the time they chased the ice cream truck about six blocks, and when they got themselves cones, realized they were lost? It took about an hour to find them."

Josey smiled, easily able to envision that, but then Jonathan's laughter dissolved. "I guess," he said, "maybe I thought the same thing would happen when they left me."

A wave of sadness washed over Josey, followed quickly by another wave, this time of confusion. He seemed so desperate. Her compassion wouldn't let her turn him away.

"You will help me?" Jonathan urged.

"Maybe," she said, squelching her skepticism. "I'll think about it. But just promise me you'll accept whatever they decide to do about this—about you."

"I will. I already know it will be hard. I'm not asking for much. I just want to be part of their lives again, as soon as possible. What's your name?"

"Oh, I'm Josey St. John."

"Josey St. John. You're a nice girl. My sons are lucky to know you. And are you just a friend to Nate, or his girlfriend?"

Josey felt heat spread across the skin on her face.

"Oh, I'd have to guess girlfriend. Well, that Nate's an even luckier man than I first thought."

The image of Nate in the shower this morning assaulted her inner eye, and she shook it away. "I'm the lucky one, Mr. Simmons."

"Jonathan, please." He put out his hand, and Josey took it. She wasn't sure what she expected—maybe a little trembling, or gentleness, but his hand gripped hers so tightly she nearly gasped. But when she looked back into his face, the sadness was there, etched into his features. "Josey, here's what I think we should do. Together."

And as he outlined his plan, Josey had to repeatedly calm her nerves. This could be the right thing. She had to try. For Nate.

Josey attacked the lettuce head with a vengeance, hoping it would ease her nervousness. Nate had unwittingly calmed her about forty minutes ago when he'd arrived at her apartment, kissing her dizzy before Derek knocked twice and walked in.

"Eww, yuck, girls are gross," he'd whined, but Josey and Nate couldn't let go of each other right away. "This is exactly why I didn't want to come here. It wasn't out of consideration for the two of you, I'll tell you that. Nope, it was for my own sanity. Who needs to watch such disgusting displays? *Blech,*" he said, handing over a bottle of wine to his hostess. "For you, darling."

Now she continued dinner preparations, and even though she'd tried to shoo the brothers out of the kitchen so she could concentrate on dinner, they insisted on helping. Which so far had consisted of chewing on half the tomatoes and cucumbers that were supposed to be in the salad.

"So where's the main course?" Derek asked, around a crunchy mouthful.

"And what is it?" Nate asked, peering over her shoulder at the countertop, looking for clues.

"It's *supposed* to be a surprise," Josey said, "but if you guys don't get the heck out of my way you'll wreck it." But the truth was, she loved having Nate so close to her now, and she wanted it all the time. For forever. The lasagna in the refrigerator wasn't much of a surprise, anyhow.

The other surprise, however... Josey's stomach dropped. She'd had an uneasy feeling all day she'd done the wrong thing. But it was too late now. A few hours ago she had panicked, and called the phone number Jonathan had scribbled on one of her catalogs from the mailbox. But after she dialed it, an electronic voice had informed her, "This number is not in service." She had dialed it one more time to make sure, and got the same response. Was it a new number he hadn't hooked up yet? Or... She didn't want to think he'd given her a fake number. No matter what, now there was no backing out.

Good thing everyone was feeling so happy. She thought of one more man in here, joking with his boys, even more laughter. Maybe once they got everything all worked out... And she'd be a part of it all, too. She tried to hold on to that thought, to keep her butterflies in check.

"If you're making anything Italian, I promise you anything you want," Derek said. "But you'll probably be as unoriginal as all the other women, and just ask for my body."

"Hey," Nate said, "watch it."

"Did I or did I not just have a date with this chick last night? She was mine first, you scoundrel. In fact, I believe you stole her from me." Derek glanced around the kitchen and snatched up a broom. "I challenge you to a duel for the hand of fair Josephine.'' He darted back and forth in front of Nate, lunging every few steps with the broom handle.

Nate pretended not to pay any attention for about ten seconds, then he grabbed a mop out of the corner and brandished it in the air. "Be prepared to back up your talk. You lose, you die.''

The brothers bounced around the apartment, which seemed too small to contain their mock testosterone battle; Josey feared for her lamps and framed prints as the two took swipes at each other. But she had to laugh when Nate cornered Derek against a wall, holding the mop up in a cross-check on Derek's chest, and growled, "You are finished! She is mine, I say!''

"Oh, don't bother trying to kill each other over little old me,'' Josey said, waving a dismissive hand and turning back to shredding lettuce. "Personally, I don't want either one of you. Nope, no Bennington boys for me. I'll just have to look for my dream man somewhere el—'' Her tongue couldn't form another word because it was suddenly entangled with Nate's, and she was so startled she would have fallen over if not for his steady hands now splayed across her back. When he drew his lips away, it was only long enough to whisper, "Just give this Bennington boy a chance.'' Then he covered her mouth with his again, and she forgot everything around her.

At least until she heard Derek's long-suffering groan, like a child whose playmate had found another friend and left him alone in the sandbox. "Ohh, here we go again. I'll be lucky if I *ever* eat now. Hello? Anyone?'' Josey felt one of Nate's hands rise from her back and make a brushing motion in the air. "Oh, so that's how it is. I get it. Three's a crowd and all that. Well!'' Derek finished with such fake indignation that Josey giggled against Nate's lips in spite of herself. She felt Nate smile, too, and she opened her eyes, so close to his, which were smoldering with a combination of happiness and lust. She sighed, and heard the doorknob turning. "That's it, I'm outta here. I'll just go around the block so you two can have each other right there on the linoleum, and when I come back I expect to get fed for my troub—"

Derek's voice cut off abruptly. After a moment, Nate drew his face away from hers again and looked beyond her quizzically. Josey twisted her back and looked there, too, at the half-open door with one of Derek's feet still inside. What was he doing? Was something in the hall?

Or…oh no, or some*one?*

Josey glanced at the kitchen clock, then squirmed out of Nate's now-relaxed arms and skidded out of the kitchen, to the living room and toward the door. It seemed to be taking her forever to get there. She'd had no idea her "surprise" would take *her* by surprise, too, a half hour early.

She reached Derek and put a hand on his stiffened back. She squeezed into the thin space between his body and the door frame, placing herself between him and her latest guest. But once there, she didn't know what to say. She looked from one man to the other. Jonathan's face was unreadable, but his eyes gleamed with something…. Josey had thought it would be tears at seeing his child again, but it wasn't that at all. Eerily, he looked a little…triumphant. A cigarette burned in one dangling hand, and the smoke drifted up into her nostrils and dissolved into her hair.

Derek's mouth was hanging open. One hand was still on the knob inside the door, and he was still in midstride. He seemed in shock, but after just one more moment, he closed his mouth and set his jaw, meeting his father's gaze and holding it. He didn't speak for the longest time, and didn't seem to ever intend to.

Josey wanted to break the tension, but with what? An introduction? Instead, she cleared her throat once, then twice.

"What the hell is going on here?"

Derek's question hung there in the hazy air, and Josey realized after a moment that it was directed at her. "It's…it's a surprise," she mumbled, all at once recognizing the weakness of her words, the foolishness of her idea and the dangerous tension between these men.

Derek blinked at her and backed into the room. "This…person is your invited guest?"

"I am," Jonathan said in a much different voice than the one Josey remembered from that morning. Then, it had been sad, a bit gravelly, strained with grief. But now it was smooth; cultivated, almost. Self-assured. And accompanied with a smile—no, a grin. "May I come in?"

Josey didn't know anymore. But Derek stood aside and nonchalantly waved him in, shrugging. "Whatever."

Jonathan dropped his cigarette butt on the floor and ground it into the hallway carpet with his heel. He stepped into the room, and as he moved toward the sofa, Josey saw him train his eyes on the kitchen doorway. She swirled around to see Nate.

His hand gripped the door frame and his chest was slowly but visibly rising and falling. All color had left his face. His eyes darted around the room as if he was desperately searching for a place to hide. He swallowed hard, and recoiled.

He lost years of his life standing there, and Josey saw him as she'd never seen him—as a little boy.

It couldn't be any clearer. He was afraid of this man.

"Hello, sons," Jonathan said, emphasizing the last word so much it came out a sneer. "Did you miss your old man?"

The only response in the room was silence. He grinned again anyway, and pulled the fabric on the front of his slacks as if to sit on the sofa.

"I wouldn't bother getting comfortable," Derek said. "You're not staying."

"Don't be rude, son," Jonathan replied, but he didn't sit down. He moved a few feet closer to Derek, and Josey was shocked to see he was taller than both his sons—not by much, but by just enough. "This apartment belongs to the lady," he continued. "So I'm sure it's up to her to decide whether or not I stay, right, honey?"

Blood pounded through Josey's temples, and she shook her head to clear it. The transformation of the stricken father in the lobby this morning to this cold man had taken away her power of speech. She hadn't been sure earlier what she was going to say when Jonathan arrived, anyway, but this was too frightening. Especially since Nate—her confident, intelligent, protective Nate—still cowered quietly in the kitchen doorway. She longed to go to him, but the tension in the room gripped her and held her fast to the floor where she stood.

"Just tell us why you're here," Derek said, his tone carrying an unfamiliar harshness. "It certainly isn't because you've been weeping over our disappearance all this time. You've got something to say? You want something? Get it out in the open and let's get it over with so you can walk the hell out that door and out of our lives again."

"A tough guy now, aren't you? That's nice. That's a nice way to talk to your old man." Jonathan raised his chin just a bit and looked down his nose at Derek. "You know what happened to me when I talked like that to my father? I got the beating of my life. You watch yourself."

Derek's body never moved, but his presence grew more threatening. "You're not our father."

"Now that's not true. Don't confuse the lady. You know how I know I'm your father? Because I busted my ass raising you. Both of you," he said pointedly to the kitchen door. Josey saw Nate shrink back even more. "And then when you grew up a little, when it came time to be grateful to your *father* for making sure you had a roof over your head your whole lives, when it came time to start paying me back for everything, you two split town. Ran off. Couple of snot-nosed kids.

"Well, I'm here figuring my two sons have grown up a little more. Enough to realize the sacrifices a man makes when he's got kids.

"What the hell's with you?" he barked suddenly. "Nathan, you've got nothing to say to me? Not a word? You're some hot-shit lawyer and you're just standing there? No objections? No charges? Nothing?"

With each "no" Nate flinched, again and again, and a little trickle of sweat trailed down from his hairline to his ear. Derek said, "Leave him the hell alone."

"Still defending him?" Jonathan kept staring down his youngest son while throwing his words over his shoulder. "What is he, thirty? And still needs his big brother around to protect him? Some things never friggin' change."

He turned to Derek again. "What do you do?" Derek didn't answer, and Jonathan repeated, louder, "I said, what do you do? Answer me. Where do you work?"

Derek began shaking his head, slowly at first, then harder. "You want money. I don't believe this. You want money from us. Of course. Did you get fired?"

Jonathan advanced a step. "You watch your tone with me."

"You did," Derek said, and laughed mirthlessly. "You got canned. I should've known. I should've known the split second I saw your face. Well, you're not getting it, *Pop.*

I'm a student. I owe more money than I may ever see at one time. So you lose. Time for you to get the hell out.''

"That's too bad for you. Rich-kid little brother isn't sharing?''

"He's no rich kid.''

"Richer than you and me right now, and I'll bet he's sharing with *you*." Derek didn't answer, so Jonathan turned on Nate again. Josey edged closer to the kitchen. "Aren't you? So you've got enough to spread around. I think it's time we talked a little business. Man to man. At least, I think that's what you are.''

Josey stepped right in front of Nate then and put up her hand. "Mr. Simmons, I believe you and I had quite a misunderstanding this morning. I really think it's time you left. Right now.''

"Oh, Josey honey, don't be that way. You know how families get. We've had our share of rough times, but we all just *love* each other *so* much. Right, Nate?''

Nate's eyes widened a little more as his father got even closer.

"Come on, Nate. Your girlfriend here thought it was a nice idea for all of us to get together tonight. The least you could do is humor the little woman. Such a pretty, sweet, kind little thing.''

Jonathan put his arm around Josey's shoulders and pulled her close to his body.

Nate lunged.

Chapter Fifteen

His only coherent thought as his hands closed around the flesh of his father's neck was that it was the first time he'd ever voluntarily touched his dad.

Then his full attention was on his fingers, constricting in a way that was unfamiliar, yet with a capability he'd known for years he surely possessed—because of who he was.

This man's son.

Then hands were on his own shoulders, jerking him back and Derek's voice was loud. "Nate! It's not worth it! That's enough!" And still Nate's hands squeezed. And still his father's eyes bulged, and then his father's arm came up....

"You'll listen to me, you little jerk! Ten years old and you think you're smarter than me? You'll listen because I'll make you listen!"

...and his hand curled into a tight ball, and his elbow pulled back...

"Now you'll listen, huh? Now you'll be grateful! Now you won't talk back!"

…and his fist arced in slow motion, closer. And Nate let go and pushed his own hands in front of his face, hard, to deflect. *Don't hurt me.…*

"Oh!" Nate made contact, and a gasp of pain burst forth from someone. But when he blinked, it was Josey who stood with her palm pressed to the side of her face. He'd hit her.

She'd stepped between him and the man who'd fathered him, and he'd accidentally hit her.

"Josey…" his voice rasped, but what else could he say? His head began to throb, and colorful sparkles danced in front of his eyes.

"It's okay, it was an accident. I'm fine, really," she assured him, but his shoulders slumped and he leaned back for support. Then his brother moved, pulling him back again. "Come on," Derek said. "Just stand in the kitchen until he leaves. Cool off."

But it wasn't done, his anger. One last explosion was in Nate, and it broke free. "Get out!" he yelled into his father's face. "Get out of my sight! Go back to where you came from!"

His father rubbed his neck with both hands, and when he spoke, his voice was deep and dangerous. "Son, you'd better start remembering where *you* came from. From me. That's why I'm here. To remind you that you owe me. It's pay-up time."

"No, your watch must be wrong," Josey snapped. "According to mine, it's time for you to get the hell out of my apartment." She crossed the living room, opened the front door and stood at the ready to usher him out.

Derek stepped forward again. "Let me show you the way, if you're lost."

"I'm going," their father said, keeping his eyes locked on Nate's. "But I'll be back soon. We haven't seen each other in a long time, but I'm sure we can work things out. After all, we *are* the same blood."

He stopped halfway to the door to light a fresh cigarette, blowing out a fetid puff before striding out into the hallway. Josey slammed the door behind him so fast it might have clipped his heels. She absently rubbed the side of her face again, and a fresh wave of nausea engulfed Nate. His knees threatened to buckle, and somehow he got to the sofa and sat down, fighting the urge to curl up in the corner in shame. He felt Derek and Josey exchange a look.

Then Derek said, "What…?"

Josey answered quickly. "I didn't know. I didn't know things were like that. I didn't even know he was…"

"…alive," Derek finished. "I know you didn't. I think I get what you tried to do here. Did you have a feeling all along it wasn't true, and what—you went looking for him? Where did you find him? In Connecticut?"

"No! I never looked for him. I wouldn't have thought to. I thought he was dead. I never even guessed he wasn't…that it was all…"

A lie. Nate completed her sentence in his head. Just a lie. But a lie he wanted to believe so badly.

Josey went on. "He found me. I mean, he found you. I met him in the lobby today. He was looking for you. He knew where you were first. I mean, he sort of knew. He knew Nate lived here, and he told me he missed you and you ran away from him. But that's true…you ran away?"

"Yes," said Derek.

"So you knew he was somewhere out there, all this time?"

"Yes."

"And…but Nate said he was dead. And I told him—

Jonathan—that. I thought he was lying, that he was some guy Nate put in jail once or something, looking to give him trouble. But he showed me pictures. Of you…and Nate.''

"Nate is in the room," Nate said then, finding the strength to stand and face his brother and Josey. "Nate has to talk to Josey about a few things right now, so maybe Derek can excuse us?''

"I didn't mean to talk about you that way," Derek said quickly. "You were just upset, detached, and it seemed you weren't even listening to a word we were saying.''

"I heard every word. How could I not listen to my—to Josey attempt to explain why she invited him here?''

"You guys do need to talk." Derek crossed the room as if to hug Josey, and then seemed in a split second to decide not to.

"I'm sorry," she said, her eyes and voice pleading. Derek nodded and touched her shoulder briefly, then left the apartment.

Neither Josey nor Nate said a word; they merely looked at each other as Derek's unusually slow footsteps retreated down the carpeted hallway. They heard the door to the stairwell open, and both flinched slightly when it slammed shut. A few more charged moments came and went.

"Are you all right?''

She looked as if this was not at all what she expected him to say, and continued to stand there looking perplexed until Nate clarified, "Your face.''

She raised her hand to her cheek again. "It's fine. It doesn't even hurt. It just feels a little warm. I won't even have a bruise.''

"That's not the point. I hit you.''

"Don't be ridiculous. You clonked me by accident. It's nothing.''

"It's something. It's everything. You don't get it at all.''

He pushed both hands through his hair, trying to gain control of the thoughts that smashed around in his brain like lawn furniture in a tornado. "It's everything," he said again. He shook his head and nothing cleared. But he shifted his line of questioning slightly. "Why did you bring him here?"

"I said I didn't know he was in town. I didn't even know he was alive."

"He showed you pictures? Of what?"

"Of you and Derek as little kids. As soon as I saw them I...I realized I had to take a chance on this man. The pictures had to be the two of you. I wouldn't have forgiven myself if he was your father and he wanted to love you again and I just booted him out the door. I couldn't do it."

"Then you believed him? You didn't believe in me anymore? You realized I lied?"

"Not a lie, more like not the whole truth. I figured there had to be a reason you'd told me what you did. Then he said you ran away from him after your mother died...." Josey's voice trailed off and Nate watched her chew her lower lip and study his face. "God, I don't know what the truth is anymore. Was that not the whole truth? Is your mother really dead or is she also..."

"She's dead." Nate felt ire boiling inside, reddening his face. "How dare you imply—"

"I'm not implying anything!" Josey cried. "I'm just trying to piece this together. You obviously haven't told me the whole truth about your past, for whatever reasons you have. That's fine, but you have to also understand that's why I screwed everything up—because I didn't know the truth. I thought I was helping bring together a family torn apart by misunderstandings. Instead, there's so much more I hadn't had a clue about. Nate, he hurt you, didn't he?

Physically hurt you, and emotionally. And you and Derek ran. After…after your mother died. Is that right?''

Nate stood then, wanting to run somewhere, but his legs just took him in circles around the room.

''That's why you were so upset that night, after the verdict. You won the case, but you realized it still hurt, that your past wouldn't go away,'' Josey said.

Nate's feet pounded on the carpet as he paced. His hands clenched tight as his brain worked hard to restrain them from punching a hole in the wall. Finally, when he was directly in front of Josey, he stopped moving and said, ''I'm not talking about this.''

''Please. Please talk to me. Was your mom sick? That takes such a hard toll on a family. Maybe—''

''I said I'm not talking about this!'' Nate roared. ''I'm not talking about this to anyone, and especially not you!''

Josey didn't flinch, and Nate had a fleeting thought that she was foolish not to. Instead, she just begged, ''But why? We're best friends. You're my—my…''

''What the hell would you know about any of this? You had perfect parents who loved you, a perfect home life.''

''Do I have to have suffered exactly like you in order to be there for you?''

''You can't understand.''

''Try me.''

''No, I won't try you! I've tried you, and you're…and I can't be with you. Don't you get it?''

''Because of what I did?''

''Because of who I am.''

''I thought I knew who that was. Don't I?''

''No. If you did, you wouldn't have let me into your—your…''

''Bed?''

''Life!''

Then Josey finally did appear stunned. "How can you say that about me? How can you say that about *you?* Doesn't anything that's happened between us mean anything?"

"It means everything!"

"Then let's talk about things!"

"I'm not going to change. People don't change people. Talking won't change me."

"I don't want to change you!" Josey shouted. "I love you!"

Nate stilled. For many, many moments, he couldn't move.

"Didn't you hear me? I said I love you!" Red-faced from her brazen, likely unplanned statement, Josey stared him right in the eye until he tore his gaze away and directed it at the floor. When she spoke again, her voice was so soft he had to strain to hear. "Why couldn't you just trust me with the truth?"

"Why," Nate countered just as quietly, "couldn't you just trust me with my lie?"

"But you can't lie forever."

Nate's eyes caught hers again. "No, you're right." They stayed like that for a few more seconds, and then he broke the spell by moving toward the door.

"Where are you going? Are you going?"

"You were right, Jose. I can't lie forever. I couldn't be with you. I tricked myself into thinking it could work."

"Please, Nate, forgive me!" Josey's eyes filled up with tears so quickly that in the same instant Nate realized she was going to cry, tears had already spilled over onto her smooth cheeks. "I'm sorry. I was so wrong, please."

"No, honey, it wasn't you." Nate checked his urge to touch her face and wipe away the wet streaks. "It wasn't what you did. I screwed up. It's so wonderful to be with you that I let myself believe it would be all right. But it wasn't. You were looking for the perfect man. You deserve the perfect man. One who will marry you and give you the family you so desperately want. But as much as I want it to be, that perfect man is not me.''

''Why not?''

''You saw what just happened. Can you imagine having to live with that, day after day, your whole life? You would have to, and I can't do that to you, all right?''

''Why would I have to live with that? It's not your father I want to be with.''

''But my father is what you'd get!''

''What?'' Josey whispered, but Nate saw in her moist eyes that it wasn't really a question. She understood. She knew, finally, what he was saying. And it was a good thing, because he couldn't say any more. He swallowed an enormous lump in his throat that threatened to choke him, and he wished it would, so he wouldn't have to say his next words.

''I'm sorry, but…I'm so sorry. But we can't be together. It has nothing to do with what you did, so don't blame yourself.''

Josey's breathing looked labored now; her collarbone rose and fell heavily. ''You're not even going to give us a chance? Even knowing how good we are, how well we get along, how we always understood each other? You think you're just a product of your upbringing? You're not. You're a separate person. You're loving, caring, compassionate, wonderful.…''

Nate turned away from her again and moved close enough to the door to grasp the knob. The brass was slippery in his sweating fingers.

''If you run away from us, you're something worse than you think you are. You're a coward.''

Nate's shoulders slumped at the new, sharp tinge in her voice. "Be mad at me if that's easier," he mumbled. "You can hate me for leaving you like this, but it's probably better for you to hate me now than for me to ruin your whole life."

"Dammit," Josey answered through her tears. "You're ruining it, anyway." She turned and ran to her bedroom, slamming the door.

Nate hesitated, but as the sounds of her sobs began to come through the wall, he quietly let himself out of her apartment.

Josey lay on her bed, crying and gasping for what was probably hours. Her misery was interrupted only once, by her mother's phone call—a call meant to be casual but one that turned into comfort and reassurance as soon as Josey had hiccuped out her whole story. She told her mother she loved Nate, and that she'd screwed it up.

"He'll come around, honey," her mother had answered. "He loves you."

"What?" Josey had asked, incredulous in spite of her despair, and her mother had responded, "Oh, Josey-Posy, as if you haven't figured that out by now. Of course he loves you."

Which had sent Josey into a fresh round of tears again and forced her to hang up.

Finally, squinting at the light of dusk peeking through her curtains, she thought of her mother at home, worried about her. She thought about how her mother would go into her father's study and drag him away from his work with her anxiety, and how her father would blink himself out of his academic haze to concentrate on her words, and how his face would crease with serious lines as he, too, worried about his daughter. Their only child, around whom the world, Josey knew, still revolved.

Then she squinched her eyes shut against the light, and in the darkness behind her lids she was able to imagine that man again, Jonathan, and his brutal, mocking gaze, his terrifying tone, and she curled her body up tight like a little girl—no, like a little boy cowering in fear as this angry giant approached, ready to lift up his arm, his fist, and strike out against soft flesh, innocent flesh....

Feeling again the hand that hit innocent flesh, Nate opened his eyes, and squeezed them shut almost immediately to close out the memories—the long-ago ones, of his father striking him, and the most recent one, of striking Josey. Nate's hand burned and itched, and he clutched it to his chest with his other hand, willing his skin to remember only the satin smoothness of the night before. He curled up tighter into a ball and tried to remember, and forget.

Chapter Sixteen

If Nate let himself count the weeks since he'd last seen Josey, he wouldn't be able to concentrate on his work. So he used the calendar above his office desk only to record and check court dates, and stayed in the present—which he strived to make as hectic as possible. Days ran into one another, a blur of papers and legal proceedings, his mental haze temporarily lifting in the courtroom and with clients. He began sleeping in his office, going home quickly to shower and change each morning, moving around his apartment hastily because if he stopped, even for an instant, he might hear his ceiling creak under her feet, and he didn't want to know she was there. Hesitant to stay long enough to even fix himself an occasional meal, he ate take-out all day long—when he actually remembered to eat. He watched no TV and read nothing but the occasional newspaper article related to his colleagues' work.

He neglected to go to Derek's two Thursdays running,

and when Derek called, Nate promised to mail him money—barely hearing Derek telling him he didn't care about the money, that he was worried. Nate just responded with a few monosyllables and hung up, and ever since sent a weekly check.

He never heard from his father—or maybe his father had tried to reach him at his apartment, and Nate didn't know because he was never there. Either way suited him fine. He preferred not to think about it, not to remember anything. Staying in the present was the only thing he wanted to do.

One morning he arrived at his office to find Jeffers waiting for him outside his door. Jeffers told him to go home. Nate stared at his mentor in disbelief, and Jeffers patted him on the shoulder, told him he'd prepared the staff to handle Nate's caseload for a while, and suggested Nate go to the Caribbean or something to relax. And he was not to return until he was himself.

Jeffers expressed his concern with a smile, so Nate wouldn't fear for his job. But Nate was afraid to face every day without his work to distract him.

Somehow he made it to the T stop, dug out some change and collapsed into a seat. He wasn't sure where to go, since home still wasn't the preferable place to be. The T passed his stop, and he blankly watched a few people get off. He thought it was odd to take the T every day and not know any of the people that got off at the stop closest to his home. It made him feel even more alone, and he wasn't sure if that was for the best or for the worst. Under ordinary circumstances, he wouldn't think twice about being alone. But his life hadn't been ordinary for a long time now.

He stayed on the T, and even changed trains at one point. Finally, an outdoor stop looked inviting, familiar, and it wasn't until he stepped onto the platform and felt the departing train's rush of air lift the hem of his jacket that he realized where he was. Two blocks from Derek's.

When he buzzed Derek's apartment, there was no immediate answer, and he leaned into the doorway, pressing his forehead to the exposed brick, feeling the roughness grind into his skin. He thought maybe he'd just stay that way until Derek came home from wherever he was at that early hour. But the door suddenly clicked open and Derek was in front of him. "Sorry, the buzzer doesn't work and I had to come down—what are you doing here? Don't you have to work? Are you all right?"

Nate slunk through the door ahead of his brother and climbed the stairs to the apartment. He brushed some papers off the living room sofa onto the floor and collapsed, closing his eyes. He heard Derek come in and close the door, and he felt Derek stand there, looking at him. "Are you all right? You couldn't have gotten fired."

Nate gave a sharp bark of laughter. "No, although I'd be carrying on the family tradition—get fired, try to mooch off someone else."

"Well, are you sick?"

"No, not sick," Nate mumbled. "Just really, really tired. Could I crash here?"

"Looks as if you already have," Derek replied. And before Nate drifted off, he thought he heard him add, "You must be tired. You didn't even attempt to straighten up the living room...."

Nate woke up shaking, his brain filled with screaming. Breathing hard, he shook his head to clear the nightmare that still echoed loudly, so loudly. But as his eyes cleared, the frightening voice seemed even closer. The harsh sounds filled not only his mind but all the space around him. The entire apartment.

He sat up with a jolt. Was his father here? In Derek's place? How could he be? Why would Derek let him in? Where were they?

Nate pushed himself off the sofa, and his limbs were stiff from sleeping in a cramped position for what must have been quite a while, as the bright morning light in the living room had since dimmed into what felt like early evening. He moved toward Derek's bedroom, and as he did, the words grew louder—berating, degrading, demanding. And just as his father finished a particularly terrible turn of phrase, Nate found his brother, alone, staring down at the answering machine. His face was expressionless, as if the voice pounding out of it was merely reading a grocery list. When he glanced up and saw Nate, he hurriedly turned off the sound. Nate covered his ears against the sudden silence.

"I'm sorry that woke you up." Derek's voice was muffled, so Nate dropped his hands to his sides. "I remembered to turn off the ringer so the phone wouldn't wake you up, but I guess I turned this thing up too high. I was curious to see what he was actually rambling on about this time."

"This time?" Nate interrupted. "This time? He's called you before?"

"Yeah. A bunch of times since that night at Josey's." The mention of her name made Nate flinch, but Derek probably didn't see it because he kept talking. "Maybe he called your house, too, but it seems you're never there, since he usually asks me where you are. I usually just screen my calls or hang up on him."

Nate shook his head.

"He was screaming to know where you're sleeping, where he can call you. Lovely phone manners. Apparently he thinks if he calls me enough nasty names I'll find you for him. So he never called you?"

"I, uh, I never got a message. No one really calls me at

home." Not since Josey stopped. "My phone's not listed, so maybe he doesn't have the number. But he never called me at work, either."

"I actually think he's afraid to call you at work, since your office puts criminals in jail and he is one. Coward. That's all he is."

Maybe. But Nate felt like the coward. His heart was still slamming into his chest at an out-of-control rate. His father was still here, still in this city, still threatening to never go away. Nate had lost Josey already to all this. And now he knew, hearing his father again when he'd thought that part was over, peace of mind might never be in his future. There was nowhere to run, nowhere to hide, no one to help him do either. No sanctuary for someone like him.

He turned to flee the apartment, to get outside where he could breathe.

"Nate, wait!" Derek dashed around him and blocked his way. "Stay here, have dinner. Come on. He'll give up. He'll give up sometime. He has to. We're not obligated to him. No matter what he says, we don't have to listen to him or give him anything. There's nothing to be afraid of. Unless...where's Josey?"

Nate shrugged.

"You broke up with her, didn't you?" Something in Nate's face must have confirmed it. "You did. When? When I left that night? Smart move, Nate. Really smart move. That relationship lasted what, twelve hours? It could have lasted forever! You threw it away, for what?"

"Don't bring this up now, all right? I don't want to discuss it with you."

"I will bring it up if I damn well please! You're my brother."

"We're not kids anymore, and you can't bully me

around, in case you've forgotten." He tried to get around him but Derek planted his hand on the door frame.

"I haven't forgotten, but it sure seems as if you have. You're acting like a kid."

"Don't pass judgment on me!" Nate yelled. "What do you know about it?"

"I know the same as you, Nate. Exactly the same as you."

"No, you don't. You don't know someone like her."

"When I do, I'll know enough not to toss her away."

"No. What you'll know is you'll never be what she deserves."

"Is that what you believe? That deep down, I'm a terrible person who can never make a woman happy?"

"No, I…"

"You think I'm just like Dad?"

"You know you're not?"

"No. I think I'm not. I won't know until I'm married and have children. But I've never been like him yet, and at least I'm willing to try life and find out for myself."

"How many times am I going to have to hear this from you? You should be on my side."

"I am on your side, Nate. You're my brother and I love you, okay? I've always been on your side. But you have to be on your side, too."

"I have to go."

"Go where?"

"Go home, I suppose. If I learned anything today, it's that I can't get away from any of this, between his phone calls and your harassment. So I may as well start hanging around the place I pay rent for on a regular basis again."

"Sure, run off. Go for it. Sit around moping your whole life. Keep dwelling on the past so you have no future. In fact, maybe you're right, after all. Maybe that's what I should be doing. Yup, as soon as you leave, I'm going to disconnect my phone, quit school, crawl into the corner there and deny myself a life. Never mind that I busted my ass for us so we could *have* that life!''

Nate's face grew hot. ''I'm repaying you, aren't I? I'm putting you through school, too, goddammit!''

''Sure, you're repaying me the money. But I'm insulted that you'd deliberately be ungrateful!''

''I was never ungrateful!''

''Then show it, you moron! Show you're grateful for your life by living it, and not throwing it away! You make me feel like it was all a waste!''

The two brothers stared at each other. And then the phone rang. One, two, three rings. Nate pried Derek's hand off the door frame, opened the door and fled.

At lunchtime on the first day of school, Josey was quite possibly more relieved than the children were. She felt so tired from standing in front of the room for just a few hours. Maybe she was getting old. She herded her kids to the cafeteria, thankful for the aides who kept order so she could go back to her classroom, sit at her desk and drop her head onto her folded arms. She'd brought a sandwich but the thought of eating a bite of it was enough to set her stomach roiling again. Instead she just closed her eyes and tried to let her mind wander.

One child in her class was absent today. Mike Crowley, the little boy whose mother had canceled tutoring sessions numerous times during the summer. The few times he had shown up he'd been restless, inattentive, with practically no recollection of what he'd learned in the previous session. Josey was concerned about his inability to concentrate, especially since he didn't seem to display any learning problems and in fact was quite bright. She'd tried to talk to his mother once about working with her son at home, and had offered to lend her some materials, but the woman had barely listened to her. Instead, she'd been preoccupied, nervous even. Josey had vowed to keep an eye on Mike this year—but how could she when he wasn't at school?

There was nothing she could do right now, so she tried to think of something else. But as usual, the perennial topic in her overloaded mind was Nate. And she couldn't mope about that right now. She couldn't—

"Knock, knock!" Ally appeared at her door. Josey hadn't heard her heels on the hallway tile outside. She wondered if she'd fallen asleep. Her brain felt murky.

"Hi, hon."

"Why aren't you eating with us in the lounge? There's a surprise there. They finally brought in a new soda machine. About time, eh? I wanted a new soda machine even more than I want tenure."

Josey looked up at her friend and smiled weakly.

"Josey, are you okay?"

"Oh, I'm just a little under the weather. I woke up feeling sick and I've been up and down all morning. I'm just grabbing a little peace and quiet."

"Do you need some aspirin or something?"

"No, but thank you. I think I'll make it through the rest of the afternoon and then I'll go right home and crash. I'm fine."

Ally perched on the edge of her desk. "Are you fine? I've barely spoken a word to you in weeks. I miss you, you know. I'm worried about you. Have you talked to him?"

Josey shook her head, dejected. She had told Ally the abridged version of her life—that she and Nate got together and broke up in a less-than-twenty-four-hour time span— but she hadn't volunteered any real details. It was bad enough to have to live the details.

As if reading her mind, Ally said, "I know you haven't wanted to give me specifics, and I won't press, but you know you can talk to me, right?"

Josey squeezed her hand. "I know. Believe me, it has nothing to do with not trusting you. It's just that it's Nate's problem and I'd feel disloyal."

"I understand. But if it's Nate's problem, whatever it is, shouldn't he want to work on it to be with you?"

"I thought so. I really thought so." Josey capped and uncapped a red pen, over and over. "But maybe everyone has something they can't get past. He can't get past this."

"Can you get past him?"

"I'm not sure."

"So you're both stuck…"

"…in the past."

"And you can't get to the future."

"And the present is pure hell."

"Josey, I'm sorry. I guess it takes real courage to face the future sometimes. I don't know Nate, but I know you, and I'm willing to bet if only one of you is capable of pulling through, it's you."

"I think so, too, actually. And that worries me. What will he do?"

"I don't know."

Josey fell silent and looked out the window at waving, lush green leaves on the trees lining the school yard. She knew from years past exactly how this view would change over the year, how the branches would drop the leaves and how snow would cover the bark and drip off in the spring sun. She'd be here, but…where would he be?

"Ally, thanks for talking to me."

"You're welcome." Ally hopped off the desk. "I'm going to eat my lunch, but I'm also going to fetch you a ginger ale from the new machine. Be back in a while."

"Thanks." Josey took a deep breath and tried to focus her mind on something. She finally tossed the pen cap across her desk and turned to her wall calendar to figure out how to schedule a few major projects she wanted the new class to tackle.

Maybe it was good to be back in school again, she thought, making a note on a Monday square a few weeks from now. She'd missed Ally. She'd missed kids, and learning from them as much as they learned from her.

But she missed Nate so badly. *Missed* was a weak word for how she felt. She missed his serious face, his common sense, his worried frown, his smile. And after only one night, she desperately missed his hands on her bare back, his lips on her throat, her breasts, her lips.

And, she realized with a jolt after examining the calendar for a few moments, there was one more thing she'd missed, but had been too stressed to notice. She counted, and counted again, flipping one page over and back, then gasped and clutched her churning stomach.

She'd missed her period.

Chapter Seventeen

The mirror offered absolutely no clue. Not when Josey stood before it, naked, and squinted at her abdomen, and not when she turned to view her lower self in profile, smoothing her hand down her own skin. Couldn't be true. Couldn't be there.

But it was. Doctor-confirmed, yesterday. And it had been reminding her of its existence by quite literally making her puke several times.

But then, maybe that wasn't the baby inside her but rather the terror that clenched her soul whenever she thought about how this baby had got there.

Nate didn't want a baby. That's what his whole life was about. Even more than he didn't want her, he didn't want a baby.

Now she had no choice but to offer him what he would never want.

She laid a protective, motherly palm over her abdomen,

a gesture she was unfamiliar with but which felt completely natural somehow, and lifted her gaze from her reflected body to stare into her own eyes. She couldn't not tell him. Late last night, sweating in bed, playing an imaginary conversation with him in her mind and wincing at his certain rejection, she had let herself entertain the idea of just not telling him. But she'd almost instantly closed off that option. She couldn't, in good faith, keep this baby from Nate.

No matter their standing now—if there was a standing anymore—he would always be the best friend she'd ever had and would ever have. Keeping a secret like this, that there would soon be a person in the world who was half him, was unconscionable. The only way to honor what they had had together was to tell him, whether he liked it or not—and he wouldn't—and whether she liked it or not. She wasn't afraid of him at all, but she was afraid of hurting him, and she knew this would hurt him more than anything in the world could.

She'd have to break it to him soon. This wasn't exactly the sort of thing she could hide for a few years.

She walked over to her underwear drawer and pulled out a pair of panties. She slid them up over her legs, and after wondering if they'd still fit her in a few months, she mused that maybe it was possible to be big and pregnant, have a baby and get him or her all the way to eighth grade without Nate ever knowing. She hadn't run into him once in weeks. How did he manage to avoid her when he lived right below her? They used to run into each other unplanned all the time. It was as if he'd dropped off the face of the earth.

The weather was such that the windows could still be kept open all the time, and she hadn't heard his television, his water running, nothing. The only thing she had heard was his phone, and when it rang, it rang endlessly, relentlessly, with no one picking it up to silence it. Where the hell was he, anyway? She was worried, but she also knew Nate had Derek, and if some awful thing had happened, Derek would be there for him. And hopefully, Derek would tell her, too—although that was probably just wishful thinking.

She stepped into a green flowered dress and cinched the waist. Then she thought better of it and loosened the belt a bit. She patted her stomach, sighed and tried to put all thoughts out of her head except where she'd dropped her tote bag. She was never late for school, not as a child and not as a teacher, and she wasn't about to start.

She found the bag conveniently next to her shoes in the living room. She grabbed the grade book that had tumbled out onto the floor, and in her hand it fell open. The list of children were there in a column, in alphabetical order. It's funny, Josey thought. There's one more child in the classroom every day now. And no one knows it but me.

As it turned out, another child finally made an appearance in the classroom that day. Mike Crowley, after missing three days, had finally arrived as a new third-grader. Even though her own problems threatened to overshadow every other concern in her life, Josey had not hesitated to notify the principal that the little boy was absent on the second day. Apparently, Mike had the flu, and his mother was very apologetic, the principal told Josey. Mike's mother was told not to worry, but to remember to call if her son was going to be sick. She called the next day, and now, on the fourth day, Mike was here.

Josey showed him to the desk saved for him, gave him all the necessary workbooks and stored his lunch on the back shelf with the others'. A couple of boys whispered his name to catch his attention, and she saw him smile back at his friends. The uneasiness she'd harbored about him began to fade.

Until the afternoon.

Josey gave the kids an after-lunch recess, knowing the children wouldn't have the luxury when the New England chill set in a few weeks from now. When she called them back to class, the kids burst through the classroom door, carrying a playgroundful of energy with them. It took a bit longer than she would have liked to settle them in, but one by one they did, the last one being Mike. Josey suggested to him that he ought to be in his seat, and when, busy examining a friend's plastic action figure, he didn't seem to take the hint, Josey moved behind him and put a hand on his shoulder to gently guide him.

He flinched.

It was a small flinch, but a definite one.

Josey's blood flowed cold through her entire body, bringing up goose bumps along her arms and legs and making her teeth chatter. A thousand reasons for suspicion swirled in her mind as she stared at the top of the little boy's blond head. The tutoring cancellations. His absence at the start of the new year. His mother's rushed, reluctant excuses.

The flinch.

Mike sat down in his seat, and in a shaking voice she couldn't disguise, Josey asked everyone to pull out their spelling notebooks. There were a few groans, lots of shuffling.

And one little boy absentmindedly rubbing his shoulder with one hand.

Leaving the rest of the class in Ally's capable hands, Josey quietly ushered Mike out the door of the music room and down the hall. It had been near agony waiting forty-five minutes for the class's scheduled music session, but

Josey thought it was the least disruptive time to shuttle Mike away. She'd remembered hearing him cough earlier that day, and told herself if she was wrong, if this was all an overreaction, she could tell his mother later that she'd heard him coughing and, coupled with his absence, she'd decided to take him to see the nurse.

But her intuition, thumping with every heartbeat, told her she wouldn't need that excuse later.

She pushed open the door to the nurse's office, and Jake greeted her. "Miss St. John! How nice to see you. Unfortunately, that usually means someone is feeling yucky." He trained his medical gaze on Mike. "Who might you be?"

"I feel fine," Mike said petulantly, gazing down the hallway in the direction of the music room.

Jake stood up from his desk in his white coat and walked toward them, smiling. But when he saw the twisted expression Josey knew must be on her face, his own smile became a little tighter. "Well, I'm sure you feel fine, pal," he said, and Josey felt relieved. Jake would help her. He'd find everything was all right.

"What's your name?"

"Mike."

"Well, Mike, you didn't throw up anywhere today, did you?"

Mike gave a half smile at the unexpected question. "No."

"That's good." Jake pulled his stethoscope from under his white coat. "Do you know how many kids throw up in school? What a mess."

Mike smiled slightly again.

"Have you been sick?"

"No."

"Mike," Josey softly reminded him, "you missed the first three days of school. You were sick, right?"

Mike gave a start as if he'd suddenly remembered something. "Yes."

Jake looked up and held Josey's gaze for the barest of moments.

"He was coughing," Josey explained, but knew she didn't need to elaborate, sensed that Jake knew why she was here. She touched her own shoulder, rubbed it in the subtlest way she could, then dropped her gaze to Mike's shoulder.

Jake nodded so briefly she almost missed it. "Well, Mike my pal, let's make sure you were feeling well enough to come back today. I bet you wanted to come back to school, huh? Pretty tired of summer vacation?"

"Yeah."

"Well, I'm going to ask you to take your shirt off so I can listen to your chest with my stethoscope here. If you have any coughing germs, I should hear them in there."

Mike looked nervous, tugged at the hem of his red shirt.

"First," Jake continued, "let's get all the girls out of here." He made a show of looking around. "Hmm. I just see one girl. Excuse me, miss, you'll have to leave now."

Josey forced a smile and went out into the hallway, shutting the door behind her.

She bit her lip, waited.

In less than five minutes, the door opened again. Jake leaned his torso out, beckoned her close, whispered into her ear.

"Go down to the principal. We'll meet you there."

The gentle tap-tap on Nate's door was just enough to violently startle him. The afternoon silence in his apartment was such that a spider starting a climb up his living room wall could jolt him out of a nap, so the tap-tap was like a double bolt of lightning.

He'd been alone in a little hole for so long, not caring, but his tired and desperate heart somehow managed to flip over and over at the sound, knowing who it was.

There it was again: tap-tap. Then Josey called, "Nate? Are you in there? Please?"

His resolve crumbled under the crushing strength of his heart, and before he had time to curse himself for it, he opened the door.

Her face, so unlike his, was at that moment very like his. Her pale skin was stretched tight over exhausted features. Her eyes showed tiny creases at the outside corners; her jaw was hard set, with clenched teeth.

She didn't make a move to come in. They regarded each other's expressions, and Nate wondered if when she spoke he'd be able to hear her, the way his pulse was reverberating in his ear. If she noticed how pathetic he himself must have looked, she gave no indication. He wondered if she wanted to kiss him. He wondered if he wanted to kiss her.

Yes yes yes yes, his heart cried. But before he could summon up strength to fight back, Josey's dry lips opened.

"I need you. I need your help. I would never have come here. I know how you feel about us. But I need your help. Please help me."

Nate shook his head briefly to clear the pounding out of his eardrums, but she seemed to mistake it for a no, because she implored, "Please. I'll never bother you again, never ever, after this, but just please listen to me and help me."

He moved aside to let her pass through, and she perched on the edge of the sofa, waiting to speak until he sat down across from her. But once she started, she didn't waste words.

"A little boy in my class is being physically abused. He missed the first three days of school because he was sick. That's what his mother said. But I touched his shoulder today and he flinched. I sent him to the nurse and when he took off his shirt to be examined, he had welts and bruises all over his back. The nurse and I told the principal and the principal reported it to the police, and now I don't know what's going on. I think they called the Department of Social Services to try to get Mike out of his house, but by the end of the school day no one could tell me what was going on. I don't want to keep calling the police, but I can't breathe, can't do anything until I know Mike is out of danger. What if the police went there and decided not to do anything, and his parents got mad that I reported it? They could do something, take it out on him...." She bit her lip and Nate could see her chin wobbling. "And that would be my fault, and I can't.... Then I thought, Nate, your office, your task force would probably work this case if they bring Mike's father or mother up on criminal charges, and I was hoping you could, I don't know, make some calls? See if Mike's all right and somewhere safe? Because I can't—"

Nate cut her off; he couldn't stand to hear this, hear her begging him, justifying her very real fright when no justification should be necessary. "Stop. Of course I will. I, um, I haven't been to the office in a couple of days but I'll put in a call to Jeffers and ask him a few questions, and when I go into the office tomorrow," he continued, planning as he talked, "I'll get a handle on this case myself. But I promise I'll get enough for you by tonight so you can sleep. Okay?"

He didn't wait for an answer; he was already up and crossing the room to his telephone. But in the middle of dialing, he glanced back at her, saw her tense shoulders droop. There were thousands of things that could have been said, by him, by her, at that exact moment, but it seemed she was going to let the moment pass, and the onus was on him. But what he said was, ''Tell me the little boy's last name, his mother's name, anything you know so I can find out the status as quickly as I can. It will be okay, Josey, I promise. You did a good thing and it will be all right.''

Josey smiled weakly. ''Where do I wish I'd heard that before?''

They looked into the darkness of each other's eyes across the room.

The phone buzzed angrily in Nate's ear, and he clicked the receiver and began redialing.

''It will be all right,'' he repeated, possibly to himself.

That night, Nate slept—not the haunted, exhausting sleep of the last few weeks, but an undisturbed, dreamless sleep that left his brain rested and lucid. Perhaps the contented night came from assuring Josey she could have the same. Several phone calls had yielded the information they'd both been hoping for—that Mike had been removed from his abusive home and instantly placed into foster care.

It was up to the courts to decide everything now—Mike's future as well as Mike's father's future. As far as they could ascertain, Mike's dad had been severely abusive toward his wife and his child, and though Mike's mom had not likely been the same way, she'd allowed both herself and her son to languish in their violent surroundings until now.

Until Josey.

Nate rushed through a shower and within a half hour was out the door to the office. He'd warned Jeffers he was coming in and he wouldn't take to another kind gesture on the firm's part to keep him home. He was ready to come back. His tone of voice was one his friend wouldn't, or couldn't, argue with.

Indeed, Lauren and everyone else greeted him with

smiles and phone messages. He grabbed them and took off in search of a few specific colleagues.

In less than twenty minutes, he shut the door to his office, sat at his desk, opened the file he'd brought in with him and dialed a noted phone number.

Dr. Jesse Moran, who'd examined Mike yesterday at Children's Hospital, had to be paged. While Nate waited, he flipped through the file, a thin folder that was bound to expand in the next few weeks with papers noting interviews and court proceedings. He got up to date quickly.

"Nate Bennington? Is that you?" Jesse had been a college buddy of Nate's, but law school and medical school demands had denied them the opportunity to see each other more than a couple of times in the years since. Still, they'd kept tabs on each other, calling every now and then. It felt nice to hear a familiar voice right then—one that didn't demand he peer into his own soul for any reason.

"Hey, Jesse, how are you?"

"I'm tired, that's how I am. Working like a dog here. I'm not sure what day it is, really."

"Trust me, I know the feeling of not sleeping."

"I'll bet you do. Ridding the streets of criminals is just as tiring, I'm sure. It's been ages, pal."

"Yeah, it has, but unfortunately, I'm calling you for something not so fun."

"Shoot."

"There's a kid I'm hoping you could give me a little info on. They would have brought him in to you last night."

He barely got the boy's name out before Jesse interrupted him. "Oh, yeah, I remember him. It *was* last night. You're involved with this one, huh? Physical trauma is definitely there. I know he is scheduled to meet with a psychologist here this morning."

"Psychologist?"

"Yep. The kid's been very reluctant to talk. It's understandable, of course, because it's been less than twenty-four hours since all this was set in motion."

"Well, we probably don't need a statement yet—"

"Oh, I'm not talking about him giving any kind of statement. I'm talking about the boy getting some seriously needed counseling."

"Oh. Of course."

"Who discovered this abuse? His teacher?"

"Why do you guess that?"

"Well, it's not his parents, and a teacher is often the next protective adult figure."

"Ah."

"Whoever it was made the right call here. Not only are his back and shoulders banged up pretty badly, there are also quite a few old scars. It looks to me like this severe beating isn't the first. Poor kid. It's rough."

Nate thanked his friend, asked if he could call in a few days, and hung up. He leaned back in his comfortable chair…and ran both hands through his hair until it felt as if it was standing on end. He'd promised to call Josey when he learned anything new, and although what he found wasn't much news at all, he found himself wishing he had more to tell so he could call her. Having her back in his life so suddenly was frightening, but knowing he was in a position to help her was a comfort. Even though with every anxious word she'd spoken to him last night he'd wanted to touch her, hold her, and he just couldn't, this was better than never seeing her. Which, when this case was over, was where they'd be back to, once again.

"He won't talk."

"What do you mean, he won't talk?" Nate was not quite

incredulous at Jesse's words, though. It had only been a few days since they'd last spoken, and he knew how long a child could keep a secret. "He talked to the police the day he was put into foster care."

"Well, he's stopped talking. Guilt, probably. Fear. He's just a little boy."

"But why force him to say anything more at all? I'd guess we have enough to prosecute his father."

"Oh, sure, you have enough to make a case, but I'm not thinking legalities now. That's your thing. I'm a doctor, and between you and me, that child is in danger."

"But he's out of that house."

"Yeah, I know. I'm not worried about his physical well-being anymore. I'm worried about his emotional state. This kid probably had been warned—likely by both his parents—not to talk, not to say anything to anyone. And he did. Now his father's been arrested, and he's been taken away from his mother."

"But that's the best thing for him."

"I'm not saying it's not. What I'm saying is, Mike's going through extreme trauma, and if he doesn't talk about it, I'm worried about the long-term ramifications."

Nate was quiet. Jesse took it as a sign to continue. "I've sent a couple of psychologists to see the child, to try to talk to him. I've sat down with the boy and tried to talk to him myself. But he shows no willingness to talk, to trust anyone. He needs to be able to trust someone enough to tell what happened to him. It's a big step toward healing emotional wounds. If he keeps everything inside him, he could be scarred for a long, long time. Much longer than those marks on his back. He's a little boy. If we can help him now, he may be able to live a normal life."

Normal life. Nate felt inexplicably frantic, seeing this

child's future slipping away, a victim of his past. Unless he could trust someone.

And Nate knew the best person. A person who was an artist at making people feel at ease and happy. A person who was hesitant to pass judgment, who had hope she could help even when it was way beyond her reach.

"Could I send his teacher to see him?" Nate asked, before he could change his mind. "If he's got any urge inside him to open up, she'll find it, trust me."

"I don't think it could hurt. He's in foster care. She might try to see him at home with the family he's staying with. Maybe being here in the hospital scares him. It certainly scares me sometimes."

"Will you ask the foster family if they'd let her visit?"

"I'll call the psychologist working with him and let her do that. I'm sure they'll cooperate. Hey, why the special interest, anyway? You have a lot of cases, don't you?"

"Yes, but I, uh, I know his teacher. She's very upset, very worried about him."

"Well, unfortunately," Jesse sighed, "she has good reason."

Chapter Eighteen

"Please, I need your help. I won't ever ask for it again."

Her own words, turned back on her, Josey realized. How quickly the world revolves. But just then, she didn't have the luxury of being philosophical. She pressed her lips to the phone receiver for a moment, then repeated what he'd just asked her. "You want me to go talk to Mike? At his foster home?"

"Yes. Please."

"Because your doctor friend told you that he's worried about this boy?"

"Yes. He says Mike could suffer long-term damage if he doesn't talk it out with someone."

"And he said the sooner he takes steps to confront this, the more likely it is he can live a normal life?"

"Yes."

It can't be possible, Josey thought, that the thick irony here is lost on him. He's too smart for that. And he must be fully aware this is the perfect time for me to say, *"See? What did I tell you? You have to talk out your problems and then a normal life is possible—a life with the family I know you could want."*

And she knew right then that this phone call had to have been an amazing act of bravery on his part, more than her visit to him was, because he was risking opening all this again—all this conflict with her—in the interest of one little boy.

And in admiration of that bravery, she chose to make it easier for him. She didn't say any of the things he must have expected her to say. She only said, "I think your friend's right. I'll do it."

"Really?"

"Of course," she replied, and the moment her words came out, inspiration burst into bloom in her head. They could help Mike, but could she solicit Nate's help with his own salvation at the same time? "Uh, Nate, you'll come with me, right?"

"What? Oh, no, that probably isn't the right thing to do."

"Why not? I mean, your office is dealing with this case. Maybe he'll say something you can use."

"No, no, whatever he says to you will be confidential. The whole point is he has to trust you."

True. "Well, I'm still hesitant to go alone. I mean, I never met the foster family. If you're there, you can assure them that I'm an okay person for Mike to talk to."

"I haven't met them, either."

Damn. "Look, I'm nervous. I've never had to talk to a child in this kind of situation before. I don't know what to expect. I'm sorry, I'm just scared." Josey held her breath. It was weak, she knew, but her fervent hope was that Nate wouldn't think too hard about it, but would follow through

on his natural protective instinct. The one that always made
him admonish her for neglecting to lock her door. The one
that made him agree to scrutinize her dates, in what felt
like lifetimes ago.

And perhaps an even deeper instinct—the instinct that
had rushed him to her doorstep moments after Derek had
left her that night. The instinct of love.

She squeezed her eyes shut.

"All right. I'll go with you if that's what you need."

"It is." I need you. "It is."

"I'll arrange it with the foster family. And I'll meet you
after work."

"Today?"

"Is there a better time? You have to try right away.
He's…he needs you to get through to him."

"Yes," she answered. "I imagine he does."

After foster mom Francine Travis had shown them into
the room Mike was using, she backed out quietly to give
Josey and Nate the privacy they needed to speak to the
little boy. Although Nate made it clear to the woman it was
Josey who'd come to talk to Mike, Josey had taken gentle
hold of his arm, making it clear she intended for him to
accompany her.

Unfortunately, she was also making it clear to herself
that she still wanted him. She didn't think it was her imagination that made her feel the pulse beating hard inside his
elbow, even through the sleeve of his button-down shirt.
The scent of him sent an erotic shock through her veins.

She steered him down a short hall toward the spare room
that Mike had been given as a bedroom. It was decorated
thoughtfully, with colorful animal prints on the walls and
a bright blue carpet. She imagined she would have liked
this room as a little girl. She wondered what kind of a room

Nate had slept in, played in. Had his mother taken care to make it a happy sanctuary? Or had his father's presence made it a frightening place instead, full of monsters?

Mike sat on the floor near the twin bed, surrounded with toys. The Lego bricks he was fiddling with were obviously not shiny new, but weren't worn out by any means. It appeared as though the foster couple's own children had grown a bit older, and had been the sort to be careful with their toys.

When Mike glanced up at Josey, nothing more than recognition was in his eyes. He showed no emotion as he picked up a blue brick and snapped it into place atop a shaky-looking tower. Josey tried a smile. "Hi, Mike. We miss you at school so I thought I'd come to see you. What are you building there?"

No answer. Josey's nerve endings were on fire. She didn't dare look at Nate, didn't want to know yet what was going on inside him. She folded herself onto the floor next to the little boy, her eyes never leaving his small, expressionless face.

"Can I help?" she asked, and Mike listlessly handed her a red plastic piece. "Should I put this right on top like you were doing? Or should I put it down near the bottom?" If a base wasn't built for this leaning tower of Lego, it was going to collapse. Mike just shrugged, so she snapped it near the bottom. "There. That looks like a good spot."

Mike just looked at the tower. Or maybe beyond the tower at something in his own mind. It was so hard to tell.

Out of the corner of her eye, she saw Nate sit on the edge of the small bed. She didn't have to turn her head all the way around; she knew his discomfort was like that day in her classroom, when her student Sara had forgotten her book. But this time, Josey guessed, he was probably even more nervous and wary, because Mike was a boy whose pain he'd known over and over again, in his childhood and in his memory.

She put her hand on Mike's arm. "I'd like you to meet Nate. He's my…" she hesitated, unsure of how Nate would like her next words, but knowing she needed to say them so Mike would feel at ease "…my best friend."

Her gaze darted to Nate, and she wondered if he'd even heard her. He and the child were quietly assessing each other. After a few moments, Nate said, "Hello, Mike," with such admirable confidence, Josey wanted to cry.

Mike still said nothing.

Josey kept her fingers on Mike's arm, trying to comfort. She thought she felt the baby move inside her, however impossible at this stage of pregnancy, and resisted the urge to lay her other hand across her abdomen. Instead, she kept talking.

"I know we haven't known each other very long, but I hope you think we're friends. I'm your teacher and your friend. You know that, right?"

No response.

"Part of being friends is that you can talk to each other about what's bothering you. Is there anything you'd like to talk about?"

At this point, Josey would have even settled for a "no." Because then, at least, she could be certain he'd heard her.

Mike reached for another Lego brick and fingered its smooth surface without picking it up off the floor. Josey looked at Nate, but his face mirrored the boy's reluctance.

She began to think this wasn't such a good idea, after all.

Her parents' faces suddenly took shape in her mind. She wondered briefly why she would be reminded of them, and then suddenly, her imagination distorted their features into those of terrorists. Her calm, gentle father's teeth were

bared in a predator's grimace, and her loving mother's spar-
kling eyes were unfocused and wild. Her relentless imagination put her at their mercy, cowering from them as their
child victim. For a split second, she shared the horror Nate
and Mike both knew.

It was as though her heart—which grasped how fate had
spared her the pain that had come to these two—had sent
her brain a message. A message to act. A chill sped through
her, down to her toes, but she forced herself to rise slowly
to her feet. She wished she could just disappear.

Both her companions looked up at her.

"I have to, ah…" She peered through the open bedroom
door. "I have to use the bathroom."

She moved to the doorway, turned her head once, caught
Nate's eye even though she didn't want to, and saw what
she knew she'd see there. Fear. A silent plea not to be left
with the little boy. She stared back at the man she loved,
willing her own eyes to reflect all the love she held for him
in her heart.

And she walked out.

Nate stared at the door Josey had not quite closed, conscious of the fact that as long as he kept his eyes on it, he
didn't have to look at the little boy now sharing the room
with only him.

But minutes dragged by, and Mike sat quietly with a blue
Lego piece, and Nate's leg began to jiggle up and down of
its own accord. Where was Josey? Had she fallen in or
what?

He felt the child look at him, and he forced himself to
meet the youngster's gaze. Mike was the first to break eye
contact, apathetically. They both studied the door again.
Nate felt guilty. It was odd, but here he was in this room
with the first person he'd met in a long while who'd ex-

perienced the kind of things he'd gone through. So he felt less alone. But Mike didn't know this, so he was still alone, locked inside by his own pain, unable to function.

It wasn't fair, really. And so Nate thought he should make it fairer, let Mike know he could have a friend.

"Do you like baseball?"

The boy blinked. Nate decided not to search the small face for reaction, but to just keep talking. Keep things normal.

"I went to a Red Sox game a few weeks ago, but they lost. Well, they're only two games out of first place. Maybe they can still win the pennant. If it wasn't for those Yankees, huh?

"When I was your age, I had a big collection of baseball cards. I had so many shoeboxes full of them. I don't have them anymore, though. When I…when I left home, I forgot to take them."

Nate slid off the bed and onto the floor, and picked up a Lego block. He snapped it onto the base Josey had built, picking up where she'd left off before she'd excused herself. A long time ago.

"Josey—ah, I mean, Miss St. John—will be back in a minute, I think. She really cares about you. She came all this way to see you. I bet she's a really good teacher, huh?"

It was apparent that the conversation was destined to be one-way.

"Well, she does care about you. A lot of people do. This family you're staying with really likes you, and I know that the doctors you saw care, and also the nice police officers."

Nate sighed. That hadn't sounded as comforting as he'd meant it to.

"Hey, everyone wants you to be safe and happy. But see, if you don't talk at all, how is everyone supposed to know what you're feeling? Well, I understand. Everyone keeps asking you to tell them how you feel, and you can't. I know how that feels.

"Because the same thing happened to me that's happening to you. When I was just a kid, like you."

Nate felt blood rush to his head, and his heart banged against his chest so hard he thought his sternum would crack. He fell silent, piling up Lego blocks as the child watched. Nate wasn't helping. Probably best to just sit quietly here and play.

"If he keeps everything inside him, he could be scarred for a long, long time. He's a little boy. If we help him now, he may be able to live a normal life...."

"Dad can't hurt us now.... You're not like him. And look what you're doing to yourself. You're letting this get in the way of you and Josey...."

"Son, you'd better start remembering where you came from. From me. That's why I'm here. To remind you that you owe me. It's pay-up time...."

Jonathan's fist, arcing through the air.

Josey reaching out in the dark that one night. Their only night.

"My father was a very bad father," Nate said. "He did lots of bad things. I have an older brother, Derek. My father yelled all the time at both of us. We always tried to be quiet, to try not to make him yell, but it didn't matter what we did, ever. He used to yell at my mother, too. Sometimes she yelled back, but not very often.

"When I was very small I remember my father hitting Derek so hard he crashed into the wall, and there was...there was a lot of blood. Then my mother took Derek away, and I thought he was never coming back, and when I asked my father where he was, he screamed at me to shut up and not ask stupid questions. I sat in my room for hours, trying not to cry because my brother was gone. But my mother brought him back. She'd brought him to the hospital to get his broken nose set. They had to wait a long time at the hospital because there were a lot of people there. He told me Mom wouldn't let him tell the doctors what really happened. He had to say he fell down the stairs.

"That kind of thing happened a few more times. His arm was broken once—actually, maybe twice. And some other things.

"But we always thought something would happen to our father. I mean, I remember we thought that's what the police were for. We were kind of scared of the police, but Dad was doing bad things to Derek and we thought the police were supposed to save us. But the police didn't know what was going on because no one told them.

"Anyway, our father started hitting me, too, a lot. I got hit a bunch of times for running up the stairs too hard and closing my door too hard, and for spilling juice on the kitchen floor. A couple of times, a friend called and my father was angry, saying my friends were tying up his phone, and he hit me for that, too.

"Mom acted like everything was normal all the time. After Dad hit me or Derek, she would leave us alone for a while, then come and offer us cookies or a chance to stay up a little later to watch TV. If one of us was crying, she pretended not to see it. She was trying to make everything look normal, I guess.

"We learned. We all learned to live with it. But then my mom died."

Nate took a breath, and his vision felt blurry from staring at the wall to see the memories again, but he could tell he had Mike's attention. And he thought the child had moved just a bit closer to him.

"She was sick often," Nate continued, "my mom, I mean. She had a part-time job as a secretary but she had to stay home a lot with headaches, so finally her boss just fired her. She and Dad got in a big fight about it and that was one of those rare times I ever heard her yell back. Then she got in bed and stayed there for about three days. I think my father stayed at the office all that time. I don't remember him coming home at all.''

Nate grew silent then, the details searing his memory. Their neighbor had come over. His mom had likely called her. Mom had taken too many aspirins, on purpose. Then she'd gotten scared—apparently she didn't want him and Derek to find her. The neighbor had come and then the ambulance that took his mom away. She never came home.

"She died," Nate said. "She left us with our father. I was twelve.

"Not too much changed after that. Dad was sad for a while, we could tell, but he didn't change the way he was. He got worse, probably because he was no happier getting stuck with us than we were with him.

"Derek and I were different. I used to stay as quiet as I possibly could, all the time, so my father would just forget I was there. I read books a lot, because it was a quiet thing to do. And I got really high grades because studying was another quiet thing to do, so I did a lot of it. But Derek was different. He knew Dad hated the music loud, and he blasted the speakers anyway, to see if he could get away with it. He never did. And if Dad was threatening me when Derek was around, Derek got between us and took the heat. I just had to stand there and watch.

"One night he and Derek had a terrible fight about college. Derek was about to graduate high school and he wanted to go to college, and Dad said that was never going to happen because it was too expensive and Derek would have to go to work instead. They argued and Dad punched Derek, and it was very bad. I saw Derek cry and I went into my room and took out an envelope with money I had hidden under my mattress. I'd gotten small jobs shoveling snow and mowing lawns and running errands around town, and I was saving up for a while and had almost two hundred dollars. So I went out and bought Derek the nicest duffel bag I could find, blue with all different pockets and things. The next night was Derek's graduation and Dad was at work, so I was the only one to go and see him. When we came home, I gave the duffel bag to him with the remainder of the money for a graduation present. I wanted him to go to college. I told him I knew he probably wouldn't need a lot of money because he was very smart and could get a scholarship and could definitely get a part-time job to pay rent somewhere, and so he could just pack and use the money for a train or bus ticket to Boston, where there are a lot of schools.

"He just sat there, looking at the duffel bag for a long time. And then he hugged me for a minute and went into his room and closed the door."

Nate stopped again, but not because he had trouble remembering. He was thinking of Derek, his brave brother, and feeling all over again the awe of him he'd had as a child. And the child next to Nate inched still closer to him on the floor.

"A few days later was Derek's eighteenth birthday. That night, he walked into my room and started putting some of my clothes into the new duffel bag. I didn't know what to say. He kept putting my things in the bag, careful to choose the clothes I liked and wore the most, and when the bag was half-full, he walked into his room and I followed, and he filled the rest of the bag with his stuff. By then it was pretty late so he told me to go to sleep. I did, and he woke me up at four in the morning and we sneaked out of the house. We bought bus tickets to Boston. We never went back to Connecticut.

"I had nightmares a lot, though, and I was always scared Dad would come after us and make me go home. Derek enrolled me in high school and convinced my teachers he was my legal guardian, and I told everyone from that day on that our father was dead.

"It took about a year, but eventually I stopped listening for Dad at night. I stopped worrying he'd break the door down and drag me back home. I was safe. I'm still safe."

Nate's throat was dry and his tongue hurt from talking, and he suddenly remembered he wasn't talking to himself. He dragged his gaze from the carpet, where it had somehow stuck a while back. As his eyes met Mike's, the child edged still closer until there weren't too many inches left between them at all. He was intently watching Nate's face. Listening hard.

"You had a tough time, too. I know you did," Nate said, "and even though it doesn't seem like it, you're luckier than me because you won't have to run away like I did. You got help, and now you won't be hurt like that again. You've been very brave. Do you know you're the first person I ever told this story to? That's because I'm not as brave as you. But now you have to be a little braver and talk about what happened to you. You can choose whoever you want. You can talk to your foster family or to a nice doctor or maybe…or maybe even Miss St. John. Because you know what? The bad things don't go away, but talking about them helps make them not so bad. And after that, you can think about the happy things you'll do in the future."

Words he'd heard countless times. But never in his own voice. Until now.

And just as he was considering how much faith he could

put in those words, Mike placed his small warm hand into his own larger one.

Nate became a believer at last.

Josey, sitting with her ear pressed to the other side of the door, sobbed gratefully.

Chapter Nineteen

Josey knew better than to make presumptions about what might happen next—to her, to Nate, to the unshared secret she kept inside her, to their possibility of a future.

Even as she said goodbye to Mike—with his promise he would talk to the psychologist and perhaps to her, too, when she visited again—and left the house with Nate, she didn't dare presume to believe everything would be all right between them, ever. She just walked at his side, breathing in suburban air. The breeze smelled green, but ripe with a reminder the green wouldn't last much longer. Josey's hold on late summer was as tenuous as her hold on the man beside her.

She had a few more days, maybe, to keep the knowledge of the baby from him before guilt would consume her, but Nate deserved some freedom just now. He'd left his past behind in the foster home, and he deserved to walk lighter for a little while, untroubled. The thinning sun slanted through the leaves overhead and gilded his hair, and Josey's heart nearly burst with emotion, but still she walked, quietly, with her best friend.

The above-ground T station wasn't very crowded, and just as they stepped onto the platform, the Green Line outbound trolley passed them in the other direction, packed so tightly the commuters inside must have been fearful for their oxygen supply. Then Nate cleared his throat, and when she looked up at him, her own oxygen was in short supply, for she nearly stopped breathing.

"I'm not going home yet."

"Oh." Josey squinted at him, searching his expression, but it was completely relaxed, his features calm, his eyes clear. Close to beatific. She'd never, ever seen him so at ease. "Are you going back to the office?"

"No, I have a few…errands to run. I have to see a couple of people. Then I'll come back."

"Oh," she said again, feeling slightly stupid. "Well, I'll be around, you know, so you can give me a call in a few days…"

"What?"

"To let me know how Mike's doing, if you find out," she finished hurriedly. No presumptions.

"I'm sorry, no."

"No?"

"No, I meant, I'm going to see a couple of people and then I'll come back to see you."

Josey blinked.

"If you're not busy."

"Busy? No—well, I have papers to grade." The hell with the papers. "I can do that while you're running your errands."

"Good. I want to talk to you. But I can't say what I

think I'll say until I do these few things. I know you understand.''

Did she? ''Yes…''

The T pulled up with a startling rumble. Josey hadn't even heard it coming until it had rolled past her, stopping a few feet ahead. She dug for change, but Nate gently tugged her hand from her bag and dropped a few coins into her palm. He closed his fingers over hers and held them closed, and Josey tilted her head up to look into his eyes again.

They were jostled from both sides by people shuffling on and off the train, but the only contact Josey felt was her hand, engulfed in his warm, smooth fingers.

''I'm waiting here,'' Nate said. ''I'll take the next train. If I go with you, I might start talking, and I can't yet. I need to finish some things. Then I'll start—'' He cut himself off with a slight, gentle smile at himself. Josey resisted the urge to lift her other hand to stroke his lower lip. ''I've said too much already. Go on.'' Before she could protest, he steered her to the trolley door. He let go of her hand and she stepped up into the train. She went to drop the change in the conductor's box, but her hand shook so much she dropped a quarter and had to scramble to grab it before it rolled under someone's foot. She plunked it in the box and fell into the nearest seat, pressing her forehead to the window. Nate stood on the platform, his hands tucked easily in his trouser pockets, watching her. Her exhalation fogged the window.

One jolt back, and the T began to roll.

No presumptions.

''Wait for me,'' Nate mouthed.

Josey took a deep breath, wondering if she had the strength.

* * *

It wasn't the black-shuttered house he grew up in. It was an impersonal brick apartment building in Allston, where in-line skating B.U. students weaved around old women creeping along the sidewalk with Star Market grocery bags. Walking up the steps, Nate expected apprehension to settle in, but resolution won out.

He had looked for the address in the Travises' phone book as Josey was saying her goodbyes to Mike. But it wasn't listed. So he put in a quick phone call to a Boston police officer he was friendly with, and obtained the address in a matter of minutes. Ironic how easy it was to find someone in a big city. Even more ironic when it was the person he'd been hiding from for half a lifetime.

The buzzer was dirty from the smudge of thousands of fingerprints over who knew how many years. Nate pressed the buzzer and waited. He didn't exactly expect the intercom to be functional, so his father's voice startled him even more than usual. ''Yeah? Who's there?''

Nate cleared his throat. ''Your son.''

He heard incredulous silence. Then the door clicked open. Nate stepped into the foyer, then heard a door open one floor up. He saw his father lean over the railing, squint into the dimness. ''Derek?''

''No,'' Nate said, ascending three steps. ''Nate.''

''Nate,'' his father repeated, and when Nate reached the top of the stairs, Jonathan had rearranged his surely shocked features into his typical sneer. ''How nice to have family living in the area. Always dropping in on you to surprise you.'' He was standing up straight, imposing, intimidating, but Nate walked right up to him, right into his father's face, forcing him to walk backward into his apartment. Nate shut the door behind them. He could feel his father's breath on his face, cigarette-stale.

And he could feel the apprehension he'd thought he'd

feel on the front steps. But this apprehension was coming from Jonathan. Because of his presence. It had a heady effect, and it propelled Nate to say what he came here to say.

"Dad." He laughed. "*Dad.* I haven't called you that in fifteen years. Well, Dad, why do you think I'm here?"

His father stared at him, and Nate didn't flinch, nor did he blink. He just stood there until Jonathan dug into the pocket of his thinning brown corduroy pants and fished out a crumpled cigarette pack and a lighter. He lit a bent cigarette and blew a puff of smoke into his son's face. Nate still didn't move.

"I'm thinking you're finally understanding your obligations."

Nate nearly laughed again. "Obligations?"

"To me. The man who sacrificed to raise two kids on one income for years."

"And, I'm sorry, that obligates me in what way?"

"Well, it means it's time for you to kick in a little to help your old man."

"And how's that?"

"I suppose it's just as easy as whipping out your checkbook."

"Do you?"

"Yeah, I do."

"So you want me to write you a check, then you'll leave me alone? And you'll leave Derek alone?"

"Yes. Until…"

"Until when?"

"Until the next time I need a little assistance. You're my son for life, you know. Your obligations don't end."

"That, Dad, is exactly where you and I differ."

Jonathan raised his voice. "Excuse me?"

"No, I don't excuse you. And I'm not obligated to you in the least. Not now. Not ever again."

"You ungrateful little—"

"No." Nate cut off his tirade. "I'm not little. Not anymore. But I *am* ungrateful, I admit, for plenty that you gave us. You think we owe you. Maybe kids do owe their parents something. They owe it to their parents to grow up right, and make something of themselves that parents can be proud of.

"Well, in spite of you, Derek and I grew up right. We made something of our lives, something good, and our responsibility to you—" he paused "—and to Mom, ends there. It's over.

"You can keep calling Derek, you can keep calling me, but I'm telling you right now, it's worthless, and maybe you'd better spend that valuable time on the phone looking for another job to pay your rent. We're not giving you a dime, because although you were never capable of taking care of us, I know you're fully capable of taking care of yourself. I hope you're listening to me, because I will never tell you this again. Because I will never speak to you again."

A muscle in his father's cheek twitched once, twice, and his jaw tightened. Then he drew himself up to his full height, but Nate was already there, and they were at eye level.

"You don't scare me," Nate said, his words low and fierce. "You don't intimidate me. You have no control of any kind over me."

His father's breathing was hard. He seemed to be searching for something to say—an argument, a threat, a profanity.

"Goodbye," Nate said.

Then he turned and walked out of the apartment, keeping

his stride steady and even. He walked into the street, into the fading summer dusk.

He walked down the block, away from his past, away from his father, for the second time in his life.

But this time, as an adult. Free.

The next buzzer he rang was his brother's. And it was still broken, apparently, because a few seconds later, he heard Derek clomping to the door in his sneakers.

"Hey," Derek said, sounding a little uncertain.

"Hey," Nate said back, and the brothers regarded each other for several moments. "Is this a bad time?"

"No. No, I'm just going through the course book for next semester."

"Any good classes?"

"Just endless public speaking courses. And I'm supposed to do an internship, so I have to start calling radio stations. I'm going to be one of the oldest interns ever hired." He grinned. "But that's all right. I can't wait, to be honest."

"You'll be the best intern they ever hired, I'm sure."

Derek sighed. "Are you okay?"

"Yeah, well, that's what I came over to tell you. I'm all right. I'm better than all right. I just had a lovely visit with Dad."

Derek froze. "He came to see you?"

"No, I went to see him at his place, in Allston."

His brother shook his head. "Please pardon me for asking, but why the hell did you do that?"

"I had to see him so I could leave him."

"Now, that sounds paradoxical."

"Not really. You know, when we left Connecticut, it was you taking me away. You were older. You made the decision. It was the right thing to do, but I didn't do it—you did. Maybe that's why you were always able to feel cut loose from him and I wasn't able to shake off his memory. I don't know. But seventeen years later, I was getting weary of his hold over my life. So I went to see him. Then I walked out on him. It's the last time. Now we're both free. You *and* me.''

Derek widened his eyes for a moment, then smiled. ''I can't believe I'm hearing this. Thanks for coming by to tell me.''

''It wasn't just to tell you that. I wanted to assure you that it wasn't all a waste. You said last time I saw you that I make you feel like it was all a waste. Well, it wasn't.'' His voice broke. ''It wasn't.'' And then he reached blindly out, through tears many years held back, and wrapped his arms around his older brother, his protector, his idol, his friend.

Derek's shoulders began to shake, or maybe it was Nate shaking with emotion, and the two brothers held on to each other on the steps for long minutes. Then Derek stood back, swiped at his eyes once and said, ''I'm glad you feel that way.''

Nate wiped his wet face also. ''And listen, I'm going to prove it.''

''How's that?''

''The way I see it, I just finally buried my past. And here, with you, I'm making peace with my present. But now I'm going to go secure my future. If that's still possible.''

His older brother put his arm around Nate. ''I think that future's a sure thing. And tell her hi from me.''

Josey might have been waiting two hours or two minutes. She had no concept of time, sitting on the floor in her apartment, wondering what Nate would come back with, uncertain she could handle whatever it would be. She put a kettle of water on the stove to make tea, but then forgot about it, and when the kettle whistled like crazy, she turned the heat off, but had no energy to get a cup and saucer from the overhead cabinet. So she just walked back into the living room empty-handed, thirsty and worried. And stayed that way, until the tap on her door.

She forced her voice to come out normal. "It's open!" She watched the knob turn, watched the bottom of the door as it swung open, watched Nate's shiny black shoes bring him into her apartment. Then she stood and looked up at him.

"Hi," he said, as if everything that had happened before today, as if everything that had occurred this afternoon, had been ordinary life.

How could she answer? "Hi."

Where have you been? Why are you here? Will you stay? "Want some tea?"

"No, thank you." He didn't move, and neither did she, and the distance between them was too great for her. "I dropped in on my father."

Josey, preoccupied, wasn't prepared for that, and she shook her head twice. "What? You went to see him just now? Why?"

"There were a few things I had to tell him."

"Ah."

"Then I stopped by Derek's. I had to clear up a couple of things with him, too."

"I see."

"I figured, you know, since I was in the talking mood, I might as well get to everyone." He glanced down at the floor and took a deep breath before straightening up, and she turned her head in the direction of the window as he continued. "I told Mike what happened to me when I was a kid…"

She had to turn back then, to tell him the truth. "I, uh, I know."

"I know you know. I guessed when we left the house and you didn't wonder out loud why he had changed his mind so suddenly about talking to people. Then I guessed, based on how long you'd left us alone together, that you'd set the whole thing up."

"Not really set it up. I was just sort of giving it a little push, hoping it would work out. I'm sorry for being deceptive about why I wanted you to go to the house with me."

Nate furrowed his brow. "Do not ever be sorry about this. Ever. It changed my life. *You* changed my life."

"No, I didn't make you say a word to that little boy. You changed your own life. I knew you could. I was—am—so proud of you."

They both fell silent then. There was so much turmoil spiraling around inside Josey's heart that she was sure he had to be feeling it, too, but his countenance remained calm. She was desperate to ask what he was thinking, but still refused to push him any further than he was willing to go.

But a smile worked its way onto his face, and he somehow knew to answer her unasked question. "I'm standing here feeling you proud of me and it feels wonderful. So, I propose continuing it."

"What do you mean?"

"I mean, I'll keep doing the right thing and you keep being proud of me. For an indefinite period of time."

They each took a step toward each other.

"No one does the right thing all the time," Josey countered with a half smile of her own. "And sometimes you think you're doing the right thing and it's the wrong thing completely. What then?''

''Well, then, I can keep feeling good because instead of being proud of me, I'll know you're at least trying to understand me. That feels just as good.''

''How are you so sure?''

''Past experience.''

Another step.

''And in return,'' Nate said, ''I can do plenty more for you. I can make sure the door is always locked so you're safe, and I can let you pick the video and ice cream flavor every time, and if anyone dares to hurt you, I'll pound them with a baseball bat.''

''My God, Nate, listen to you trying to convince me. Don't you know I know you're perfect?''

She thought she saw his lips tremble, but she wasn't certain. So she took another step closer.

''It's my turn,'' she whispered. ''Let me try to convince you I can be perfect for you.''

''You already have,'' Nate answered hoarsely. ''When we met, and then over and over again countless times since.''

Josey's eyes filled with tears that spilled over onto her cheeks when Nate took the last two steps between them, reached out and wrapped his arms around her back. He slid one hand up and cradled her head before bringing his lips down on hers. She entwined her arms around his neck and grasped at his silky hair with all of her fingers, pressing him deeper into her, and sighed, tasting his promise.

When he pulled away, his eyes were bright, and he looked at her only for a moment before dropping his head again to inhale the skin of her neck, and to trail damp kisses down the curve of her shoulder before tracing the same line back up with his tongue. He caught the tip of her earlobe with his teeth, nipping once, and his breath was hot in her ear. "I love you."

She gasped, and he continued, "And I'll love you forever."

She closed her eyes and let the long-awaited words echo through her, and then she leaned her head back to look into his face. "And I'll love you forever. We…we both will—love you forever."

"What does that mean?" Nate raised his eyebrows and began to laugh. "Something you're not telling me? You're really a twin and there are two Joseys?"

"No, I'm—I'm pregnant."

Nate froze. His hands tightened on her tensed shoulders. Her suddenly frightened expression was proof she wasn't joking. Pregnant. A baby. His baby.

His—and Josey's.

Her hands had fallen away from his body, and she wrapped her arms around herself, but he didn't allow her to stand alone like that for more than a split second. He gathered her into his arms and walked her to the sofa, where they sat, and she curled herself into him, burying her head in his chest. He stroked her hair for a few moments, bracing for his fear to overtake him.

But shockingly, happily, it didn't. It was just a flutter inside.

"I haven't hidden it for long. I only just found out. And I was going to tell you, no matter what.…"

"Josey," he said, rocking her gently, "when I ran back here to you tonight, I wanted to get started on our future right away." His heart banged hard, and Josey must have felt it under her face, because she reached up and laid a hand over his breast pocket. "Well," he stated, "it looks like we already did that, without even realizing it. But I'm ready."

"You are?" Josey's voice was muffled, and she pulled back to look at him once more. "Because I am. You really are?"

"I'm ready for everything in our future."

Her eyes shone, and her expression of pure joy was one Nate vowed to keep there, always. "Well, if that's the case," she said, winking, "then get ready to kiss me again."

And still scared, but filled with more strength than he'd ever possessed, Nate kissed his best friend again. And again.

* * * * *

SPECIAL EDITION™

presents

DOWN FROM THE MOUNTAIN
by Barbara Gale
(Silhouette Special Edition #1595)

Carrying scars from his youth, forest ranger
David Hartwell had fled his home and settled in
the sanctuary of the Adirondack mountains.
But now, called back to deal with his father's will,
he was faced with temporary guardianship of
Ellen Candler—beautiful, innocent and exactly
the kind of woman David had always avoided.

Only, this time he
couldn't run away.

Because Ellen was blind.

And she needed him.

Follow the journey of
these two extraordinary
people as they leave their
sheltered existences behind
to embrace life and love!

Available February 2004 at your favorite retail outlet.

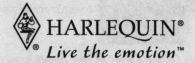

The legend continues!

New York Times bestselling author

DIANA PALMER

MEN
of the
WEST

**A Collector's Edition containing
three classic Long, Tall Texans novels.**

Relive the spellbinding magic of Harden, Evan and
Donavan when the spirited women who love these
irresistible cowboys lasso their elusive hearts.

Look for MEN OF THE WEST in March 2004.

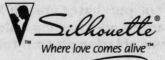

Silhouette®
Where love comes alive™

Visit Silhouette at www.eHarlequin.com   PSDP880

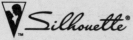

COMING NEXT MONTH

SSECNM0104